The Seeker

***

Sharron McClellan

ImaJinn
Books

The Seeker
Published by ImaJinn Books, a division of ImaJinn

Copyright ©2004 by Sharron McClellan
Printed and bound in the United States of America. All rights reserved. No part of this book may be reproduced in any form or by any means (electronic, mechanical, photocopying, recording, or otherwise) without prior written permission of both the copyright holder and the above publisher of this book, except by a reviewer, who may quote brief passages in a review. For information, address: ImaJinn Books, a division of ImaJinn, P.O. Box 545, Canon City, CO 81215-0545; or call toll free 1-877-625-3592.

ISBN: 1-893896-25-0

10 9 8 7 6 5 4 3 2 1

PUBLISHER'S NOTE:
This book is a work of fiction. Names, characters, places and incidents are products of the author's imagination or are used fictitiously. Any resemblance to actual events or locales or persons, living or dead, is entirely coincidental.

Books are available at quantity discounts when used to promote products or services. For information please write to: Marketing Division, ImaJinn Books, P.O. Box 545, Canon City, CO 81215-0545, or call toll free 1-877-625-3592.

Cover design by Rickey Mallory

ImaJinn Books, a division of ImaJinn
P.O. Box 545, Canon City, CO 81215-0545
Toll Free: 1-877-625-3592
http://www.imajinnbooks.com

The quest they were on was dangerous, but not as dangerous as Lore was to her heart . . .

"Where was I?"

"In my vision," she whispered.

He pressed the heel of his hand against his forehead. His blond hair fell forward. "It was horrible. Medea. She . . . I killed . . ."

"It is over."

Lore shook his head. "I was there. I felt you beneath me as I killed you."

"It was a vision. Nothing more. Do not let it make you doubt what is truly real."

"Real?" Without blinking, he reached out to her, as if testing reality.

Her instinct was to turn away. To flinch.

She held the urge at bay. He needed to touch her. Feel her. Know she was alive.

His hand, large and calloused, traced her cheek. His thumbs skimmed her lips. Sculpted her brow.

She closed her eyes, and with a slow inhale, she turned to his palm.

Above her, Lore groaned, and then his lips were on her. Tasting her skin. Marking her with their heat. "I thought I killed you." His whisper was as heated, but she heard the relief in it, as tangible as his hands on her hair.

She needed to stop this.

But it felt so good. Like water after a long run she had thought would never end.

To be touched, loved.

It had been too long.

She could not stop him, even if she wanted to.

To Corey Cowan.
Our journeys have taken us on paths we never imagined,
but I am always glad when they cross.

Other Books by Sharron McClellan
The Given

Prologue

Medea contemplated killing the man across the table from her. It was not that he was a Reaper. She could live with thieves and cutthroats. No, the problem was his attitude. He knew something. Something she did not.

She hated that.

However, the tavern was full of citizens who might protest the spilling of blood. It would be easiest to hear Kole out—for now.

Raising the heavy metal goblet to her lips, she sipped the dark red wine and gestured for her companion to do the same.

He raised his chalice. The wine sloshed over the side, staining his tunic.

Medea smiled at the slip. "Do I make you nervous?"

"No." He took a long draught.

She did not challenge the denial. Did not need to. Men were such poor liars. They thought they were better than women. Smarter. Stronger. Oh, so brilliant.

However, it only took one woman, and a well-honed blade, to prove them wrong. She patted the knife that rested under her skirts and against her thigh. For now, it was enough to know her presence affected Kole. Made him clumsy.

It should. Kole knew her from before—when she was Mako's mistress and lady of his Keep.

But that was before the Keep fell—before she killed her lord and lover.

Such a pity. Not a pity that she had knifed Mako in the back, but that she had not managed to kill her whore of a replacement.

Enough. Looking back never brought her anything but regret. Now was the time for moving forward, even if it involved listening to Kole's proposal.

With luck, he would not bore her.

Medea leaned back against the rough wooden wall and let her hands fall to her lap. "You mentioned the Orb of Dalis. Tell me why I should care about some local legend."

Kole rolled the half empty goblet between his open palms. "I have seen drawings. A crystal sphere resting on a pedestal of dark stone."

Medea wove a strand of her black hair through her fingers.

"I can find crystal spheres from a vendor on the street."

"Perhaps, but they will not give you what the Orb of Dalis can."

"What is that?"

"Power."

Medea raised a brow.

Kole continued, "Legend says that when the Season of Renewal passes a hundred times, the Orb will fill with power. Enough energy to do the bidding of one who is smart enough to obtain it."

She yawned. "While this sounds interesting, what makes you think this Orb is anything more than a tale made to entice fools."

Kole grinned, his teeth stained dark. "There is a local man. Very old. When he was a boy, his father attempted to pass the first test. He watched."

"And?"

"His father failed."

This was it? "You waste my time." Medea sneered at her drinking companion. "You bring me the ramblings of an old man as if it were truth. Bring me proof, and I might allow you to babble at me a while longer."

Rising from the table, she downed the last of her wine.

Before she walked away, Kole grabbed her wrist. "He spoke truth. I swear."

Pleased with his reaction, Medea did not struggle. Kole was loathsome, and she would eventually kill him, but until that time, she wanted a man who knew how to beg. Who knew her importance. Who would do anything to keep her.

She saw that man in Kole. "How do you know he did not lie out of fear?"

Releasing her, Kole touched the long, wicked knife that hung at his waist. "Because I encouraged him otherwise."

Medea granted Kole a smile and sat down on the bench next to him. If this was true, it was possible the Orb did exist. Still, there were questions. "You said the Orb would do its master's bidding. What do you mean?"

Kole swallowed the last of his wine and wiped his mouth with a dirty sleeve. "I mean it will do as you wish. Do you want to kill your enemies? Become the lady of another Keep?" He grinned again, but the artificial smile never made it to his eyes. "It can help you."

Outwardly, Medea did not react to Kole's tale, but on the inside, she glowed at the possibility.

She needed power. Craved it like most people craved food and water. With true power she could become a Queen. Maybe a Goddess.

All would bow before her. Her enemies would die. Not simple and not well, but they would die.

With practiced indifference, Medea circled the rim of the goblet with a long fingernail. "Tell me how to find this Orb."

"The old man spoke of a field ten suns from here. It is where the tests begin." Kole stopped her hand, taking her fingers in his. "We have little time, and you will need a guide. Someone who knows the backcountry. I can help you. I can be your companion as you ride."

Kole's hand was hot and sweaty, as he stroked her skin. It took all of Medea's will not to slit his throat for touching her, but he was right in that she needed him. At least until she obtained the Orb.

She managed one of her best smiles. The one that said, Do as I ask and I will give you anything. Including a bedding like you can only imagine.

Leaning into him, she pulled him close. "You will help me?" She whispered the question against his ear like a lover whispered a promise. "You will assist me on my quest?"

He squeezed her hand in answer.

Satisfied, she pushed him away. "What do we need, and how soon do we need it?"

Kole leaned back and crossed his arms. Superiority oozed from his pores. "We need mounts and supplies. Food. Heavier cloaks."

His arrogance annoyed her, but arrogant men were easier to manipulate so she held her tongue. Pulling a small sack-purse from a pocket in her dress, she tossed it on the tabletop. "This should be enough."

He hefted the bag in his hand. "You do not worry I will take your coin and leave you to travel alone?"

If there was one thing she understood, it was men. Especially repugnant, deceitful men. He might try to abandon her, but it would not be until after he bedded her. "You could, but then you would never taste me." Her tongue darted over her upper lip. "You do want a taste, do you not?"

Kole watched her mouth, mesmerized. "You make a good

argument. I will return soon."

Medea did not signal the bar maid for more wine until Kole was through the door. How unfortunate that she needed him.

Luckily, it would not be for long. Soon, she would obtain this Orb, and then all would pay.

She would see her enemies suffer, cry, and weep for mercy.

The first to die would be the one who ruined her life. The Trancer whore who stole her lover.

Iliana.

One

"We do not serve your kind here."

Iliana pulled her cloak around her body. The tavern was ill lit, dank, and the only one open in the small town of Mardid. "All I want is a bit of sweet wine. Maybe some food." She jingled the small pouch of coins at her side. "I can pay."

The barkeep's gaze traveled up her frame and back down. The sneer never left his face. "You are Mako's Trancer whore. I do not want your money."

Mako's Trancer whore? It was not as if she could deny the accusation. Perhaps the whore part, but even if she did, the barkeep would never believe she had managed to stay untouched while she was Mako's prisoner.

Even in death, the Reaper Lord managed to draw her blood.

The barkeep waited.

Not bothering to reply, Iliana turned on her heel. She was a fool to think the villagers would forgive her. With deliberate steps, she made her way through the thicket of chairs. The doorway loomed ahead of her. She hesitated, knowing she should walk through it—

She was tired of running.

A small wooden table was to her right. She pulled out a chair and took a seat. Her back to the open doorway, she faced the bar, daring the barkeep to deny her service.

It was early evening, but there were three other patrons in the small tavern. They quieted, watching, waiting too see how the barkeep would respond. Iliana did not need Trancer senses to know what they thought. They hated her. Despised her for living when so many of their women had died at the Reaper's hands, or worse.

They would never forget what she was, but then, neither would she.

The silence intensified. She felt their hot gazes on the back of her neck. Her skin. The smell of their fear and loathing permeated her nostrils and filled her head.

She did not move.

The barkeep threw down the piece of dirty cloth he used to clean the tabletops and walked over to her. Though he was thin, and his hair was peppered gray with age, Iliana was sure he was still stronger than she.

He stopped in front of her. "Get out."

Iliana took a deep breath, held it, and let it out. "All I want is some food. That is all."

"Your kind always wants more."

"My kind? You mean Trancers?" He would not be the first person suspicious of a Trancer's empathic abilities.

"No, I mean traitorous Reaper whores."

His vehemence was not a surprise. "I am neither traitorous, a Reaper, nor a whore." She met his gaze, willing him to believe her. "Please," she whispered. "Wine and food. That is all I ask. Just a bit and I will leave."

He did not respond but went back to his bar and through a door.

"Hey, Trancer," one of the men called to her. She did not acknowledge him, but the hairs on the back of her neck rose, nonetheless.

"Spread your legs like you did for Mako and maybe Allar will give you a piece of bread."

A barrage of laughter followed the comment.

Iliana set her jaw and refused to show any emotion to the taunt. She would be strong.

The kitchen door opened again, and the barkeep came out with a plate. She straightened in surprise.

Maybe there was forgiveness. She almost wept at the thought.

He threw the plate in front of her with a clipped laugh.

It was not food. It was garbage. Moldy bread. Vegetables that had taken to rot days ago and smelled like a swamp. A chunk of meat that resembled the bottom of her boot.

Her gloved fingers dug into the tough cloth of her leggings, and she forced back bitter words from her lips.

Unflinching, she met the barkeep's eye, picked up the meat, took a bite, chewed, and swallowed the dry hunk of flesh. "It is wonderful. My thanks."

With pointed deliberation, she wiped her mouth with the back of her hand.

The barkeep stormed back to the kitchen, the door swinging shut behind him.

The scrape of chairs on the floor signaled that the three men were moving closer. Trying to ignore them, Iliana took another bite of the meat. All she wanted was too be left alone. It sounded simple enough.

"Want some company?"

Apparently, it was not meant to be.

She looked up. She was surrounded. Citizens of Mardid. Upstanding workers. Good people.

Good people who wanted her out of their tavern and out of their city. She lowered her gaze, hiding her face with her dark hair. "No."

They pulled chairs out and sat down.

Iliana grabbed the bread, picked the mold off, took a bite, and gagged. Setting her jaw, she refused to show any more disgust.

"I got something for you that might taste better." The one closest to her, his brown hair cut short, placed his hand on her knee.

Iliana flinched away from the touch and knew immediately it was a mistake.

In a heartbeat, all three were on her, trying to pin her to the table.

With strength born of fear and memories not faded, Iliana kicked out and made contact with someone's groin. A roar of pain followed, and the brown-haired attacker fell to his knees. Iliana rolled off the table and landed on her back.

The remaining men grabbed her feet and pulled her towards them. Desperate, she gripped the table legs and held on to them like a ship's mast in a storm.

Although she lay halfway under the table, she saw the rage in her attackers' eyes and heard their breathing—quick and shallow—as they pulled at her legs, trying to force her to let go.

She knew what they would do to her if they succeeded. Knew because it was the same thing the Reapers had wanted. They wanted to break her. Hurt her. Make her cry and beg.

Her Trancing skills fought to emerge from behind the dark wall that surrounded her mind, but the barrier refused to crumble or crack or allow her access.

Although unable to use her power, Iliana felt it rolling like a thick storm in the back of her head. Sticky. Black. Lethal. It hammered at her, desperate to emerge and destroy those who would harm her.

Desperate or not, the making of the wall was not her conscious decision. She knew its fall would be equally unexpected.

She both prayed for the fall and feared it.

The men pulled harder, their thick fingers digging into her thighs as they tried to pull her out and across the wooden floor.

Iliana held back the scream that threatened. She would not give them the satisfaction.

"I see you are making friends."

The comment was low and without a hint of humor, a bright light in the dark of her mind.

It was not made by her attackers.

Heavy footsteps hurried across the floor, and within seconds, a body accompanied the voice. The merciless tugging stopped. Chairs were flung out of the way to crash overhead.

Her attackers followed.

Except for her own quick breathing and the groans of the men, silence filled the room.

Relief roared through Iliana. A hand reached down to help her to her feet. "You are safe."

Iliana did not look up to meet her savior. She did not need to. She knew who it was. Lore, a Warrior, and her self-appointed guardian.

Ignoring his hand, she used an overturned chair for leverage and struggled to stand on shaky legs.

"Are you all right? Did they hurt you?" Lore watched her with concerned eyes.

Iliana met his gaze, knowing she should be grateful, but angry that she needed to be saved. Her eyes narrowed. "I had the situation under control."

He grinned. "I suppose you were hiding under the table to give them a false sense of security?"

Iliana bit her lip. As much as she hated it, he was right. With no Trancer powers and no training, she was defenseless.

***

"I want you to train me to fight."

Iliana stood in the center of the training field, practice sword clenched in her gloved fist. A few bruises from yesterdays attack marred her skin, but they were easily ignored. Her cloth leggings, a size too small and dull with dust, itched. A trickle of sweat rolled down her back in reaction to the midday heat.

More galling than the clothes and bruises was asking Lore to help her, but there was no one else. He was the best. The Master of Many Skills.

And the only Warrior Trainer in the Keep.

She waited, praying he would not laugh at her request. If

he did, Warrior or not, she vowed she would beat him for the insult.

The new recruits trained around her, completely absorbed in their lessons. Behind her, the thunk thunk of wooden swords slowed, telling her that the sparring of two boys was about to end.

Lore flipped an abandoned shield up with his foot, caught it in midair, and strode towards the edge of the field. "You are a Trancer, Iliana, not a Warrior. Yesterday proved that."

His laughter would have been preferable to his immediate rejection of her request. Iliana hurried after him, not about to be denied. "As you well know, I am a Trancer no longer, and it is because of yesterday I ask this of you."

"If you would stop going places you should not, incidents would not happen."

And live her life in the Keep? A virtual prisoner? "I go where I choose."

Reaching the stone wall that encircled the courtyard, Lore set the shield down and out from underfoot of the recruits. Standing, he hesitated then shrugged. "You are still a woman, and women are many things, but they are not Warriors. Not fighters. That goes against all that the Goddess has taught us."

Iliana trembled at the comment and wished she could stop the shaking. He might misunderstand and see girlish behavior when that was not the cause of her quivering.

It was not weakness that made her tremble. It was anger. "There is nothing in her teachings that says a woman cannot be trained as a Warrior."

"True, but—" Something behind her caught Lore's attention, and he stopped mid-sentence. Excusing himself with a nod, he walked past her. She followed.

He stopped in front of two recruits. Hot and sweaty in their padded shirts, they were overripe.

Lore shook his head at the youngest. "Adrik, you must hold the sword with a gentle, yet firm, grip. Like you hold a woman."

"Like a woman? Is that what you teach your students?" Iliana rolled her eyes. Leave it to Lore to equate a sword with the female form.

Lore glanced over his shoulder at her, his eyes crinkled. "I seek concepts that interest them."

Iliana could only manage a snort of disgust.

Lore turned back to his student. "Remember, this is not just a weapon. In battle, it might be your savior."

The young man hefted the instrument in his hand, confusion on his face. "Master Lore, it is wooden."

Lore laughed. A great, deep chuckle that Iliana envied.

He clapped the young man on the back. "So it is, but if I gave you a real one you would hack poor Seth to pieces." Taking the training weapon, Lore demonstrated how to hold it. "Do you see?" He flipped the sword around in a circle. Once. Twice. Despite its woodenness, it buzzed through the air. "Light enough to give movement. Firm enough as to keep control. Like the current of water as it holds a leaf in its grasp."

Adrik sighed. "I shall try."

Lore handed the training weapon back and motioned the two boys to continue.

Lore's back still to her, he stretched. His muscles strained the seams of his dark green tunic. The tiniest of smiles played on Iliana's lips. Despite her general feelings about men, he was pleasing to her eye. His thick, dark blond hair reached down between his shoulder blades and almost to his waist, where he held it tied back with a Warrior's leather cord.

With his broad shoulders, she saw why the girls of the village giggled like children when he walked past.

She moved to stand next to him and get a better view of the boys as they sparred.

Lore glanced down at her, and her breath caught in her throat. He might be handsome, but it was his eyes that held her attention. Not the blueness—although they were an amazing shade—but the depths she perceived in them. Depths she was sure she could swim in if she just let herself open up . . .

No. She shut the temptation down before it grew stronger.

Lore was a Warrior, an amazing swordsman, and a good teacher. That was all. Nothing more and nothing less.

The teaching skills mattered, not the shell that contained them.

He raised a brow. "You are still here."

Her smile died. "How observant of you."

Now both brows went up, and he grinned. "It is why I am the teacher."

She ignored his attempt at humor. It was always his first defense when he wanted to win an argument, and she would not let that happen. Not this time. "Then we can discuss my training?"

Lore shook his head again. "There is nothing to discuss. Warriors are fighters, and Trancers are not. If you take up the sword, it is doubtful you will ever regain your gift. We both know this." He reached out to touch her hair. Twined with a plain cord, it fell across her shoulder, just touching the top of her breast.

Instinctively, she flinched from him before he could touch the dark black strands.

With a shake of his head, Lore crossed his arms. "I will not be a party to such a loss."

Her abilities did not matter to her. Not any more. Once, she had considered them the gift Lore spoke of. The power to read the currents of the air, to touch minds and thoughts, was her life. What she was born and bred to do.

Now, she knew the darkness that was the twin to the good. Tasted it and was grateful she could not access it. "It is not your decision. It is mine."

Lore closed the gap between them. "You are being selfish. We have only Aria to read the currents, and with the impending birth of her daughter, we shall need your skills more than ever."

It was true. With the Mistress of the Keep hindered by her pregnancy, there were no other Trancers to watch for signs of trouble or help the sick.

Except her, and she was useless. "Skills?" Iliana mocked. "What skills?"

Lore frowned. "You helped Aria with Tarik's birth. I know she hopes, we all hope, your Talent will return if you are able to help with Roam."

She shook her head. Her short braid whipped her cheeks. She would not take the chance. Not with Aria and certainly not with a babe. She still remembered what had happened the last time she tried to force her skills to wake. Luckily, the sick child felt nothing, but she had ended up screaming with pain until she passed out. Next time, she feared that neither the patient nor herself would be so fortunate.

"Do you not remember what happened before?" She reminded Lore.

"It was an accident. Your first try at Trancing since . . ." he hesitated.

She both appreciated and loathed his hesitation. No one liked to speak of Mako and all he had done, but ignoring what had happened would not make it less real. She prompted Lore to continue. "Finish your sentence. Go on, speak it."

He looked her directly in the eye, his expression soft. "Since we rescued you from Mako."

It was truth but not the crux of her problem. "You mean since Mako kidnapped me and tried to make me his woman."

Lore's face reddened. "Now is neither the time nor the place to speak of such things."

"Tell me, Lore, where and when shall we speak of my kidnapping?"

Lore's lips curved downward. "Why speak of this at all? It is over and done, and you are safe."

He did not understand. No one could. "I will never be safe. I will not even be able to walk the streets alone, not until I can take care of myself."

"By taking care of yourself you mean gaining the ability to kill."

She hesitated, and then she tilted her head up a notch so she could meet his eyes. As tall as she was, he was much taller. "If it comes to that, yes."

He uncrossed his arms and stared at her. Hard. "You are not a killer, Iliana, and even I cannot teach that. Nor would I want to. I train boys to grow with honor. To defend. To protect. I do not train them to kill without reluctance or regard, which is what you are asking." His jaw tightened. "If you do not know that, then you are not ready to be trained—even if you were a man."

Turning on his heel, he walked across to the other side of the large courtyard where two more boys went at each other with long, blunt-tipped spears.

Iliana let the wooden sword drop from her hand. It landed with a thud, raising a small cloud of dust around her feet. She touched her face, praying that her anger and embarrassment did not show. The heat of her cheeks told her otherwise.

She blinked. Once. Twice. Then she brushed back the tears that threatened.

A bell sounded, signaling the end to the training and the beginning of the midday meal. Training weapons still in hand, the boys filed past her and towards the great hall.

They were so young. So eager.

And like her attackers and Lore and everyone who thought they knew her, they were unaware of what she truly was. Blind to the darkness that burned in her heart and threatened to consume her and everyone she loved.

***

"I hear Iliana asked to be trained as a Warrior."

It was early evening, and heavy cloth covered the windows, keeping the evening chill at bay.

Oil lanterns lit the great dining hall and all Warriors—from Apprentice to the Blooded—were gathered at the long table, enjoying the final meal of the day.

"Yes." Lore had hoped to keep her request silent, but it was not a surprise Talon knew. As Lord of the Keep, he seemed aware of everything—even when Lore would prefer otherwise.

Focused on their meal and bragging about the day's sparring, the other Warriors ignored the conversation.

"What did you tell her?"

Lore broke off a chunk of bread from the loaf between them. "I refused, of course."

"How did she take it?"

"She was . . . unhappy . . . with the decision."

Talon chuckled at the comment. "I am guessing she was more than unhappy."

Lore shrugged. "I understand her desire and might even accommodate it under different circumstances, but not now. Not while she is ruled by anger." He broke off another piece of bread. "I will not give her a weapon to give her anger form."

"You are right in your assessment, Master Lore."

Lore turned to see a pregnant Aria waddling towards him and Talon. Her hair, a mass of bright red curls, fell to her waist, and her skin glowed. Even close to giving birth, she was a great beauty—if not more so.

Taking a seat on the bench across from Lore and to Talon's right, the Mistress of the Keep continued, "But that will not make it any easier for her to understand."

"If she could get past her anger . . ."

"If she could, she would not want to train as a Warrior. She would be happy to pursue the skills the Goddess gifted her with."

Lore picked up his goblet and raised it. "Point taken."

Aria smiled at his agreement and began her meal.

A young girl walked into the room with Tarik, Talon and Aria's son. Barely walking, he struggled in the girl's arms. She put him down, and he toddled over to his father, arms outstretched. Smiling, Talon whooshed the child into the air and onto his lap. One hand tickling his son, Talon's other hand reached out to touch his wife's rounded belly, rubbing it like a talisman.

Despite the sliver of jealousy that pricked his thoughts, Lore could not help smiling. It would be wonderful to have what they did. Talon and Aria's love was the kind bards sang about, and one he did not see for himself.

Unlike Talon, he was raised from infancy as a Warrior. With that lifetime of training came obligations and tradition.

Duty.

With a sigh, Lore set the goblet down. Following Talon was a breach of tradition, and if he had not owed Talon a life debt, he sometimes wondered if he might have stayed behind.

Now, seeing his best friend happy with his mate, Lore knew he had done the right thing.

"Hello, Lore."

Lore looked up to see Iliana standing next to him. With a scowl on her lips and a flick of her braided hair, she rounded the table behind Talon and took her seat next to Aria, nodding acknowledgment.

Tarik held his arms out. "Nana. Nana."

Iliana smiled and held out her arms to take the toddler onto her lap.

The little boy kissed her on the cheek. A wet, sloppy toddler's kiss. Iliana touched it with gloved fingers. Her lips curved upwards, the pain fell from her face, and her eyes sparkled. For a moment, Lore was sure this was what she must have been like before Mako.

"You are good with him, Iliana." He could not take his eyes off the tableau. "You will be a good mother one day, Goddess permitting."

"Perhaps." Iliana's smile died as suddenly as it had appeared. "I would rather train to be a Warrior."

The girl was as stubborn as a *rohha*. "Now is not the time."

"You seem to say that a lot." Taking a moment to untangle Tarik's chubby fingers from her hair, Iliana turned to Aria. "Talk to him." She glared back at Lore. "Make him understand."

Aria shook her head. "He is the Warrior trainer. For me to command his compliance would not only be overstepping my role, but it could be dangerous." She shifted in her seat. "If he has denied you training, you might want to listen to the reasons."

"I know his reasons. He is bound by his upbringing and is unable to see me as anything more than a Trancer or a breeder of small children."

Color flooded Aria's cheeks.

Lore leapt to his feet. How dare she speak such words to her friend and Mistress of the Keep?

The very pregnant Mistress.

He leaned across the table. "I am bound by nothing other than good judgment. You, however, have a sharp tongue that you would—"

Talon cut him off, his voice harsh. "Iliana, you would slight Aria, after all she did for you?"

"Enough." Aria silenced her husband with the single word and focused her gaze on Lore.

Both men sat back down. Lore took a deep, cleansing breath, briefly wishing Iliana were one of his students. If she were, she would be running the sticks by now.

Thoughts of her walking the rungs over a pit of mucky water made him smile. A vision of her falling in made him grin.

"Are children such a bad thing?" Aria's question interrupted his brief but pleasant daydream. He watched for Iliana's response.

The Mistress of the Keep waited for her friend to reply, her hands resting on her pronounced belly.

Iliana reddened. "No. I have nothing against children. I love Tarik. You know that."

"I do. I understand much about you."

"Then let me train."

Aria managed to offer a sad smile. "It is not my decision to make."

Iliana opened her mouth and then snapped it shut again. Lore knew this was not the end of the conversation. Not by far. The dark-haired Trancer was nothing if not tenacious, but tenacity bordered on obstinacy when it came to this topic. He rose. "Iliana, I would speak with you. Outside."

Iliana glared at him, her cheeks still flushed. Deliberately, she handed Tarik back to Aria and picked up a wedge of fruit. "After I am finished eating."

The table grew silent.

Lore reminded himself that she was wounded. Emotionally scarred by her ordeal and either unwilling or unable to heal herself.

The reminder did not diminish the urge to yank her from her seat and drag her outside.

The silence deepened as all waited to see how he would

react.

To show anger at Iliana's defiance and react to that anger would only lessen him in the eyes of his charges.

And rightly so.

He also trained his Apprentices to command any situation. Any of them would be dragged from the hall for showing such disrespect. She wanted to be an Apprentice? He would show her the reality of such training.

Pushing back from the table, Lore walked around the end, past Talon and Aria, to where Iliana sat.

Keeping his voice even, he stopped behind her. "We will have this conversation now, or not at all."

She did not acknowledge him but picked up her goblet.

He grabbed her by the scruff of her collar and yanked her to her feet. The goblet flew from her hands.

She flailed at him, fists flying.

Holding the shrieking Trancer at arm's length, he neither hurried nor slowed down as he made his way out of the dining area, dragging Iliana behind him.

Screeching in anger, she stumbled backwards, trying to keep up. "Let go of me!"

Her shriek went up a notch as she ran into a chair.

Lore gritted his teeth and held on to her collar, hoping the cloth held. If not, he would throw her over his shoulder, but one way or another, she would learn manners.

Slamming the door open, Lore dragged Iliana into the hall, slammed the door shut and tossed her towards the far wall.

She came at him, teeth bared and fists flying. "You big, overgrown barach. You did not have to embarrass me in front of the others."

He grabbed her hands and pulled her close to keep her still. "I could say the same."

She struggled, trying to push away from him.

He let her go, knowing how she hated to be touched.

She glared at him but did not leave.

He waited. Silent.

Finally, she managed a curt nod. "Agreed."

She had the graciousness to admit fault? It was a step forward and one that surprised him. "Iliana, I have told you my reason for not training you. I am reluctant to train a woman much less a Trancer, but those are not the main issues, as you well know."

Her arms clasped around herself, the anger in her eyes began to fade. "Teach me duty. Teach me honor. Teach me to be as you."

He shook his head. Duty and honor could not be taught. One either carried the potential or one did not. There was little gray in that area. As for Iliana, she would have to find them on her own.

"Why not?"

Her voice caught on the question. A tiny catch that he was sure hid a deeper pain. The male part of him roared to life, wanting to soothe her hurt, wanting to take her in his arms and stroke away her sorrow.

The Trainer half denied him. Hurt or not, beautiful or not, he could not help her if she refused to help herself.

"Iliana, I wish—"

The sound of approaching footsteps stopped Lore before he finished. This was not a conversation for others.

A boy, on the brink of manhood, strode toward them. A Warrior, acting as guard, followed.

Lore put Iliana behind him. A hand on the dagger at his waist, he motioned the Guard to hold while he met the stranger. "Who are you?"

The boy dropped to his knee. "I am here to see Lord Talon. I bring news."

"Of what?"

"Medea."

Two

"I know as much about Medea as you do, Talon. You cannot leave me out of this conversation." Iliana shoved her leather-clad foot between the wooden door and its jamb to keep it from closing.

She neither missed the annoyance that flared in his eyes nor blamed him the hesitation as she waited. He knew Medea, and he knew her. She was sure that Aria had told him enough to make him wonder if it was wise to mix the two.

Would he deny her entry? It flashed through her mind that it might be better if he did.

Beyond him, she spied Lore. Arms crossed, his face was expressionless as he leaned against the wall, waiting. He would deny her entry if it was left to him, of that she was certain.

Perhaps he was wiser than she thought.

With a growl, Talon opened the door. "You may listen but no more. A word and you will leave."

Iliana slid in before Talon changed his mind or her feet decided otherwise and took her back down the hall and to her solitary room.

Avoiding Lore's heavy gaze, she made her way past a low table. What am I doing here? She should listen to her feet and run. Run far and fast, before Medea's evil brand of insanity spilled over onto her—again.

Instead, she took a seat by the fireplace, shuddering despite the heat that beat against her cheeks.

The door slammed shut.

Taking a moment, Talon escorted the pregnant Aria over to the couch across from Iliana, settling her with a gentle hand.

When he straightened, all gentleness was gone, and in its place was a hardened Warrior.

Hands clasped behind his back, Talon nodded towards the young messenger. "Benn has information. Part of it he has already told me. There is an artifact, an Orb, with great power. Medea seeks to obtain it."

So much for an introduction or niceties.

For a brief moment, passionate anger cracked the stoicism of Talon's expression. "Whatever this Orb is, we must keep it from her."

Or for listening to the entire problem before making a

decision.

"Do we know if this Orb is a true threat and that Benn brings us correct information?"

Iliana turned towards Lore's voice. He still leaned against the far wall, but the nonchalance he displayed was far from real. The tenseness of his jaw and stiffness of his shoulders were obvious, even in the dimness of the shadows.

And his tone. It sounded deeper. Darker. Far different from his usual teasing self.

An icy chill made its way through her body. In her head, she knew that Lore was capable of great darkness.

Now she knew it in her heart as well.

The Warrior Trainer pushed away from the stone and walked towards Talon. "Perhaps she let slip the information, knowing that it would make its way to you."

He stopped in front of the messenger.

Benn stared at his feet.

Taking a moment to look the boy up and down, Lore's eyes narrowed. "Or, perhaps Benn works with Medea, and this is just one of her twisted games."

"I . . . I would never bring you false information."

"Not knowingly, perhaps," Lore countered.

"My brother is your Apprentice, Baine. I, too, would train with you one day. I bring you the truth." Benn's voice cracked. "That is all. The truth."

He took a step towards Lore, and Iliana bit her tongue to keep from speaking. It was unkind to push the boy. He looked either ready to cry or go at Lore with clenched fists.

"Be calm." Talon held up his palm, silencing both Lore and Benn before the heated conversation escalated into a brawl.

Iliana settled into her seat, glad to find that control reigned once again.

Talon motioned the boy to come to him. "I am going to have my mate see if you speak the truth. Do you submit?"

"See?"

The tremble in the lad's voice was obvious.

So obvious that even Lore softened. "She is a Trancer, Benn. Talon's mate. Surely, you know of her."

The boy nodded and glanced towards the women.

With a broad smile, Aria held her hand out to the young messenger. "It will not hurt. I promise."

Benn shuffled over to them. Iliana noticed that he cast a

wary eye her way as he passed. Hesitating, he settled next to Aria.

Across from her, Aria laid a hand on Benn's shoulder, took a deep breath, and shut her eyes. Though Iliana could no longer surf the currents, she knew the precise moment Aria stepped from reality and into the shifting light that surrounded all living things.

She knew it, and she envied it. Envied Aria's utter control of her talent. Envied her power.

Most of all, she envied her faith. When Aria used her talent, there was no doubt that what she did was right.

A few heartbeats later, Aria blinked and returned. "He speaks the truth."

The boy expelled a noisy breath and grinned as if to say he had told them so.

Talon nodded. "There is no question. We must obtain the Orb before Medea."

Iliana did not know it was possible for their Lord and Leader to look more serious, but he did.

"Talon, we do not even know what this Orb does," Lore argued. "Perhaps it is but a bauble the witch uses to taunt us and drive us to action."

Iliana bit back a retort. Medea did nothing without purpose. Lore understood many things, but not this. She took a deep breath, forcing herself to remain both calm and silent. Knowing that any other action would get her tossed from the room.

"If Medea searches for it, rest assured it is lethal in some fashion," Talon countered.

Iliana let her shoulders drop in relief. Lore might be unaware of the danger, but Talon was not.

"Benn," Talon continued. "You are from this region, tell us of this Orb."

"I only know the legend. Rumors."

"It will have to be enough," Talon replied. "Continue."

"There is not much to tell. It is said the Orb was created by the Goddess to serve the world, but an evil man, Dalis, took it and used it for harm. People died. Many people." He sank into the cushion, as if seeking shelter from a great malevolence.

Aria patted the boy's shoulder in assurance. Benn relaxed. Again, a thread of envy shot through Iliana. If she did the same, there was no doubt that her touch would do anything but relax the boy. On the contrary, he would be more likely to shoot out of his seat and run away.

Benn continued. "Dalis proclaimed himself a god. It was a bitter time."

"What happened? How was the Orb taken from him and hidden?" Talon asked.

"It is said that many tried to wrest the Orb from Dalis. It is also said that many died. In the end, it was a Trancer that undid him." The boy cast a shy, admiring glance towards Aria.

"How?" Talon asked.

"She called upon the Goddess and begged her assistance. The Goddess listened. Upon seeing her creation misused, the Goddess killed Dalis, banished his spirit to the dark, and reclaimed her Orb."

"Interesting." Talon tapped a thumb against his chin as he thought. "What makes Medea think she can take the Orb from the Goddess?"

"The Orb is perfect and eternal. In her wisdom, the Goddess made it possible for the Orb to be returned to the realm of man, but only if one was worthy enough to win it."

Talon nodded. "How does one win it?"

"The Season of Renewal will pass a hundred times and a portal will open. Therein lay the trials. Pass them all and the final door is revealed. The Orb rests within, ready to do man's bidding once again."

Iliana bit her tongue—again. The legend sounded like every other tale. Trials. Great danger. Probably death.

In other words, a quest that only the brave or foolhardy would undertake.

"How does one find this portal?" Talon asked.

"I am not sure. I was told it was in the Field of Sceton, where the Goddess took the Orb back, but I know of no one who has ever seen the portal."

Talon frowned, and Iliana knew he was losing what little patience he carried. "Benn, what can you tell us about the tests?"

The messenger shrugged. "A childhood rhyme, nothing more."

"Recite it."

"The elements of my land arrive to take you to the other side. My breath. My bones. My blood. My beating heart.

Talon gave a single nod. "Anything else?"

"Legend says that the first portal opens with the moon and closes with the sun."

"And?" Talon prompted.

"No one has ever passed the first trial. They all died."

***

Benn left, after offering a Warrior's vow of silence.

The tension in the room did not leave with him. If anything, it grew larger. Stronger. It loomed over the small group like a blackened sky.

Lore saw it in the way Aria rubbed a pinch of her skirt between her thumb and forefinger.

And in Iliana's silence. As if at a loss for words, the dark-haired beauty stared into the flames, neither blinking nor speaking.

She barely breathed.

Opposite of Iliana, Talon paced—long, slow deliberate steps that took him from one side of the small room to the other.

Lore waited. Training his students had taught him much, but the biggest lesson was patience.

Finally, Talon stopped his restless walk, but the tension still showed in the way his right hand flexed, as if ready to pull a blade. "Lore. What do you think of this story?"

Lore wished he could lie, but as Talon's friend and tactician, he could do nothing other than give a truthful answer. "Benn thinks he speaks truth, but his words are born of legend and fear. We have no physical proof that the Orb exists."

Talon frowned but nodded for Lore to continue.

"We all believed in spirits under the bed when we were young, and then we grew up to find they were phantoms of our imagination. This might be much the same. A phantom. A story handed down to scare would-be warlords into submission. A fable to teach a lesson about ultimate power. A legend."

"All legends have a basis in truth," Aria countered.

"True," Lore agreed. "But rushing in to claim this legend might be more a fool's journey that will get Warriors killed. Is it not better to watch Medea? Let her run this errand. If she manages to find and gain the Orb, we can take it from her before she does any harm. Tactically, this is the best choice."

"It would, if this were a normal battle."

The comment was whispered, barely heard, but it was there. Iliana?

Still sitting by the fire, she seemed calm. Or was it numb? It was difficult to tell in the shifting light of the flames.

But the flames could not hide the drumming of her fingers

or the way her body hunched into itself.

She continued, her voice almost inaudible above the hissing and crackling of the wood, "This is a battle with Medea, Lore. Not an army. Medea is not a man or a clan that fights with honor and blood. She is a Reaper. A witch who would rule the world. She fights with convenience. With subterfuge and lies."

Iliana sighed, a heavy sound. "If the Orb is as powerful as told, would we be able to wrest it from her grasp?"

She was convincing, but it was not her words. It was the slump of her shoulders, like one who bore a burden too heavy to lift. Her knowledge and pain caught Lore's attention.

He was sure it caught Talon's attention as well—not that his friend needed any more convincing.

Talon cleared his throat. Lore knew the decision was made.

"Iliana is right." Talon glanced towards the young Trancer.

She continued to stare into the flames, neither acknowledging Talon nor his agreement with her.

He continued. "We cannot take chances. Not when it comes to Medea. She is evil. Make no mistake about that. If there is any possibility that this Orb exists and will give her power, she must not be allowed to obtain it."

Lore did not agree, but it was not his place to second-guess. Once Talon's decision was made, he would support it. He was the Destro. Talon's right hand and blade. The one who would do what Talon, as Lord of the Keep, could not.

In this case, it was going on an impossible quest that would probably get him killed.

Lore nodded acceptance. "As is your wish. I will leave tomorrow."

Talon frowned. "My wish is that you will stay here. I will be the one to stop her."

Lore shook his head. "I know you consider it your duty to stop Medea, but I respectfully say it is no longer your place to do so."

Talon moved to argue, and Lore held up his hand. "Please, let me finish."

With a growl, Talon clamped his jaw shut and gave an abrupt nod.

Lore managed to repress his smile. It was unusual for Talon to let anyone, besides his mate, argue with him. He continued. "You sacrificed the right to quest when you took over the Keep and pledged the safety of its inhabitants and the town of Mardid.

You have a duty here. It cannot be ignored because you want to settle an old score."

"It is more than an old score. Much more."

Lore shrugged. There would be no arguing Talon's point. "Perhaps, but that does not change the outcome. The recruits are new. They need you here."

"You are their trainer. They will follow your lead."

"No, they will not." Lore stepped forward. Face-to-face and foot-to-foot with Talon, he knew he must make his friend understand. "I would give my life for you. My blade is yours, but I more than a friend. I am your advisor. As advisor, I remind you that you are now Protector to many people, and Protectors do not leave their charges."

Meeting Talon's hard gaze, Lore spoke with deliberate slowness, punctuating each word. "I am their teacher. You are their leader."

Talon did not blink. "They are Warriors. They will understand the need for me to pursue this quest."

Lore fumed in frustration. "You listen but do not hear my words. At this rate, I will have to truss you up like a bird before you do something foolish."

"You are welcome to try," Talon snarled.

"Talon."

Both men turned towards Aria.

"Lore is correct. You cannot go." Pale, even in the firelight, the Keep's Mistress held a delicate hand out to her mate. Aria rarely stepped in to counter Talon's decision, but when she did, her decision was the one that won.

Talon took Aria's hand in his and sat next to her, wrapping her in his arms. "If you are worried about the babe, do not. I will be back before she is born. I promise." He laid his other hand on her stomach. "I missed Tarik's birth. I will not miss Roam's."

Iliana glanced at the couple then away.

Her glance caught Lore's attention, and as quick as it was, it was enough.

Enough time for Lore to notice the longing in her eyes before she looked down at her gloved hands.

How long had it been since a man touched her in such a way? Palm to palm. Skin to skin. The kiss of a lover. The simple gestures that reached inside and caressed the soul.

"That is not where my concern lies." Aria laid her hand

over Talon's. Lore turned back to the conversation.

Talon stroked her cheek. Aria leaned into his touch, even as she spoke. "The Warriors here are young. They may not look to you for training, but they look to you for example."

"Which is why I must go."

"No, it is why you must stay." She kissed Talon's palm. "To show them that they must sacrifice their own desires for the benefit of all."

She made sense. Spoke the words Lore said, yet said them where Talon would listen.

The fire hissed as all waited.

With a sigh, Talon leaned back into the cushions, drawing Aria's head to rest on his shoulder. "As always, you are right."

"Not, as always, but mostly." She grinned and winked at Lore.

Lore returned the gesture. She was an amazing woman.

Talon took Aria's hand in his. He kissed her palm. "So, my mostly right mate, who shall we send?"

"Me," Lore answered.

Talon shook his head. "You are the Warrior Trainer. I am wont to lose my best teacher."

"And I am wont to lose a student or another Warrior on a fool's quest."

"You think this a fool's quest?" Talon asked.

Lore shrugged. "What I think matters not. What matters is that someone must go, and that someone is me. You know it as well as I."

***

"I tell you, if Iliana stays, she will get us all killed. Did you not hear about the fight in town yesterday?"

"She is the Mistress's best friend; you should not say such things."

Sitting sideways on the wide stone ledge of her window, hard stone against her back and pushing against her feet, Iliana listened to the two Warriors talking in the courtyard below her as they made their night rounds. Out of the corner of her eye, she saw that the two moons had peaked in the sky. It was late, and with the exception of herself and the two below, all were asleep within the Keep's wall.

"Where would you have her go? No one will take her. Besides, is it not our job to protect her?"

Thank you. She shut her eyes as she listened.

"She is a traitor and has been treated better than she deserves. It is not just myself that thinks so. Others feel the same way. Perit even went to Talon yesterday and told him of our concerns."

They went to Talon? Did they loathe her so much?

She knew the answer. Saw it in their eyes and the way they backed off when she walked past, but to hear it hurt more than she thought it would.

With a sigh, Iliana rubbed a hand over her gritty, tired eyes. She would go to bed to forget, but sleep rarely offered comfort anymore.

The creaking of her bedroom door caught her off guard. She tightened, but just for a moment. "Hello, Aria."

Her friend shut the door. "You are troubled. I felt you in my sleep."

Light footsteps and her friend stood beside her, both a comforting presence and a reminder of what she was not.

"I am sorry if I woke you. I would try to shield my thoughts, but . . ." she shrugged, knowing she did not need to explain to Aria.

"I do not mind. We are sisters bound by a friendship that has weathered death and destruction." She smiled. "Even your ill-temper. I would share your pain if you would let me. Ease your burden as you once eased mine."

It was a kind offer, but Iliana could not accept—even if she were able too. "No thank you."

Aria accepted the decline with a polite nod. Waddling to the bedside settee, she fell onto the small couch, settling into the overstuffed cushions and sighing with obvious pleasure. "You realize I will not be able to rise?"

A weak joke and an even weaker attempt at setting Iliana at ease. Iliana worried her bottom lip. Aria was here for a reason. She did not need Trancer senses to know that. She could take Lore's playing with her but not Aria. Not her best friend. "Aria, why do you play games? Speak your reasons for being here."

"You know why."

Iliana swung her legs around so they were in the room and jumped off the window ledge, landing on the floor with a thud. Her feet silent on the woolen rug, she walked to Aria and took a seat on the opposite end of the settee.

The words of the men came back. If she stayed, she would get them all killed. They had spoken to Talon.

Iliana blinked back the tears that threatened. Even without the Warriors sharp words, she had known that this moment would come. The moment when Aria would ask her to leave.

No one was safe while she lived with them, and that included Aria and her children.

Now, with Medea's return, the Trancer witch would be out to kill Iliana and all she loved. To keep Aria and her family safe, there was little choice but to leave. She knew this.

It seemed Aria knew it as well.

Still, the knowing did not ease the pain. Iliana ran a hand through her dark hair. "Yes, I know why."

Aria managed a weak smile. "I want this no more than you, but I cannot fathom another course. Can you?"

"No." Her head bowed, Iliana shut her eyes. She would not cry. Would not make this more difficult than it needed to be.

Patting the cushion next to her, Aria motioned Iliana to come closer.

Iliana denied her with a shake of her head. Aria only made this harder for both of them.

With a sigh of exasperation, Aria reached over and snatched Iliana's hand in hers.

Iliana flinched but did not pull away.

Aria laid Iliana's hand on her rounded belly. "She is much like you. Dark hair, blue eyes. Stubborn."

The baby kicked at her hand.

Aria continued. "She will also be born soon. You were there for Tarik's birth, and I would have you with me for Roam's." She let go of Iliana's hand. "But I imagine that even with you at his side, Lore will not complete the tests in time to see her enter this world."

Iliana pulled away, confused. "What are you talking about?"

Aria held up her hand. "Let me finish. I know you do not want this burden, but you and I both know that Lore cannot do this alone. A Trancer saved the world from the Orb once. It will be a Trancer who will do it again."

Confused, Iliana turned away, then back. "You are asking me to go with Lore on this quest? You are not asking me to leave because it is dangerous to have me around?"

"What?"

"You are not asking me to leave because my presence is dangerous to you and the children?"

Aria's cheeks turned pink and then pale. Her eyes widened

in shock. "How can you even think such a thing?"

Feeling both awkward and relieved, Iliana shrugged and manage a small, "I do not know."

Aria shook her head and wiped her eyes with the back of her hand. "I do not ask you to leave and never return. Quite the opposite. I expect you to find the Orb, have a grand adventure, and return to tell me all about it."

Despite it all, Aria was still her friend. Iliana sighed in relief. There was little in life she wanted, but Aria's friendship was at the top of her mental list.

But to go on a quest? "I appreciate the faith you have in me, but I think it is misplaced. I cannot do as you ask."

Aria shook her head, bright red curls falling about her shoulders. "Yes, you can. Once, I asked you to save my son. You did. Our Tower fell to the Reapers, but you did as I asked, and in doing so, you saved both me and Talon."

Iliana shut her eyes. If Aria knew the truth, she would not be so quick to praise her.

Aria continued. "Now, I have another favor to request. Do the same for Tarik's sister. Do not let her be born into a world where Medea rules."

Iliana heard the fear in her voice. Terror that Roam would not just be born into a world under Medea's rule, but that her daughter would die in it as well.

"Please," Iliana whispered. "Do not ask this of me." She could not do this. With no powers, she would fail them all. Fail her friend.

"I have no one else. The nearest Trancer is four suns ride, and Lore must leave before then." She met Iliana's gaze.

Iliana scooted away. "Lore will not let me travel with him. You may be blind to his opinion, but I am not."

"Leave him to me. Once he understands there is no other way to obtain the Orb, he will cooperate."

Iliana's heart pounded in her chest. Aria made it sound so easy. So acceptable.

It was not. It was not just the Orb. It was Lore.. To spend time alone with him both excited her and made her queasy. "Please do not ask this of me. Find another."

"There is no other." Aria squeezed her hand. "You are our last hope."

Iliana swallowed hard. They were doomed.

Three

Iliana kneeled at Medea's feet, trembling. Sweating. Waiting to find out what the Dark Queen would do to her.

Using her foot, Medea tilted Iliana's chin up.

With the orb in her possession, the once simply beautiful Reaper witch now possessed a terrible splendor. She smiled. A dark grin that chilled Iliana's blood. "You thought you would destroy me?"

Iliana shook her head. Behind her, a baby cried out. Roam.

"Do not lie to me, Trancer whore." Medea took her foot away.

Iliana let her head drop back down. The carpet was rough against her forehead. Itchy. She dared not scratch.

Medea continued. "I know what you tried to do. Tried to do and was as unsuccessful as you have always been."

Silence and then footsteps approached and stopped. Turning her head, Iliana saw the owner stood next to her.

She recognized the boots. Dark brown leather. Plain with the exception of a strap that held a throwing knife.

Lore.

The baby cried out again.

"Shut that brat up," Medea barked.

The sharp swish of steel sliced the air. The cry cut off.

Oh Goddess, Roam! Iliana's stomach dropped. She had failed worse than she thought. Lore was her last hope. He was close enough that if he tried, he might snap Medea's neck and free them all.

"Look at me, Trancer."

Not sure if it was her fear compelling her to obey or the power of the Orb, Iliana raised her face.

"Lore, come stand beside me."

Perfect. Here was his chance.

"Aww, little Trancer, I bet you thought this Warrior might save you." Medea pouted, but her expression was anything but disappointed.

Her eyes never leaving Iliana, Medea caressed Lore. Her delicate hand sought a path up the front of his shirt. One quick motion and she ripped the pale cloth, exposing his chest.

With a sly smile, Medea let her fingers follow a path from Lore's chest, down to his navel, and to the top of his leather breeches. Still grinning at Iliana, she let her fingertips skirt the edges.

Iliana swallowed. Why did he not kill her?

It was then that she noticed the vacancy in his eyes. The slackness of his jaw. This was Lore's body.

Lore was gone.

Eyes still on Iliana, Medea tugged at the front of Lore's breeches, drawing him closer. "Kiss me," she commanded.

His hand buried in the Queen's dark hair, Lore bent down and pressed his mouth against Medea's.

No. No. No. Iliana pressed her forehead onto the carpet to shut out the awful sight.

"Look at me, whore. Look at me now!"

Medea's command sounded like thunder and was as undeniable.

Hot tears burned Iliana's cheeks. How could she have let this happen? Let Medea get the Orb?

Choking on her fear, Iliana raised her head.

It was no longer Medea who sat on the throne.

It was herself.

With a cry, Iliana bolted upright. Her heart pounded. Her face was damp with sweat. She wanted to throw up.

Her nightshirt in a tangle about her waist, she took a great, heaving breath, gasping until the queasiness faded.

It was a dream. A sick, sordid nightmare brought on by her earlier talk with Aria. She swung her legs over the side of the bed and lit the oil lamp that rested on the floor next to her bed. Elbows on her knees, she cupped her face in her hands and tried to block out the horrible vision. She was not the Dark Queen. Would not become her.

It served her right for giving Medea power over her. She might pretend to the others that she was able to handle the witch, but she knew in her heart she could not.

Even if she could use her powers to kill Medea, what kind of choice was that? Any Trancer who killed with her thoughts joined her victim in death.

She did not want to die. She wanted to be free of Medea. Her past.

Herself.

The bedroom door slammed open.

Iliana jumped and pulled her bed covers around herself at the same time.

Lore.

He barged into the room. His feet and chest bare, his attire but a blanket with one end tucked around his waist to hold it on.

A drawn sword was in his left hand.

In seconds, he was at her side, his weapon raised and ready to defend her.

He glanced around the room. With a snort of disgust, he lowered the weapon. "There is no one here."

Iliana took a deep breath. She should be angry. Most likely, her door was broken from being kicked in, Lore was barely dressed, and he waved his sword like a mad man.

But anger was a poor relation to the interest, the desire, which pounded through her veins. Lore was almost naked, and she had never seen him so. His body sculpted. Muscles bunched and stretched as he raised his weapon again and took one more hard look at his surroundings.

If she reached out, she might touch him. Feel him. Just a little bit . . .

Lore turned towards her.

She snatched her hand back.

"What are you doing?" He grinned down at her. His sword settled on his shoulder, the flat against his skin.

"Nothing." Iliana took a deep, shuddering breath. She had heard of this strange desire before. After a battle or a great fright, the body reacted with passion.

Another breath and the heat in her skin began to subside.

"Are you sure? I thought I saw you reaching towards me." He raised a blond brow. "Maybe you like what you see."

Iliana glared at him through narrow eyes. He knew. He knew her blood pounded. He knew she felt a desire brought on by fear.

He knew, and he teased her.

Snatching a pillow from the bed, she lobbed the cushion at his head. "Get out."

He caught it and tossed it back, hitting her.

She held the pillow up again, taking aim.

"Can you two ever play nicely?" Talon stood in the doorway. Dressed much like Lore and with sword in hand, he glared at them.

"Talon." Lore saluted him with his weapon. "Iliana apologizes for waking you."

"I do not need you to apologize for me." Iliana pulled the covers up around her, suddenly aware of her own state of half-dress.

Lore continued. "I will investigate the problem, but be assured there are no attackers."

"Dreams?"

Talon sounded angry.

Lore shrugged. "I will let you know, if that is your wish."

If it were possible, Talon looked more annoyed. "My wish is to go back to sleep beside my mate."

"Then go." Lore waved him on. "And shut the door behind you. I have no desire to wake the rest of the Keep."

The door slammed shut.

She would kill them both. Flay them alive and leave their hearts for the *katah's* to feast upon.

"How dare you." She scooted backwards until her back rested against the headboard.

Lore sat down at the foot of her bed. The stuffing shifted with his weight. "Would you like to tell me what this dream was about?"

"How do you know it was a dream? Maybe my lover was here and climbed out the window as you came in," Iliana shot back.

"I can recognize a cry of fright from a cry of pleasure, Iliana. Besides, if he climbed out the window I would have heard another shout—the one as he fell to his death." Lore chuckled. "If you wish to goad me in to anger you will have to do better."

Heat fanned Iliana's cheeks. She turned away. He was right—at least about that.

"So tell me, what was so horrible that you cried out in your sleep?"

Iliana replied with a shrug. Did he think she would confide in him? Tell him her thoughts? If she did, there was little doubt that he would use it to tease her with later.

"You are a strong woman. It must have been something horrible to make you call out my name."

He thought she was strong? She smiled, but just for an instant, as she realized the rest of his comment.

She had called out his name?

***

"I called for you?"

"Uh huh." Lore grinned.

Iliana winced. Why could she not have called out for someone else? Anyone else. "Maybe you misheard," she suggested, desperate.

Smiling his "You are not going to slip out of this that easily" smile, the Warrior trainer laid his sword on the covers between them. "I know my name. Besides, if it was not my name, what was it?"

Iliana worried her lower lip. Any other man, any other Warrior, would understand that she did not want to discuss such a subject and would have dropped it by now, but not Lore. No. Instead, he seemed compelled to torture her.

She seemed compelled to reply, even as the rational part of her mind told her to shut up and make him leave. "Anything. Chore. Gore. More. Anything."

"I doubt it was chore unless your nightmare involved cleaning the stable." He chuckled. "Gore? Maybe."

The sword still between them, he leaned forward until their lips were inches apart. His breath was warm against her mouth. His scent musky. She knew she should lean back, retreat from his heat.

She froze.

He leaned still closer. So near, that his lips were but a taste away. "Now, *more*. That holds promise. Promise that leads back to me whether you called my name or not."

Desire died. She would kill him for this. She would honest-to-Goddess take that sword and lop off his head. Or maybe just the parts he implied. "I think not, Master Lore. *More* might lead to many things, but it will never lead to you."

The retort failed. She knew it even as it left her lips. With her angry reply and verbal riposte, she had given him the battle.

Lore leaned back, setting space between them again. With a sigh, he ran a hand over his hair. "Iliana, I tease you, but understand that beneath the jest, I am serious. You called for me. Now tell me why."

Was he mad? Did he think he could take verbal jabs at her and when finished, continue onwards with a sane conversation? "I had a bad dream. Nothing more. Perhaps I called for you, but do not place too much importance on it or yourself."

"I am your Protector. The importance is not on me. It is on you."

"My Protector?" Lips tight, Iliana wondered if she could push Lore off her bed. He was close to the edge. "I neither asked for nor want your protection."

"You need it."

"If you trained me, I would not."

"We have already discussed this," Lore replied with a groan.

"True, but that does not mean we cannot discuss it again."

She started ticking her complaints off on her fingers. "You act as if protecting me is your sole purpose. If I take a walk, I know you are not far behind. You sit near me at meals. I heard you punished an Apprentice for speaking ill of me. You follow me when I go into town."

"I saved you from a mauling."

Iliana continued as if she had not heard him. "Now you barge into my room and want to discuss my sleeping habits." She crossed her arms. "Know this, even in my dreams, I would fare better from being able to use a blade."

Lore crossed his arms as well. "You are missing my point. I did not come here to debate the issue of your training. I came here because I thought you were in danger. I came to help."

"Now I ask you to leave." She glared at him. Defiant. She did not need him.

Taking his sword in hand, Lore leapt off her bed and made for the door, mumbling as he stalked away.

Did he always have to have the last word? "If you have something to tell me, Master Lore, speak."

Turning on his heel, he glared at her. "I said that going after the Orb would be a relief from arguing with you."

"It will also be your death."

"Perhaps, but Aria, Talon, our world—even you—are at stake. I hoped to ease your fears before I left, but I now know that any compassion or caring where you are concerned is a mistake."

Lore flung up a hand in mock defeat and stalked away. "I am going to bed. If you have another bad dream, do me a courtesy and do not call my name, as you have made it clear I am the last person from whom you would seek help."

She could not let him leave. She did not need him, but he needed her—whether he believed her or not.

Whether she liked it or not.

"Lore."

"What."

She hated this. Not the arguing but the guilt. By the Goddess, sometimes she wished she was more like Medea. If she were, she could walk away without looking back. Without caring about Lore or Tarik or Aria or anyone.

She did care, even if she did not want to. That was what the dream was about.

With a sigh, Iliana got out of bed and walked over to where Lore waited at her door. "If you leave tomorrow, you will fail."

Lore put a firm hand on the door handle. "Thank you for your concern, but that will not happen."

"Yes, it will." Iliana pushed against the door, closing it. "I saw it."

"Was that what your dream was about? My failure?"

"Yes and no." She did not want to say this. Did not want the responsibility.

"What do you mean?"

There was no choice. The Goddess would not give her one, no matter how she tried to avoid her fate. "Yes, you failed, but it was because of me."

The look of shock on Lore's face almost made the guilt worth it.

***

"What do you mean, it was because of you?" Confused, Lore waited for her answer.

Iliana sighed. "What I mean is that you will not succeed in retrieving the Orb. Not without me."

So, that was what this was about. Iliana wanted to come with him. A bit of a shock, considering how much she claimed to loathe his presence, but not entirely unexpected. She was unhappy here.

Both the people of Mardid and the Keep's inhabitants might love Aria, but they did not know what to make of Iliana. She was a Trancer. Mako's captive. Perhaps his whore. Perhaps not.

No one knew the truth. Not even Aria.

What they did know was that when the great battle was fought and Mako fell, it was due to Aria and Talon. Aria might be a Trancer, but she had been willing to sacrifice her life for strangers.

When they looked at Iliana, they saw a Trancer who had had the exact same chance as Aria but had failed.

In their eyes, she was not just a coward, but a traitor as well.

He did not view her that way. He saw her as so much more. A survivor. Strong. Beautiful.

Even tender, when her guard was down.

Mainly, he saw a woman with emotional wounds that went all the way to the bone. Wounds that refused to heal. Wounds that were killing her, giving her a slow death.

Wounds that gave her a most un-Trancerlike temper.

Iliana continued. "Lore, you must listen to me. The key to passing the trials is not just in a Warrior's skill, but in a Trancer's ability to read the currents."

"What makes you say that?"

"Aria. I did not want to believe her, but—"

"The dream changed your mind," he said, finishing her sentence for her.

Iliana nodded. "I think—no, I know it was the Goddess telling me what I must do. I must go with you." She ran a hand over her sleep-tousled hair, pushing it away from her face. "Without a Trancer you will fail."

Lore frowned. This scenario felt wrong. Too convenient. "Why now? Why are you and Aria the first to figure this out? Why have not others come to the same conclusion and retrieved the Orb?" As much as he wanted to help her, accompanying him was not the way. This was not just a mission into unknown territory, but also a mission into magic. Her inexperience would only get them both killed. Her hostility might cause inadvertent harm to others or even failure of the quest.

Iliana shrugged. "I do not know. I only know I speak the truth."

To Iliana's credit, she did not appear to be self-satisfied at the revelation. On the contrary, she looked angry. Betrayed.

Lore scratched his chin. None of this made sense. If a Trancer was required, why go at all? Aria must realize this? "If what you say is true—"

"It is."

"Why take on the quest? Let Medea try for the Orb. She will fail, and we will be free of her."

Iliana shook her head. "My dream told me otherwise."

She shut her eyes as if in pain, but she continued, her voice a whisper as she related her thoughts. "I do not know how Medea succeeded in capturing the Orb. I do know that my vision was of the future. Or at least a possible future."

She opened her eyes, and for a brief moment, all her agony was as obvious and tangible as if he carried it in his own breast. Lore shuddered. How could she live with such sorrow?

Then, the pain was gone, replaced by her usual glare of anger. "It was a future that no one should experience. Least of all Medea."

He shook his head. Even with Aria's agreement, he could not take Iliana. She had had a dream. A nightmare brought on by word of Medea and Aria's well-intentioned interference. To give such a nightmare substance would not help her heal.

Iliana cocked her head and stared at him. "Are you saying no?"

"I cannot take you with me. It is too dangerous."

"I told you—"

"You told me of a dream." He wished she understood that a dream held only the power you gave it. "Not a reality."

"I told you of a vision."

"You cannot be sure."

She stomped her foot.

Lore held his tongue. Emotionally, she was a child. She did not react with the maturity of a Trancer but with the demonstrative turmoil of a girl barely out of maidenhood.

He could no more take her with him than he could one of his own Apprentices. The foot stomping solidified the decision in his mind.

He could not say the same about Iliana's.

"You will fail without me, Lore. You need a Trancer."

"I can get another Trancer. It does not have to be you. Please," he kept his voice as gentle as possible, not wanting to point out the obvious. "Let this go."

"The closest Trancer is far from here and in the opposite direction."

"Iliana . . ."

"By the Goddess, do you think I want to go? Is that what this is about?"

"Do you not?" Now this was an unexpected twist.

"No." She turned away from him. "I am frightened."

"Of what?"

"Myself."

"Why?" He whispered the question, a part of him not wanting to know the reason.

"I cannot tell you." Her shoulders trembled. "All I know is that the Goddess commands me."

"Perhaps it is not the Goddess, but your inner guilt, that leads you to this decision." Taking the chance, he touched her shoulder. She flinched, widening the distance between them.

Lore knew what needed to be said, but the knowing did not make the words any easier. "Iliana, as you pointed out yourself, you are a Trancer no longer. Your powers are gone. Locked away in your mind."

She nodded. "I know."

"If what you say is true, how can you help me?"

"I am unsure, but the Goddess commands and even you cannot—"

A gurgle cut off her words, and Iliana's eyes rolled upwards, until only the whites were visible. She toppled backwards.

With a Warrior's instincts and speed, Lore dropped his weapon and caught her before she fell to the stone floor.

Holding her in his arms, he hurried over to the bed, laid her down, and shook her shoulders.

No response.

He shook her again, harder and more insistent. "Wake up."

It was useless. She was beyond him.

He had seen a Trancer work before, and this episode looked similar only in that she was unresponsive to the external events around her.

Otherwise, what was happening to her was nothing like the tranquility of Trancing.

Instead of a dreamy smile, pain twisted her lips. She did not take calm, deep breaths, but panted as if running or struggling.

This was anything but Trancing.

With a sudden shriek, Iliana arched upwards, her arms reaching outwards, grabbing, thrashing, and then clawing at her own skin, raking her short nails down the side of her face.

She is going to hurt herself.

She fought him, but Lore managed to grab her hands. He pushed them back down by her sides—

And was catapulted out of reality and into her vision.

Both terrible and beautiful, it was as real as the world. He tasted. Smelled. All colors were bright.

But mainly, he felt. Fear. Anger. Helplessness.

He looked down at his hands. Manacled together, he wore little else besides the irons.

Medea stood before him. Iliana crouched at his feet like a feral animal. Dirty. Mindless. Her dark hair matted with dirt and Goddess-only-knew what else. Moaning, she clawed at the bugs that crawled on her grimy skin.

He knew Talon was dead. As was Aria and her children. All he cared about were gone. His Apprentices. His Warrior brothers.

Just he and Iliana remained, captives of the Dark Queen—kept for entertainment value. Nothing more.

He breathed deep. The stench of burnt flesh stung his nose. The gut wrenching stench of the dead.

Shrieks pierced his ears, and he knew that if he turned, he would see people dying. Tortured.

Medea laughed and motioned him to her. His legs walked forward, while his mind shouted for him to run. No matter. He walked. Walked and kneeled at Medea's feet.

"My pet." She reached out and ran a hand through his hair.

Her touch was like the touch of death. "P . . . please." He managed to get the word out, despite the mental lock on his speech.

"P . . . please what?" Medea mocked. "Please me?" With a flick of her wrist, the manacles fell away. She pulled a knife from a strap on her thigh. "I thought you would never ask."

The knife whipped through the air to land beside him.

"Pick it up."

The command was undeniable, and the knife was in his hand.

Medea nodded towards Iliana. "I am bored. Kill her."

No. He was a Warrior. Iliana's Protector.

Nonetheless, he walked towards where Iliana kneeled on the floor, keening. Flipping her over, he straddled her, pinning her down.

Forgive me.

He could not say the words, but he prayed she heard them.

Recognition flickered in her eyes then disappeared. She did not fight him.

"Do it!" Medea commanded.

His mind screaming, Lore ripped open Iliana's filthy shirt, baring her chest.

He raised the knife.

Four

Iliana emerged from the vision, and her first reaction was panic. Someone, a man, straddled her, a hand beside either of her shoulders and his naked thighs pressed against her hips, as he pinned her to the bed.

With a frantic shove, she tried to move him. Nothing. With a body of solid muscle, he was twice her weight.

He groaned and lifted his head.

Lore? Why was he on top of her? She pushed at him again. He must have brought her to the bed when she fell into her vision. "By the Goddess, Lore, get off of me."

"Forgive me. Please forgive me." His response was a whisper. A murmur.

Something was not right.

He groaned as if in pain. "Goddess, let me die. I beg your mercy. I cannot live with what I have done."

It was then that she noticed his eyes. His beautiful blue eyes were vacant. Distant and unseeing as he looked down at her.

He was here but not here.

With a sickening feeling, she realized where he was. Her vision.

She shut her eyes, trying to remember, but all she saw was Lore over her and his knife plunging towards her chest. Then, she was awake.

He must still be in the vision of the potential future—living through the moment of killing her.

She had to rescue him. Get through to him that the world he was in was not real.

She had warned him the Goddess would not be denied. "Lore, wake up!"

His response was another moan.

Lore's pain almost broke her heart. "Please wake up. I live." With a grunt, she managed to push him up and away from her. His face twisted in grief, and she knew he saw her death, not her life.

With all her strength, she backhanded him across the mouth.

His head jerked sideways from the force of the blow, but when he looked down at her, his eyes were aware. He had returned.

"Iliana?"

She nodded. "Are you all right?"

"Where was I?"

"In my vision," she whispered.

He pressed the heel of his hand against his forehead. His blond hair fell forward. "It was horrible. Medea. She . . . I killed . . . "

"It is over."

Lore shook his head. "I was there. I felt you beneath me as I killed you."

"It was a vision. Nothing more. Do not let it make you doubt what is truly real."

"Real?" Without blinking, he reached out to her, as if testing reality.

Her instinct was to turn away. To flinch.

She held the urge at bay. He needed to touch her. Feel her. Know she was alive.

His hand, large and calloused, traced her cheek. His thumbs skimmed her lips. Sculpted her brow.

She closed her eyes, and with a slow inhale, she turned to his palm.

Above her, Lore groaned, and then his lips were on her. Tasting her skin. Marking her with their heat. "I thought I killed you." His whisper was as heated, but she heard the relief in it, as tangible as his hands on her hair.

She needed to stop this.

But it felt so good. Like water after a long run she had thought would never end.

To be touched, loved.

It had been too long.

She could not stop him, even if she wanted to.

Instead, she reveled in the path he left across her shoulder. The small kisses that made their way to her brow.

Almost of their own accord, her hands drifted down his sides, under the edges of the blanket that still clung to his hips and to his breechclout—the thin piece of material that separated them.

He urged her onward with a moan.

She loved the sound. The power that came with knowing he wanted her. She moved her hands upwards, tracing his spine. His muscles danced, as she skimmed them with her fingertips. She had known they would feel this way. Hard. Hot. As chiseled as a statue.

Fisting her hair in his hands, he tilted her head back, exposing her throat. He whispered her name like a chant. A benediction. A prayer as he nipped her with his teeth.

She responded, arching into his touch. All that mattered was here and now and the way Lore made her feel.

Wanted.

He cupped her breast, torturing it with promise.

Someone groaned. Perhaps her. Perhaps Lore.

He pulled his hand away, taking the heat with him.

She opened her eyes. He lay on her, his legs still straddled her hips as he propped himself on his elbows. With a sweet slowness, he traced her cheek again.

His eyes held her. She wanted to fall into them. Drown in their depths. "So blue."

"So are yours," Lore whispered. He pushed a strand of hair away from her forehead. "Iliana, we cannot do this. I want to make love to you, but not like this. Not as comfort to my guilt." He kissed her forehead. "You deserve more."

She felt like a fool.

"Get off of me." She spoke through gritted teeth, beating back the hot tears of anger that threatened her. She would not cry. Not in front of him.

He rolled sideways and onto the other edge of her bed. His back to her, he leaned forward, forearms on his knees. "Please accept my apology for taking advantage of you. I have no excuse, other than it was my joy at seeing you alive."

Taking a moment, he rubbed his eyes as if checking reality one more time. "You have already been through so much, and to think it was my blade that took your life . . . I cannot describe the guilt. The hopelessness." He looked at her over his shoulder. "Then there you were. Under me. Breathing and very much my Iliana."

Iliana pulled the covers close. "You overstep yourself. I am not your anything."

He flashed her the familiar, if weak, grin. "If you say so."

She pulled the covers tighter. "You need to leave."

The grin faded as quickly as it appeared. "I will, but first, we need to talk." Shifting his body, he turned until he faced her, one leg crooked under him.

She refused to look at him. "About what? Are you going to apologize again?" Why did he not just go? It was clear he did not want her, and his presence mocked her.

"No. We need to talk about the quest."

"I do not want to." All she wanted was for him to leave her alone in her humiliation.

"Iliana, you were right in that you must accompany me. I do not understand why this must be, but as you pointed out, the Goddess commands it, and I cannot ignore her."

He shuddered. "I have seen what happens if I refuse, and that is a future I would not wish on the world."

All feelings of humiliation fled. She was going? She was unsure if she should be pleased or nauseous. "When do we leave?" The question was a whisper in the silence.

"On the morrow. We must reach the Field of Sceton by the time the moons rise side by side. Can you be ready in time?"

Four suns to ride such a distance? She nodded.

Lore stood, and all evidence of trouble disappeared from his expression as he rose. He towered over her, a Warrior sure of himself, his actions and his purpose. "Good. We shall stop to purchase a *rohha* for you to ride. Otherwise, there will be little time for rest."

She nodded.

"Understand, Iliana, I accept this as what must be, but that does not mean that it will be easy."

Iliana rolled her eyes. She knew this voice. Recognized the stern tone as the one he used on his students whenever he was about to give a lecture.

He continued, "What happened between us cannot happen again." He softened for a moment. "It is not that I do not wish it or that I do not want you. I do. You are a desirable woman, but any entanglements . . ." The sternness returned. ". . . will hinder us."

"You mean hinder you."

Lore frowned. "No, I mean us. We both have our parts in this adventure. I wield a blade. You wield your mind." He paused. "If it comes down to it, I do not want you to hesitate in letting me go, not if it would save the world."

"What do you mean, let you go?"

"Most quests require the shedding of blood. That is what I do." Walking towards the door, he picked up his fallen blade. His hand tightened around the hilt. "If it comes to it, I do not want you to hesitate to let me pass on to the next life. I fear that an entanglement between us would hinder you."

How could he even consider such an option? "Do not ask this of me."

The firm set of his shoulders and unyielding set of his jaw strengthened. "I can and I do. If it comes to such a choice, you cannot stop it. I want your word you will not try."

"If I do not give you my word, what shall you do? Leave me behind?"

His frowned deepened. Darkened. "Your word, Iliana."

Her mind raced. By the Goddess, she wanted this, and as manipulative as it seemed, she knew now was her opportunity—perhaps her single one—to get what she wanted most.

"I will give you my word, but you must give me yours that you will teach me the ways of the blade."

Immediately, she knew the asking was a mistake.

Lore shook his head. "I am tired of this. I will see you in the morning."

She could not let him leave. Not now. Not when there was so much at stake. "Lore, please."

He stopped. "What?"

"I need this."

His back to her, he nodded. "I know why you persist, Iliana. I have seen your fear, but you make a mistake in thinking that a sword will conquer it. A sword invites danger." His shoulders slumped. "A sword will get you killed."

He did not understand. Not really. "What if I promise not to fight unless you ask it of me?"

"No. You ask the right to kill, the choice to take a life, but you are not willing to learn the means and motives behind the skill. You want the greatness of a Warrior with out the wisdom."

"Then teach me."

"I cannot. You are a Trancer. If nothing else, I have an obligation to tradition. To duty."

She closed her eyes. Tradition. It was a bitter thing. It was also her ally. He would—could not—not deny her when he clung to tradition with a closed fist and used it with such convenience. "I call on the tradition you love so much." She took a deep breath and held it. Then she let it go and took the plunge. "I demand the Ritual of Acceptance."

***

"This is a waste of time." Lore rubbed his eyes. Instead of sleeping and gaining strength for the quest, he had spent the rest of the morning arguing with Iliana.

And lost.

Now, the sun was high overhead, and the rest of the Keep was present. An excited murmuring rippled through the crowd.

"Possibly," Talon replied. He stood with Lore at the edge of the arena. In the middle, Iliana kneeled, head bent, as she waited.

Talon glanced from Lore to Iliana and back again. "But she did ask, and I think it would be best to accommodate her."

"It would be best if we were on our way." Lore replied. He was not comfortable with this. To his knowledge, no woman had even taken the Ritual of Acceptance. It was reserved for those who came to the Warriors late in life—like Talon. As was customary for those past the Apprentice age, Talon had taken the ritual to show his strength, endurance, resolve, and quickness of mind.

Maybe that was why his Lord was willing to let Iliana participate. She was like him—another with a troubled past.

"Are you worried she will succeed?" Talon asked.

Lore shook his head. "No. She is a woman, the weaker sex in strength, but I would not have her hurt or humiliated for trying."

Talon raised a dark brow. "You may know many things, Lore, but you do not know women if you think they are weak."

Lore scanned the crowd. Apprentices and blooded Warriors waited. They looked eager for the ritual to begin. "Regardless of my knowledge, or lack of knowledge, about women, I know this is a bad idea. Tell her to stop. Tell her to accept her place in life."

"If I did, she would continue this throughout your quest and beyond," Talon replied. "Besides, if you think she will not succeed there is nothing to worry about." With a shove, he pushed Lore into the arena.

Lore strode towards Iliana and stopped in front of her.

She did not look up. Clad in her usual leggings, she had forgone her heavy tunic for one without sleeves. Her feet were bare.

He hated to admit it, but a part of him admired Iliana's nerve in asking for this. It would hurt them both when she failed.

Feet apart, Lore nodded towards the dark wooden box resting in the sand between himself and Iliana. "You have asked for the Ritual of Acceptance."

Iliana nodded.

"We will grant your request."

She smiled.

Stubborn girl. He would save her the humiliation if she would let him.

He continued. "There are three parts to the ritual, strength of self, balance and wisdom. You must pass all three."

Iliana looked up, her blue eyes bright. "I am ready."

With a sigh, Lore knelt and flipped open the lid of the box. "We begin."

***

Lore pulled two black stones from the box and held them out. Iliana took a deep breath. There was no turning back.

Her hesitation lasted a heartbeat, and then she took the stones, one in each hand. She flexed her arms, testing the weight of the black rocks. Round as a ball and with the glossiness of a still lake, they filled her upraised palms.

The stones were not heavy. Yet. She knew they would be before the test was over.

Without a word, Lore motioned towards one of the Apprentices. The boy, barely more than a child, carried out a staff. Carved from feriswood, it was as glossy and black as the stones. One end was sharpened to a point, the other end blunted. With a small bow, he handed the staff to Lore and walked back to his place.

Lore jammed the staff into the ground in front of her.

"Are you sure you want to go through with this?"

His voice was a whisper, and she knew she was the only one who heard him.

"There is no shame in ending this," he said when she did not respond.

She wished she could but knew there was little choice. Not if she wanted to lay this demon to rest. "If I did, I would never find peace." She met his expectant gaze.

He nodded and marked a line in the sand. Straightening, he addressed the crowd. "When the shadow meets the mark."

"When the shadow meets the mark." The crowd repeated the chant as one.

Turning back to her, Lore motioned her to begin.

Upright on her knees, she raised her arms until they were out from her side and perpendicular to the ground.

She took a deep breath, wondering what the trick was in holding the stones for an extended period. Was it brute strength?

She hoped not. She did not have that. All she had was her will to succeed and her desire to wield a blade.

She prayed it would be enough.

Countless heartbeats later, she was not sure that either strength or sheer will was enough to hold the stones. Her arms were as heavy and lifeless as the feriswood staff. Sweat dripped down her face, stung her eyes, and trailed down between her breasts.

The sensation was maddening. She would give anything for a good scratch.

She glanced down at the shadow in the sand. Had it even moved?

Maybe Lore had moved the stick when she closed her eyes. She shook the thought away. It was foolish, and while Lore might wish her failure, he was an honorable man.

A deep breath and Iliana shut her eyes. The thudding of her heartbeat sounded like a drum and was easier to listen to than the thoughts in her head.

Her eyes stung. Goddess help her, the sweat was annoying.

She realized it was not sweat. Tears stung her cheeks. She opened her eyes again. Lore stood in front of her. "For the sake of the Goddess, stop this madness."

She saw the concern in his eyes and heard it in his voice. For a moment, she almost agreed. Almost.

She pressed her lips together. His concern would not move her. "Has the shadow met the mark?" Her voice sounded thick. Dry.

"No, but if you could see yourself, you—"

"I will continue."

"The trembling in your arms says otherwise."

He might be right, but it did not matter. If she failed, she would accept her fate. If she let the rocks drop because of a few tears, she would wonder the rest of her life if she gave up too soon. Letting go the breath she held, she shook her head. "Ignore the trembling. I will."

Hands clenched into fists, Lore stalked away.

Iliana shut her eyes again. Tears did not matter. Pain did not matter.

She could overcome both. She would not fail.

Another deep breath, and she resumed counting, letting her mind drift while her body fought the battle.

The weight lifted. Her eyes flew open. Lore stood in front

of her, the stones in his large hands.

Anger flared in Iliana, racing through her blood like a flame. With a grunt, she staggered to her feet.

The muscles in her body spent, she fell backwards onto the ground. She groaned as she rolled over onto her stomach and propped herself up on her hands. "How dare you? I said I did not want to give up. By the Goddess, Lore, you presume too much."

Lore let the stones fall to the ground. "You passed."

"I passed?" She fell back into the dirt, not caring that it coated her sweat covered skin and hair. Relief rolled through her. Excitement at success gave her new strength. "I passed."

"The first test," Lore cautioned. "There are two more."

She ground dust into her hair with a nod.

"Then get up. There is no resting." Lore held his hand out, but he snatched it back before she could even think of accepting assistance.

A smile played on Iliana's lips. He still reacted as if he were her Protector. If she succeeded today, maybe she would get the chance to be his. With a grunt, she rose, staggered, and caught herself before she fell again.

The crowd groaned, and there were a few chuckles as well. Iliana ignored both.

Lore was already walking away, and she hurried to catch up. He stopped at a pit of muck. Iliana followed his gaze as he looked upwards. Normally, the sticks—a series of ladders the Apprentices ran over—rested over the pit.

Today, the sticks were gone. Fifteen feet above the mire a beam, no wider than her hand and held up by sturdy poles with a ladder at each end for access, was perched.

Lore jammed the staff back into the ground and drew a line in the dust. Unlike the other test, this one was close to the shadow. Too close. She would have little time to accomplish this task.

Lore motioned her to turn around. Her back to him, she looked up the ladder one last time. Fifteen feet looked fifty, and once up, it would be her job to cross the beam blindfolded.

Lore put the blindfold on her. Then, hands at the sides of the ladder, Iliana climbed upwards as fast as she dared. Reaching the top, she grabbed hold of the beam. It remained steady under her hand. With a careful grip, she straddled the beam and managed to get her knees under her.

She stood. Shaky, but she was vertical. She grinned.

"You might want to hurry," Lore called.

His comment made her heart beat harder. Was he serious, or was he trying to make her rush and fall? It would not be the first time he had tested someone's patience.

How close was the shadow to the mark?

"It does not matter," she murmured to herself. The only thing that mattered was winning.

Because once she won, Lore would have no choice but to train her.

She put one foot in front of the other. She felt a slight bobble as vertigo gripped her, but she recovered.

Arms outstretched for balance, she took another step. And another. A few more, and she knew she must be over the muck.

It would be a long fall and a messy landing if she slipped. In her mind, she saw the pit, filled with mud and straw. Worse, she could smell it. She choked on the stench of decaying organic material.

Thinking about the pit would not help her in her quest. Only feet that moved fast and sure would bring her success. "One at a time, Iliana," she murmured

She took another step.

And slipped.

***

Iliana screamed, and Lore rushed towards her.

Arms flailing, she caught the beam in midair. He stopped mid-step.

Around him, the surrounding Apprentices and Warriors surged forward. Never, in all the testing, had this happened.

When would-be-Apprentices fell, they hit the muck.

Not Iliana. Whether by luck or skill, she managed to catch the beam. Now, hanging on with her hands, she kicked her legs, trying to find her way back up.

Around him, the others were silent, but tension hummed in the air. Would she manage to get back up? If so, would she make it to the end before time ran out?

With a grunt, she swung her legs upwards, wrapping them about the beam.

"Well?" she shouted, clinging to the beam like a *pilta* on the hull of a ship.

"Can she do that?" Talon murmured.

While Lore's heart cheered Iliana's ingenuity, his head was

not so forgiving. If she passed, he would have no choice but to teach her the way of the blade.

Still, there was no rule on how to make it across the beam, just that it must be done. No matter his trepidation, he would not offer her less than a fair chance. It was her right and his duty. "As long as she makes it down the ladder on the other side, she will complete the test."

Talon grunted acknowledgment, and Iliana began shimmying her way to the end of the beam, legs and arms wrapped around the thin piece of wood.

Lore glanced down at the stick. The shadow was almost at the mark. Maybe she would not complete the test in time.

As if sensing his thoughts, Iliana shimmied faster. She reached the end of the beam. Letting her legs drop, she probed the ladder with her feet, found the rungs, and with a dexterity that surprised Lore, she managed to move one hand from the beam to the ladder.

She would make it.

At the bottom, she yanked the blindfold off and held it up in triumph.

The crowd both roared with approval and groaned in disappointment. Lore ignored both responses. The opinion of the crowd meant nothing.

He stepped forward, both dismayed at the thought she might be the first female Warrior and proud at the same time. He managed to keep both emotions under a stoic expression. Neither was appropriate for the Ritual of Acceptance. "Well done."

She flashed him a grin. "I did it."

Yanking the stick from the ground, Lore nodded towards a table and chair that were placed apart from the rest of the trial. "Do not let success make you cocky, Iliana. You are not an Apprentice yet."

"Yet."

She spoke the single word as if it were a challenge, sauntered over to the table and sat in the chair.

Lore followed. Her cockiness would be her downfall if she were not careful. If she passed, it was something she would need to work on.

A smug Warrior was a dead Warrior, and he would not see her blood spilled.

Standing on the other side of the table, he thrust the stick back into the ground. He glanced skyward, made the estimate, and drew the mark.

An Apprentice brought over another dark wooden box and handed it to him.

"What is that?" Iliana's dark brows rose in curiosity.

"It is your test." Lore dumped the contents on the table. Carved pieces of wood scattered like sand. "Put it together."

The color drained from her face. "My test? Where are the steel loops? That is the final test."

He did not grin, but it was a fight to keep his lips from curling upwards "This is a test of wisdom. How your mind works under pressure. Why would I be so foolish as to give you a test you have already seen?"

She hesitated then managed a shaky nod. "What am I suppose to do?"

"Put it together."

"What is the shape?"

Lore shook his head and stepped back to watch. Hands trembling, Iliana gathered the pieces in a pile. She picked one up, examined it, set it down, and grabbed another.

Lore hid his satisfaction behind a stoic mask. The carvings on the pieces were not random, and if she figured out the mathematical riddle of their numbering, she could put them together with ease.

She would also be his Apprentice, and the war between his heart and head would continue instead of ending. He reminded himself that, apprehension or pleasure aside, her winning was not his to decide.

A slight movement in the crowd caught his attention. Aria. She stood by her mate's side, her small hand engulfed in Talon's larger one.

Iliana glanced up. Lore glanced at Aria, and she mouthed the words, You can do this.

He turned his gaze back to Iliana.

It was as if the four simple words were all she needed. She took a deep breath. Her muscles relaxed, and she continued to study the pieces of carved wood in front of her.

He glanced downwards. The shadow was closing in on the mark. Either way, the decision would not be long in coming.

"I have it!"

Lore watched in both awe and shock as the seemingly random wooden pieces interlocked with each other forming a perfect sphere.

Iliana jumped to her feet, arms upraised as she crowed in triumph.

It was done. She was his to teach. Lore's heart both soared and sank.

Once again, the crowd roared.

What had he done? He should never have allowed her to take the Ritual. She was cocky. She was insecure. She was untouchable. She was a Trancer and a woman.

She was his Apprentice.

Five

Iliana groaned as her *rohha* stopped in the middle of the forest path. Above her, the leaves muted the sun's light, creating deep shadows all around her. An animal's call, high-pitched and quick, broke the silence of the forest, and the sweet scent of *ici* flowers tickled her nose.

She was living her dream. She was away from the Keep and the animosity and insecurity that came with her name. Only none of it mattered. What mattered was getting her *rohha* to move. Her hands gripped its pale brown mane. She kicked it in the side with her heels. "Walk, you ungrateful beast."

Lore rode up beside her. His own battle-trained *rohha,* Lev, came to a stop. "Having trouble, Apprentice?"

Iliana bit her tongue before a stream of sarcasm spilled forth, and she wondered again if she had made a mistake in wanting to be Lore's Apprentice. Since the Ritual of Acceptance and their departure from the Keep, he had done nothing but make her take care of Lev, cook, clean their camp, and ride the nag he dared name Qi, the Paxxon word for intelligent. And the way he called her Apprentice . . . It made her want to poison his stew.

Still, he could only taunt her for so long. At some point, her training would begin. Lore had given his word, and for him, his word was more valuable than his opinion.

He poked her with a stick. "Apprentice, I asked you a question."

She snatched the stick from his hands. "No trouble, and stop hitting me!"

Lore placed his hand over his chest. "You wound me. I would never hit you, Apprentice."

She shook the stick at him, jarring loose the few remaining leaves that decorated the end. "What do you call this?" She stuck him in the side with the end of the stick.

Lore grinned. "Poking."

She gritted her teeth. "Poking?"

His grinned broadened. "Poking."

With a growl, she snapped the short limb into two pieces and tossed it to the ground. "Whatever you call it, stop it."

"Of course, Apprentice, since it bothers you so, but you might want to consider working on your patience."

"And stop calling me Apprentice," she growled. "My name is Iliana."

He laughed, and she knew she had lost whatever game he seemed to be playing. It would at least be nice to know the rules next time.

She kicked Qi in the sides again, and the *rohha* began plodding along the wide path.

Lore brought his mount into a walk beside her. As if sensing her impatience, Lev nudged Qi's shoulder, pushing the smaller animal forward.

"Thank you, Lev." Iliana reached over to pat Lore's mount with her fingertips. He was a magnificent animal. Trained. Majestic. She hoped she would merit such a mount one day. "I do not think Qi is inclined to listen to anyone, including you."

Lore frowned. "You make a good point, Iliana."

She held her tongue. Maybe if she stopped reacting, he would stop taunting her.

Lore continued, "As much fun as it is watching you try to control Qi, if you cannot manage to make her go faster, we will have to leave her behind."

Iliana glanced at Lore out of the corner of her eye. "Promise?"

"And you will have to ride in front of me." Lore patted the space in front of him.

She would have to sit between his legs? Heat burned Iliana's cheeks. Without bothering to respond, she gave Qi another kick. The *rohha* sped up to a teeth-jarring walk.

Within seconds, Lore was beside her again. "Need help?"

"No," she replied. The jarring of Qi's hooves made her words chatter. "I . . . I . . . Am. Fine."

"Really?" Lore laughed. His mount moved smooth beneath him. "You would not mind racing?"

Race? Was he mad? It was the last thing she wanted. Her thighs, already tender from riding and Qi's lack of grace, were starting to burn.

"Of course, Apprentice, if you are not up to a little physical challenge, we might also want to forget your training for this evening as well. I would not want to tax your strength."

Iliana perked up. Despite her every instinct telling her not to step into the trap, she found herself asking, "Where to?"

"The Field is not far—"

She slapped Qi on the rump before Lore finished. The *rohha* shot forward. By the Goddess, she would beat Lore if it killed both her and Qi. Clinging to her mount's mane in a bid to stay saddled, Iliana urged the smaller beast to hurry.

She glanced over her shoulder. Lore was behind her and coming up fast. She looked ahead. The opening was not far.

Then Lore and Lev were beside her. Tied with a Warrior's cord, Lore's hair whipped behind him.

He flashed her a wicked grin, and Lev shot forward, faster than Qi, faster than any *rohha* she had ever seen.

She gave Qi another jab with her heels. The petite beast gave another burst of speed. It was not enough. Iliana watched in both admiration and annoyance as Lore and Lev reached the meadow ahead of her.

***

It surprised Iliana that Lore managed to make it though the evening meal without a single remark, verbal jab or taking yet another poke at her with a stick.

Perhaps they were past the "let me taunt you until you scream" part of their relationship. Either that or he was planning something. She eyed his plate. He moved the food around, but there was almost as much as when she had served him.

It would serve him right if he thought it poisoned. She gestured towards his half-touched meal. "Are you not hungry tonight, Master Trainer? The food does not taste funny, does it?"

Cleaning his *cuchil,* his short knife, off in the grass at his feet, Lore slid it back into the strap on his boot. "The food is good, but I prefer to spar on an empty stomach."

She leapt to her feet, her own platter falling to the ground unnoticed. "Spar?" But she had lost the race.

He nodded. "Some. Just to give you a feel for the fight, but mainly, we will work on balance."

Balance? She quelled the urge to roll her eyes, fearful he would pull away the opportunity as quickly as he had offered it. "Is this because I fell during the ritual? I was blindfolded."

"There is no need to become defensive, and I neither want nor asked for an excuse."

She bowed her head and silently berated herself for offering one.

Lore continued, "All Apprentices start with balance. Balance of body, mind and emotion." He poked her in the sternum. "You need to work on emotional balance."

"What do you mean?"

"Many things. The most obvious is your anger. It is unfettered. Unfocused. You do not control it. It controls you." He hesitated. "It was why I did not want to train you."

Her anger was uncontrolled? She opened her mouth, but instead of replying, she bit her tongue, wanting to train more than she wanted to argue. The faster she completed the basics, the quicker she would hold a sword.

Besides, he made a good point, and she regretted some of the things she had said. When she remembered the thoughtless comments she had made to Aria, she wanted to cringe.

As for Lore, her only regret was not winning more of their verbal sparring matches.

"Do you disagree?" Lore asked.

She shook her head. "What would you have me do?"

"Sit"

She sat in the grass, legs crossed in front of her. The sun set behind her, lengthening her shadow. The grass around her glowed a fiery gold around the edges.

Lore stood in front of her, over her. "Shut your eyes."

Shutting them, she placed her hands on her knees, palm up, thumb touching index finger, creating a circle.

The grass rustled as Lore circled her, talking. "Unchanneled anger kills Warriors. It might give you a sense of power over a situation, but in actuality, it does the opposite. Anger dissipates power by clouding your mind. It weakens your body by impeding your judgment."

He crouched down behind her, his lips near her ear. "Do you recognize anger?"

Iliana jumped at his sudden nearness but refused to open her eyes or turn her head. This was not unlike Trancer training, and she knew there was a certain degree of control expected. "Of course."

"How so?"

She did not want to tell him the truth, but there was no other answer. "I feel it. The heat. The darkness."

Lore's breath was warm on her neck. "Before the heat, how does it make your body feel?"

Her body? "I am not sure. I never thought about it."

"Admission of ignorance is a good start."

She smiled. The air behind her moved as Lore stood and walked back around to face her. "I want you to call upon your anger, but instead of giving in to the emotion, I want you to pay attention to your body. Your skin. Your heart. Your muscles. Everything."

Her right brow shot up. "You want me to conjure up anger on command?" It was unfortunate he did not ask her to do this right after he won the race.

"Yes."

The single word gave no indication as to his state of mind. What was he doing? Frowning? Smiling? His voice gave her no clue, and she wished she knew. "Can I ask why?"

"Emotions motivate action—especially strong emotions. Anger. Love. Hate. In battle, this will get you killed.

What I want you to do is recognize your anger before it takes over your emotions. Feel your body. Learn it. Become its master before it becomes yours."

The air changed again, and the grass rustled as he sat down in front of her. "Right now, you are relaxed. Describe it. Physically."

She took a deep breath. The sun was on her back. A breeze blew. "Warm."

"You heart. How is it beating?"

She cocked her head but neither felt her heart nor heard it. "I do not know."

"Good enough. Now, think about anger. The heat. The racing of your blood and thoughts. Let your body fall into it."

This was another silly test. No one got angry on command. "I do not think this will work." She cracked open one eye. Lore was hazy through her lashes.

He snorted in disgust. "I knew it was a mistake letting you take the Ritual."

"What?" A mistake? They had just started training!

Both eyes shot open. Lore still sat in front of her. His hands tented in front of his lips, he stared at her as if he wished she were anywhere but here. With him.

"A woman and a Trancer," he sneered. "I knew you would not be able to live up to Apprenticeship standards, much less a Warror's. I make a simple request, and you do not even try." Rising to his feet, he turned his back to her.

"I passed the Ritual of Acceptance." Iliana leapt to her feet to follow. She would not let her training end. Not like this. "You have a duty to me, Lore. You are my Teacher."

He turned on his heel to face her. "I cannot teach you, Iliana.

You fight every step. Every suggestion. You do not listen. You will never learn." He looked down his nose at her. "You are many things, but you are not a Warrior and never will be."

Heat raced through her. "How dare you." She closed the small gap between them. "I have been through too much to give up now. Either you will teach me or I will find someone who will."

"Do you feel that?"

"Feel what?" She would poison his stew. She would poison it, finish the quest alone, and find someone who would teach her what she wanted to know.

"Your body. How the muscles tighten and the power surges? Your heart. How it races, pounding in your ears louder than the world."

Understanding dawned. "You said all that to make me angry?"

He did not reply, did not need too. Sitting, he motioned her to do the same. He reached for her and hesitated. "May I?"

She nodded, knowing that his touch was necessary in her training.

He placed her hand over her heart and pulled away. "Shut your eyes."

She shut them.

"Now, do not focus on your emotions. Ignore them. I want you to concentrate on how the anger affects your body."

Reining in the desire to pound her mentor into the ground, Iliana focused on herself and listened. "My heart pounds. It beats against my chest like an animal beats against the bars of a cage."

"Keep going," Lore urged.

What else? "I am hot. Feverish. Sitting still is torture. I am ready to jump out of my skin. I want to move. My muscles are screaming for action. They twitch." She tilted her head as the song of a night bird caught her attention. "And sounds. They are stronger. Louder."

Time passed as she listened to herself. Touched the angry, hot emotions she had avoided for so long. The darkness in her head did not matter. Not at this moment in time.

She heard Lore as well. His breathing. Deep. A little quick as he watched her, waiting. His scent. Clean sweat. The smell of the fire. Grass. It was all there. All these sounds and smells—heightened by the heat of her anger.

"Your emotions," Lore asked. "Describe them."

"Better."

"How?"

"I cannot describe it, but I can say that I no longer want to brain you."

Lore chuckled. "Good. It is a beginning. Now let us spar a little and put your energy to good use."

They rose. Lore walked over to Lev and pulled something from one of the saddlebags.

A short wooden training sword. Her heart raced as Lore came towards her with it.

He hesitated. "I know you are excited, all Apprentices are. But just like anger, you must restrain your excitement. Rule it."

He held the weapon out.

She took it. The wood was heavy in her hands. Warm. She ran her hands up the edge, reveling in its smoothness.

His own weapon at ready, Lore stood a few feet to her right. "The first lesson is to learn the positions. Follow my lead. I will go slowly."

Blade in left hand, he lunged forward.

Despite Lore's caution, excitement flared in Iliana. This was the first step towards a new life. One where her skill would be in the blade and people would respect and admire her instead of fearing her.

She mimicked the move.

And the ground opened under her feet and swallowed her.

***

With a scream, Iliana dropped from Lore's view.

She was dead. The thought was not so much in his head but in his heart as he rushed to where she had stood moments ago.

What he did not expect to find was Iliana hanging onto the edge of a black pit by her fingertips.

Fingertips that were losing their grip. She looked up at him, her eyes wide with fear. Her mouth open in a silent scream of terror.

Reacting before thought, Lore grabbed her wrists. He pulled. Her feet scrambled against the dirt walls as she tried to make her way to the top.

It was also loosening his grip. "Stop moving," he shouted, his voice harsh with fear. If he dropped her . . .

She went limp. Muscles straining, he pulled her straight up.

Her feet touched the grass, and with her pressed against his chest, he backed away from the gaping hole.

He had almost lost her!

Time stopped as he held her. The only sound was his heartbeat, and the only sensation was the trembling of the woman in his arms. He tightened his grip, wanting to sink into her. Needing to feel her skin. Her heart. Her breath. Anything to confirm that she lived. He kissed her hair, savoring the texture.

Goddess help him, if he should ever be so careless again.

Although they had the rhymes and legend to lead them, Lore had not truly believed the tests were real. He would have to be more cautious now that he knew they were not a myth.

He pushed a strand of hair away from Iliana's cheek, tucking it behind her ear. He was grateful she did not stop him. Much like when he woke from her vision, he needed to touch her, feel her skin, to believe she was truly safe.

A dusting of dirt smudged her cheek. A shallow scratch marred her jaw. He brushed it with his thumb.

He would not put her in harm's path again.

She reached up, her hand coming to rest on his, stopping him. "I think we found the first test."

He barely heard her. Instead, all he could focus on was her hand. Two of her nails were torn and bleeding. If she would let him, he would wash them in cool water. He knew she would not allow it. "You are hurt."

She pulled away, out of the circle of his touch. "It is nothing." Edging past him, she walked over to the pit.

He followed. What had opened up under her was more than a doorway. As wide as he was tall, the edges of the pit were smooth. How she had managed to catch the side and avoid falling to her death was as amazing as when she fell off the beam and grabbed hold. "You may not be a Warrior as of yet, Iliana" he murmured. "But you have the reflexes of one. Actually, better than most. I will admit that much."

"Thank you," she answered. "I lost my training sword."

"You are welcome, and I will buy you a new one," Lore replied. Staring into the dark hole in the ground, he could not see its bottom. Perhaps it went on forever.

Iliana wiped her bloodstained palms on her leggings, flinching as one of her jagged nails caught on the rough fabric. "Do you know what we are to do?"

Lore glanced at Iliana out of the corner of his eye, expecting fear. Uneasiness.

Instead, her cheeks were flushed. Her lips parted in a half-smile.

By the Goddess, she enjoyed this. Her reaction surprised him. When death touched one and pulled back, most reactions were dramatic. He had seen men cry, freeze in fear, and even laugh.

With Iliana, he had expected anger—her usual reaction to anyone or any situation that was stressful. This excitement was unexpected.

But there was no time to speculate on the "why" of her reaction. The sun was set, and what little light remained faded fast. He did not need to turn around to know the moons rose behind him. According to Benn, when the moons completed their path across the night sky, the entrance to the test would close, and he and Iliana would either be on the surface in their success or trapped below the earth.

His Iliana trapped? A vision of her screaming, as the weight of the world caved in on them, flashed through his mind.

He shuddered. It was a horrific scenario, and one he refused to take a chance on. "What are we to do? We are doing nothing. I am climbing down alone."

"Alone? What about me?"

"You will wait here and guard the camp."

Iliana's eyes narrowed. "I will not."

She was no fool and recognized that she was being put off. The recognition did not change his decision. "You will. As my Apprentice, you have no choice but to do as I bid."

"As your traveling companion and partner in this quest, you cannot tell me to stay behind," she countered.

There was no time to argue. Without replying, Lore put his fingers to his mouth and whistled for Lev. The *rohha* clopped over and pushed against him.

Lore gave the beast a pat on the shoulder. "Now is not the time for play, my friend. We have a job, and your strength is needed."

As if in understanding, the *rohha* quieted.

Quickly, Lore grabbed his rope from one of Lev's packs. He hefted it in his hand. Thin and light, it was still strong enough to support him.

Was it long enough?

There was one way to find out.

A delicate hand on his wrist stopped him. "You cannot go without me. I am as much a part of this as you, or have you forgotten the visions already?"

A picture flashed through his mind of Iliana under him, his knife in her chest. One equally disturbing—her cries of fear as death claimed her below the ground—followed. "No, I do not forget, but I will not take a chance with your life. You know this. We discussed it."

"No, you told me how it would be, but there was no discussion." Her grip tightened. "This quest is not about you or about me, and I am a part of it, whether you like it or not."

He shook her off, tied the rope to the horn of his riding seat, and tossed the other end into the pit. "Keep her safe," he ordered Lev.

The *rohha* tossed his head in answer.

"By the Goddess, Lore, you will fail without me. Do not be so stubborn."

He did not answer. After she calmed down, she would understand. He lowered himself over the ledge of the pit and started his decent into the dark.

Ten hand spans below the surface, a small breeze tossed the edges of his tunic and tickled his skin.

Another step and it grew in strength. Bits of debris pelted him, obscuring his vision.

He stopped his descent. It made little difference. The wind screamed and became a circular force that threatened to loosen his hold and beat him against the rough, dirt walls. There was no choice but to return to the surface.

Hand-over-hand, he reached the top just as his feet were beginning to lift with the force of the gale.

With a sigh of relief, he rolled onto the grass.

"I told you I needed to go with you." Iliana stared down at him.

Rising to his knees, he rocked back on his heels and stared into the pit. Dirt and rock, caught up in the whirlwind, circled the edges. "I think we have found the Goddess's breath," he murmured as he pulled the rope back up. To attempt to descend now would not be foolish. It would be lethal.

"What do you want to do?" Iliana leaned over his shoulder. "I do not think climbing down is an option any longer."

He stood. Was the quest over already? Was failure so quick to come? There was another way. There had to be.

After all, this was a test. He managed a wry smile. "I do not know, but I am willing to listen to any suggestions, should you have them."

She shrugged. "Perhaps if I had gone with you . . ."

She was most likely right, but he would not give up. Not yet. "We will never know, but I do know that this entrance is no longer an option." Taking a small cloth from Lev's pack, Lore cast about, gathered up a small branch, wound the cloth about the end and lit it from their campfire. "There has to be another way down. Perhaps a secret entrance."

Iliana rolled her eyes. "This is the secret entrance."

"I know," he snapped. Taking a deep breath, he let it out slowly. Frustration would not help. "It is also the most obvious way and a trap. We must look for another. One that will not kill us."

She sighed. "I suppose you are right."

"I shall look around. Perhaps we missed something. You stay and watch for changes. If the whirlwind dies, we can try to descend."

"We?"

Silently, Lore cursed the slip. "Maybe." He would not promise.

Torch in hand, Lore scouted the field and the edge of the woods. In the bright moonlight, there was little other than dark and shadows.

"Lore!"

Iliana's call carried across the field.

She was in trouble. Torch in hand, Lore bolted across the field, adrenaline surging through his blood. If she was hurt, someone would pay in blood and pain.

He rushed into camp.

Alone, Iliana sat at the edge of the pit, her legs crossed with a large pile of stones by her side. She was quite alone and quite unharmed.

"Why did you call me?" Lore replied, trying to keep the frustration from his voice. "I thought you were being attacked."

Iliana glanced over her shoulder, shaking her head as if she thought him dim. "If I were in trouble, you would hear more than a single shout." She picked up a large stone and hefted it in her hands. "Watch."

She tossed the stone into the middle of the whirlwind.

It floated, caught in the air as if by an unseen hand.

Lore stared, mouth open, all frustration vanished. "How did you do that?"

"I was curious," Iliana said with a small laugh. "Being a Trancer taught me that not all is as it seems. Much is invisible. I tossed rocks into the wind. When I tossed one into the middle, it did not fall." She tossed in another large stone. "I think I found our way down."

Was she mad?

Iliana stood, her skin pale in the moonlight. "I know you think this is suicide, but to walk the true path, sometimes faith is required." Her voice lowered. "Maybe that is what this is about. What better way to begin a quest than to test our level of belief in the Goddess and ourselves."

"To leap into nothing is a fool's test." Lore shook his head in disbelief. "The whirlwind might float a stone, but we both weigh a good bit more than a rock."

Iliana turned away. "That is where the faith comes in. Lore, I lost many things when Mako took my Tower. I lost my friends. My family. My sisters. My Trancer abilities. And yes, my faith.

"Perhaps that is why I need to do this. I need something to hold on to. Something to believe in. Even if it is just my belief in the Goddess, it is a start." She looked back at him, her eyes dark in the moonlight. "Whether you choose to go with me or stay behind, I will take the leap."

Lore jammed his fingers through his hair in frustration. "I cannot let you do this."

"Would you restrain me?"

Tie her up? As much as he wanted to keep her safe, even he would never resort to such methods, especially with Iliana. He shook his head. "You will die if you do this. It is my job to protect you."

"Then go with me." Turning, she took two steps and stood on the rim of the pit. Beneath her feet, the wind groaned and screamed. She glanced at him over her shoulder. "You know I am right."

He did. He knew it. He hated it. He moved to stand next to her. "We do this my way. We jump together. When we reach the middle, I will pull you to me to minimize the space we occupy. Keep your head down. I do not want you addled by a flying rock."

"I suppose your skull is so thick you do not think it will be a problem."

Another brief flash into the Iliana of the past? Perhaps. Lore grinned. "You made a joke."

She shrugged. "Do not get used to it."

He would not, but it was good to find that a sense of humor lurked beneath her more volatile exterior.

He hoped he would get the chance to experience it again. Lore took a deep breath. He glanced down at her. She looked scared. Confident. Prepared to give her life.

He took her hand in his. "Ready?"

"Yes."

"One, two, three . . ."

They leapt.

Six

Medea stood in the shadows at the edge of the field and watched as Iliana and the Warrior jumped into the pit.

"Fools." She muttered what she hoped was an epitaph under her breath. She had been more than a little annoyed when she watched the pair ride into the clearing earlier in the day.

She did not have to be a witch to know they were after the Orb. Somehow, they had found out about it, and if they obtained it, who knew what the Trancer would do with it.

Medea stepped out of the shadows.

Sensing her presence, the Warrior's *rohha* looked over.

She stopped. This was a battle beast. Trained for more than simple defense. Silently, she stared at the animal, willing it to leave. She wanted, no needed, to see if Iliana was dead.

The *rohha* pawed at the ground and tossed its head.

"Would you like me to kill it?"

Medea jumped at the voice behind her and whirled to face it.

Kole grinned at her. In his right hand, he held a leg of cooked *falku*. A few burnt feathers clung to the end. In the other hand was his short knife.

"You were supposed to wait for me in the forest," she snapped.

With the air of a man who has time, he sliced off a strip of meat and offered it to her.

She slapped it from his hand.

He shrugged. "If you want to see the portal, I suggest you let me take care of the beast."

Before she could answer, he dropped what was left of the falku leg on the ground. Knife still in hand, he approached the *rohha*.

The beast pawed at the air as Kole approached, his blade a bright sliver in the moonlight.

A part of Medea prayed the *rohha* would kill her companion. Kole annoyed her, and his stench was overwhelming.

But she needed him. His strength. His muscle.

For now.

"Stop."

Kole glared at her over his shoulder and kept walking towards the *rohha*.

She glared back. "If you harm the animal, you will announce our presence."

He hesitated, and then he sheathed his blade. Turning on his heel, he walked back to her, the grasses and leaves rustling as he left the clearing.

He grinned. A knowing grin. One she was familiar with, as she had seen it before on her Lord and Master, Mako.

Realization struck her like a heavy stick. Kole knew this would happen. Knew Iliana and the Warrior were here and had not told her. Knew the beast would attack if provoked, and knew she would stop him.

Anger coursed through her, tightening her muscles, making her hands ache with the need for vengeance. He would suffer for keeping this knowledge from her. For using it to manipulate her.

But again—not yet. Kole was clever. More clever than she thought. That meant he might be smart enough to withhold even more.

She would need that information before she gutted him.

"You knew they were here. You planned it."

He nodded. "Of course. You did not think I was going to take a chance with my life, did you?"

That was exactly what she had planned—have Kole go through the trials. She would have to be more cautious in their future dealings and remember that the only thing holding Kole in check, beside the thought of wielding the Orb's power, was her own promise of letting him bed her.

Uncrossing her arms, she wrapped a dark curl around her finger, toying with it. "Why did not you tell me?"

"I knew the Warriors would suspect you, and I did not want to give them any reason to think we might be setting them up." He crossed his arms. Grinning. Pleased. "I made sure they got wind of our quest and then waited. I am sure they have their suspicions, but in the end, I knew they would do this. How could they not?"

Medea gave a slow nod, evaluating his words. What if Iliana and the Warrior had not taken up the quest? It was certain she would be the one in the pit. After all, while he wanted her, she was sure he did not offer to bring her just for her abilities to please a man.

She would let him live.

Besides, she liked this plan, now that it was in play. It kept her out of danger, and it let Iliana and her Warrior take the chances. Even if they failed, she would win with Iliana's death.

"I like the way you think." She went to him and skimmed a nail down his chest. "What happens next?"

"We wait. If they are not back by morning, they have failed and will be buried alive."

Medea shivered in delight.

Kole continued, "If they succeed, we will be waiting in the woods and will follow them." He licked his thick lips. "What shall we do to amuse ourselves in the meantime?"

He grabbed her hand and pulled her closer "I know your pleasures, Medea. I know what you like."

She gazed at him through heavy-lidded eyes. Neither his intelligence nor his desire would buy her body, but it might be useful to let him think so. He had fooled her once. It was time to return the favor. "You do? Tell me."

"You like it rough. You want a man who is forceful enough to satisfy your appetites." Gripping her hair, he tried to kiss her.

She turned her face away. "You know nothing about me." His grip tightened. She refused to cry out. "Do not assume that because your little plan worked that you have earned the right to bed me."

He nipped her ear. "I do not need to earn anything. I take what I want."

Leaning into his grip, she smiled up at him, her finest seductive smile. "You think to take me?"

"Why not? Mako took you, and you reveled in it."

She took a deep breath. The rise and fall of her chest brushed against the man who wished to be her master. "You are not Mako."

"He is dead."

"By my hand. He betrayed me. Lied to me." She jerked from Kole's grasp and took a step back, closer to the edge of the pit. The wind sounded like an animal at her heels. "Do not make the same mistake. You withheld your plan, and with that you lost any hope of bedding me this night."

Seven

Time seemed to hesitate, almost stop, when they reached the center of the pit. Iliana held her breath. They did not fall.

She exhaled, and time roared back into existence, along with the swirling winds. Her feet rose behind her as the cyclone pulled at her clothes and hair. Her fingers slipped from Lore's hand. She screamed.

His blue eyes narrowed, Lore grabbed her tunic and yanked her back into his arms. Wrapping himself around her, he held her close, burying her face against his chest.

The descent began. Her head pressed against his shoulder, Lore squeezed her as if to say it would be all right.

It did not feel all right.

Her heart pounded in her chest. Her ears ached from the sound. And it was unnerving to be held aloft by nothing other than air.

She clung to Lore as they descended deeper into the pit. The light of the moons above them faded, and the darkness became complete. Soon, the only sensation was the sting of sand. The only tastes were bitter fear and dirt.

The only noise was the screaming of the winds.

Then another, more familiar, sound emerged from the black. THUMP thump. THUMP thump.

Lore.

She pressed her hand against his chest. His heart beat beneath her palm, a reminder of life as they made their way into the underworld. A comfort to cling to as she faced the endless eternity of descent.

The wind ceased.

Still caught in Lore's embrace, Iliana tensed, twisting in midair even as Lore fought to place himself under her. She screamed again.

Impact cut off her shriek, and she found herself stunned, unhurt and lying on top of Lore, his arms still tight around her waist.

Limp with relief, she could not move. They had passed the test. They had jumped into the pit with nothing more than faith, and by the Goddess, they lived.

She started to laugh.

Shoulders shaking as she tried to rein in her amusement,

Iliana propped herself up on her elbows to make sure Lore was all right.

Still beneath her, he managed a pained smile. "Next time, I want to be on top."

Guffaws burst forth, and she fell back onto his chest. His arms still about her, he joined in, his laughter echoing off the stone walls that surrounded them.

She managed to prop herself back up. Their eyes met, and their laughter died as suddenly as it began. He smiled up at her. His mouth was perfect. Though their kiss in her bedroom had not lasted long, she remembered the heat of his mouth on hers. The tenderness. The need.

As if reading her thoughts, he brushed her hair back from her face and cupping her cheek with his palm. She did not flinch. Did not feel the need. "You are beautiful when you laugh."

She took a deep breath at his touch and closed her eyes. By the Goddess, why did she have to travel with Lore? It would be simpler if her companion were someone she did not crave.

He might want her, but she also remembered why the last kiss ended. He did not want any entanglements.

She was starting to understand why.

With a groan, she rolled off him and onto her back.

Lore sat up, dusting the dirt from his clothes. "That was . . . intense."

Did he mean the moment or the leap? Did it matter? Both were over. "Agreed."

She held her ribs, painful from both the unrestrained laughter and Lore's hold as they had descended, and watched as the winds above them swirled like a maelstrom in the water, circling them like a predator with rocks for teeth.

She blinked hard as she realized she could see. The darkness of descent was gone, and in its place was a strange, yellowish light. With her eyes, she followed the glow to its source–the walls of the cavern. Rolling onto her knees, she rose and walked over to get a closer look at the phenomenon. The light came from a plant that coated the stone. She ran a gloved finger through it, a dark trail marking her examination.

"And the Goddess provides," Iliana murmured. She wiped her glove off on her leggings, leaving a smudge of light.

"That she does." Lore's voice, close to her ear, echoed the sentiment. "Which is good, as I suspect that a flame would not work under these circumstances."

He was right. It was windy. Not overly so, but more so than when she was lying on the ground.

She turned her gaze to Lore. With his Warrior's height, he was just ten hand spans from the lethal winds. Despite the fact that his long hair was bound behind him, it rose and swayed.

It made her nervous. What if a rock hit his head?

As if sensing her uneasiness, Lore hunched over. "Better?"

She gave a quick nod.

"Good." His hand went to the hilt of his sword, and his expression darkened. "We need to finish this as fast as possible. There is little time."

The fine hairs on the back of Iliana's neck rose at Lore's sudden transformation. All kindness in his expression disappeared, and in its place was the same darkness she remembered from the Tower when Benn had appeared to tell them of Medea and the Orb.

What frightened her more was the reason. "Sunrise?"

Lore gave a curt nod. "Yes."

***

Iliana ran both her hands over the walls of their stone prison, looking for something, anything that might suggest a way out of the pit. It was horrible to think that they survived the test only to be buried alive.

She glanced up at the ceiling of wind overhead, but no moonlight penetrated the swirling earth. How long had they been looking for freedom? She could not tell. Between the steady yellow glow and the howling of the wind above, she had lost all perspective on time.

She looked over her shoulder at Lore. Intent on his task, he was once again the dark Warrior that she both admired and somewhat feared.

Reminding herself to focus, she returned to her search. She peered down the length of one of the many crevices that cracked the wall of the pit, but the deep shadows were impenetrable.

She would have to use her hands as her eyes.

Teeth gritted, she felt down the length of the crevice, praying no bugs resided in its depths. Anything with more than four legs seemed wrong somehow. Her fingertips touched something hard. She stopped, her heart racing. Was this it? She ran her fingers over the object. Smooth and round, it was most certainly made by the hands of man.

"Praise the Goddess," she muttered. She tried to pull on the object but it was wedged tight in the compact earth. Whatever it was, she was not strong enough to free it. "Lore, I found something."

He sprinted towards her. "What?"

"I am not sure. It is wedged in the dirt." She stepped back, pointing to the area.

Quickly, Lore reached in, found the object, tested it with a tug, and pulled. There was a snapping sound, and he stumbled back. "Goddess!"

Catching himself, he held out what was left of the object.

A bone. Knobby and old with what was, perhaps, dried flesh stuck to the end, it was almost unrecognizable.

Almost. Iliana knew what it was. Or, rather, what it had once been.

Human.

A small multi-legged creature crawled out of the broken end and across Lore's hand.

He grimaced and tossed the bone away.

Iliana's stomach clenched into a knot. Bile rose, and she held her hand over her mouth.

He glanced at her, his expression softening. "Are you going to be ill?"

Shaking her head, she forced her stomach to calm.

Lore gave a nod of approval. "Keep searching." As he went back to the opposite side of the room, he looked neither angry nor disappointed.

Iliana wished her control were as complete. She pressed her lips together, wondering if this was what battle was like. No light. No humor. Just the chill of death breathing down one's neck.

She trembled. She did not want to die. Not like this.

"Iliana!"

"What did you find?" She ran across the circular cavern to where Lore kneeled, grateful for the interruption, even if it proved to be false.

"I am not sure, but I think it is what we seek." He gestured towards a crevice in the stone.

She prayed he was right. Hunkering down beside him, she peered into the crack. It went almost an arm's length into the wall. Nothing but shadow met her gaze. Disappointed, she rocked back on her heels. "It is too dark to see anything."

With an exasperated grunt, Lore moved. "Look again."

Taking his place, she looked again. Hidden in the crack was something shiny. She turned her head, and it gave off a dull glint when a sliver of the yellow light washed over it. Metal?

"Can you pry it loose?" She spoke to Lore over her shoulder.

"No." He held up his hands, and she understood. He could not reach it, not with his large palms and thick, muscular arms.

It was up to her to find out if this was their salvation, and it looked like a tight fit, even for her smaller hands. Taking off her gloves, she set them beside her.

At least it is not another bone.

Her hands scrapping the sides of the rock, she reached for the object. Something skittered across her bared knuckles. With a shriek, Iliana yanked her arm out of the hole.

"What is it?"

She shuddered. What was she going to tell him? That she wanted to be a Warrior—as long as it did not involve small multi-legged animals? "Nothing."

Eyes squeezed shut, Iliana wiggled her arm back into the crevice, determined not to shout or pull her arm out. She was not going to give Lore any reason to doubt her.

The edges of the rock scrapped her skin. She winced.

Something ran over the palm of her skin, followed by a friend. How many more nasty little creatures were there? She shuddered, fighting the reflex to scream. Keep going. Keep going.

"Iliana, you might want to hurry."

"I am doing the best that I can." She spoke through gritted teeth.

"I know, but . . ."

A rhythmic thudding drew her attention. She did not need to turn around to know more rocks fell from the ceiling. The force of their circular journey was not tossing them.

They dropped as the winds came to a halt.

Dirt rained down on her. She choked on the grit.

With a grunt, she shoved her fingers past the rock, past the pain, as she sliced her hand on the sharp edges, and past small creatures of her nightmares.

More dirt poured down on her, obscuring her vision. There were things worse than bugs.

The rain of soil stopped. She took a chance and looked up. Grim faced, Lore bent over her, protecting her.

Their eyes met. Locked. Spoke the words she could not say

aloud. *I do not want to die.*

"You will not," Lore said, obviously reading her mind.

She turned back to her task. A little farther, with the rock biting into her forearm the entire way, and she was at the object.

She moved her lips in silent prayer, beseeching the Goddess for help. Praying that whatever this object was, it would somehow stop the cavern from closing in on them.

Her heart beat loud in her ears, as Iliana concentrated. She had to get it free. Quickly, she felt around the edges. It was wedged tight.

She would have to make room. Biting her bottom lip, she jammed her already broken fingernails into the hard soil at the edge of the object, forcing them under its rim.

Using what little leverage she had in the confined space, she pulled.

The object moved.

Eyes squeezed shut, she pulled harder. It fell into her palm, warm and smooth. She yanked her hand out, ignoring the rock, the pain and the roof coming down on her head.

She opened her fingers. Diamond shaped, the piece of metal was the gray of a stormy sky.

It looked of little consequence.

Lore pulled her to her feet.

She did not look up. Did not need to do so to know that the hole was closing in upon them.

She clenched the talisman in her fist as the world went dark around them. The winds stopped howling. Another, more ominous sound, took its place. A great cracking. A groaning. A thunder that shook them as the earth moved, closing in upon itself.

Iliana wrapped her arms around Lore's neck but knew even he could not protect her.

Not from this.

White light shattered the black. Crystal-blue rays spilled through the Iliana's finger like so much water.

The talisman. The white light illuminated Lore's face.

He looked as surprised as she felt. The glowing increased until it was so bright it burned. She blinked, and when she opened her eyes, there was nothing left. No fear. No death. No Lore.

Just light.

***

Lore woke. His body felt heavy. Like he had run for days and could no longer lift his head, much less move his feet.

The warmth was magnificent. He savored the morning sun on his face and listened to Iliana's breathing as she lay next to him. He did not need to open his eyes to know she was unhurt. Her breathing was the slow, even sound of one who slept with peace. Probably for the first time in many suns.

They lived.

He smiled.

Something gooey, and somewhat smelly, touched his cheek. He opened her eyes, and a large pink tongue came at him. Again.

He patted Lev's velvet-soft nose, pushing the *rohha* away with a gentle shove. "I am glad to see you, too."

Standing at his head, Lev snorted and pushed at Lore. With a groan, Lore rolled over and up.

Satisfied, the *rohha* gave another snort, tossed his head, and went back to grazing.

Lore stretched. Looking at the placement of the sun overhead, it was early morning, but he felt as if he had slept for a full night.

He was tempted to think that the test was just in his mind, but the grit in his mouth proved otherwise. He spat out as much as possible then retrieved a water skin from their camp to wash out the rest. Taking it to Iliana, he hunkered down on his heels and waited for her to waken.

With a small sigh, she turned over to lie on her back, her arm flung over her head. Her dark hair stuck out in matted clumps. Covered with dirt, her skin was a mottling of brown, dark earth and pale flesh.

Her clothes needed to be burned.

He stared at her, unable and unwilling to turn away. He wanted to remember her in this unguarded moment.

For once, he wished he were an artist, not a Warrior. An artist could capture this moment in stone or in paint and preserve it for all time.

"By the Goddess, you are a beauty," he whispered, knowing she was not awake to hear the words.

He brushed a strand of hair from her cheek.

Her eyes opened, blue made brighter by her dirt-darkened skin.

He snatched his hand back.

She smiled. "You are filthy."

"So are you." He held the water out. Taking it from him, she drank deep then wiped her mouth with the back of her hand, leaving a streak in the dirt.

Lore rose and offered her a hand up. To his surprise, she accepted.

Their eyes met, and for a moment, it was as if he knew her thoughts. Felt the energy surging through her. The excitement. The thrill of beating the test.

She blinked, her long, black lashes covering her gaze, and when she opened them, the connection was gone.

Still, he saw the excitement in her stance. The way she bobbed on her toes as she held out her hand and opened her fist, palm up.

A talisman winked at him in the sunlight despite the smudges that tried to hide its beauty.

"It does not look like much, does it?" Iliana said. "But it is of the Gods. Even now, I feel its energy surging through me."

Reaching out, Lore ran his finger over its surface. Smooth to the touch, it seemed to be polished. Under the dirt was an inscription or perhaps it was a symbol. "May I?"

Iliana hesitated but handed it to him.

It was warm, and he understood what she meant. Whatever this object was, it almost hummed with life.

Using one of the few clean spots on his tunic, he rubbed at the metal until it was cleaned. Etched into the center was a circle bisected with a single line. Three straight lines were offset to one side. *Tralane.*

"You recognize this." She traced the marking, leaving a smudge of blood from her wounded fingertips.

He barely heard the comment, did not care that his expression betrayed his knowledge. Her damaged hand demanded all his attention. He took it in his. Her fingernails were broken so far down they bled. Her fingertips looked like raw meat. "These will have to be bandaged."

She pulled away from his. "They are fine and look worse than they feel. Lore, I can see you know this mark. What does it this mean?"

Lore pressed his lips together. He was not ready to speak of the next trial. Not when he had just come so close to losing Iliana. "It is nothing you need worry about. Not yet."

Iliana's blue eyes darkened in anger. "I am not just your Apprentice. I am your partner, Lore. My need to know is a right, not a privilege you can hand out on a whim."

Lore hesitated. Her words were true, but that did not help in the telling when his every instinct told him otherwise. She was not just a partner and Apprentice. She was a Trancer. His job was to keep her safe, not lead her straight into the mouth of the Beast of Tralane.

He ran a hand over his matted hair. Iliana was so many things to him that he was unsure of how to react any more.

"Tell me what you know." She pressed for an answer.

He knew he had hesitated too long. Perhaps Iliana's Trancer skills were buried behind a wall of dark fear, but she still carried an almost empathic ability to know what he thought.

With a sigh, he handed it back to her. "It is the mark of the Forest People of Tralane."

She rubbed the talisman between her fingers. "I have never heard of such a people."

"That is because they are all dead."

Despite the dirt that covered her skin, he knew she paled.

"Dead?" She put the talisman in a pouch at her waist. "How?"

"There is a beast in their forest. One of legend. One of nightmares." Lore rubbed his jaw as he weighed his words. "It is said to possess attributes of both beast and insect. As tall as two men, it has eight legs but is covered with fur. It has a tail with a venomous tip and fangs that can slice a man in half."

Iliana's dark brows rose. "You have seen this creature and lived to tell of it?"

"No, but I have seen its aftermath. The death. The blood." He kept a steady gaze, praying she inquired no further. "This mark is a death mark. A sign the people of Galion posted to remind people to beware the forest and heed the myths." She might want to know all, but she did not need a recount of the horror to know that the beast was dangerous. She did not need to hear how a group of merchants from Galion had not believed the tales and paid with their lives.

He was a new Warrior when he saw the carnage, but even now it was as clear in his mind as if it had happened yesterday. And he did not want to remember the broken bodies.

Or the air stained by screams of the dying.

As if hearing the silent plea, she gave him a single nod and straightened her shoulders. "We must be prepared when we come upon it. Ask questions. Be smarter than all who came before us and died."

Goddess help him, he liked the way she thought. She was beginning to see the value of thinking ahead. Planning.

Strategy.

Was it only five suns ago that they were in her bedroom and she lay beneath him, dark hair spread across the pillow and her blue eyes bright with worry?

Now, her eyes brightened with something else. The desire for a challenge. The need to prove herself.

A courage that few commanded.

One day she would make a fearsome Warrior.

If they lived.

Eight

Thrust. Block. Lunge.

Iliana shivered in the cool air and watched Lore practice another sequence of fighting techniques. Three suns on the road, and while they rode hard, he still made time to train every morning.

Since her wooden sword was left in the pit, she was unable to participate. She had asked about using a stick, but Lore refused, saying the balance was wrong. Now, she was left with watching Lore and lifting rocks to strengthen the muscles in her arms.

Lore stopped. "Are you finished, Apprentice?"

"Uh, no." She picked up the large rock and curled her arms upward.

"Good." He wiped the sweat from his forehead. "Because you have the arms of a small child."

"I do not." She made a muscle, pleased with the firmness. "I am quite strong." She gave him a sly smile. "Maybe even strong enough to knock down a big over-winded Warrior."

He sheathed his sword, unbuckled his scabbard and laid it on the ground at his feet before gesturing her over with the crook of his finger. "Come try."

She let the rock drop from her hands and rose to meet the challenge.

Standing in front of him, she looked up the length of his body. From his calves to his shoulders, he was solid muscle. A body honed from years of fighting and training others to do so. There was little she could attack that would make him flinch, much less harm him or bring him to his knees.

Except maybe his crotch. She hesitated. He would be expecting such a move from a female, she was sure of it.

Perhaps his jaw, but even that looked immobile.

He strove to teach her control over her anger and her fear. What she needed was control over her mouth.

With a sigh of resignation, she dusted her hands off on her leggings. Then she closed her fist and came up swinging.

He moved fast. Too fast for her to follow. She hit the ground with an "oomph." When she opened her eyes, she looked up at him from the ground. Catching her breath, she wobbled to her feet. "What happened?"

Lore chuckled "What always happens when one strikes with

no purpose. You lost." He crooked his finger again. "Now, come at me again, slowly, and I will show you what I did."

Easing her clenched fist towards his jaw, she watched as Lore stepped aside, grabbing her arm as it went past. Instead of stopping her, he pulled it in the direction it was going, forcing her to lose her balance.

She ended up on the ground again.

This time, she leapt to her feet. "That was amazing. You used me against myself."

"I know." He smiled, obviously pleased with her grasp of the concept.

Her skin warmed at the small sign of pleasure. She smiled back. "Can we do it again?"

The morning was well under way by the time Iliana managed to throw Lore to the ground.

He looked up at her, grinning, and she thrust her arms up in a victory salute.

She stopped, sniffed, and wrinkled her nose. "I smell."

"No more than me," Lore said, as he began loading their few supplies onto Lev. "And there is little time to bathe. We have already spent more time than I planned this morning, and I would like to get to Galion by midday."

She wiped her face as best she could with her sleeve and tried to ignore the thin film of mud that came away. "Would it do any harm to take but a moment to bathe? There must be a stream close by."

"There is."

"Why not take a few moments to prepare ourselves?" She pushed a lank strand of hair from her face. "I would prefer not to frighten the people with whom we need to speak."

He shook his head in response. "The city uses the spring's water in making their wine. They say it gives the wine certain aphrodisiacal properties. I doubt they would want us bathing in it."

"We are close to this city?"

"Yes." He gestured towards a green patch at the edge of their vision. "That is the Forest of Tralane. Galion lies just to the left."

A combination of fear and excitement swept through Iliana, making her skin tingle. "That is the home of the beast? This is where the trial will take place?"

Lore raised a brow. "You look forward to the next test?"

She hesitated, and then she decided to answer with the truth.

"I am not sure. I feel excitement, but I feel fear as well. Trepidation. A little queasy."

Lore nodded. "That is what I expect of any first year Apprentice who has tasted the possibility of death. Much like your anger, all these feelings will require your control."

"I will try." He spoke so easily of control. It was as if he turned off his emotions with a thought and expected her to do the same.

"That is all I ask. For now."

They rode in silence. As they grew closer to the green border of the forest and Galion, the fields to her right changed from tall grass to wine-fruit.

She eyed the small shrubs laden with round, yellow fruit and licked her lips. "Maybe we can pick some to tide us—"

"They are not ripe."

Iliana's shoulder's sagged. Lore did not look thirsty, hungry or the least bit concerned. How could he remain so calm, knowing what waited for them?

His request that she control her emotions whispered to her. Refused to be quiet. She was not sure that what he asked was possible. Control over her anger was getting easier, but to ask her to control the rest of her emotions seemed like an impossible task.

"Lore?"

"Yes?"

"How does one control all emotions? Do you never feel excitement before battle? Fear? Anxiety?"

Lore smiled, his blue eyes bright with laughter. "If you must know, I threw up at my first battle. And not before. During."

His confession gave her some comfort. "Now?"

"I can honestly say that I have not thrown up during battle in many suns."

Iliana raised a brow. "How did you get past the fear? The excitement? Both burn so bright I feel as if I could run to Galion."

"Years of practice and honing my skills. You do not have such a luxury, but I know you have the talent."

"How do you know?"

He hesitated. "I do not like to talk of your past. I know it is painful for you."

Her eyes burned, remembering those dark times. The nights she sat with a blade in her hand. Too scared to end the pain. Too scared not to.

Lore continued. "There was a time, after your rescue from Mako that I was not sure you wanted to live. Your only emotion was anger at yourself. Life. Everything. And a guilt so deep and dark that I thought you might never find your way out, but you overcame the anger."

She snorted in disbelief.

"To a degree," he said. "And as much as you have shied away from the world, you took on the responsibility of the quest."

"I did not want it," she whispered. "None of it. Not the quest. Not the Orb. Not the responsibility."

"I know, but you did it anyway."

Heat rose to her cheeks. He made her sound so grand. So strong, when she had little choice. One did not disobey the Goddess.

Though in truth, she rode now not just because of duty. She sought the Orb, but she sought herself. The woman she was. The woman she would be.

Without this knowledge, she was dead inside. A would-be Trancer with a black wall blocking her from the skills that once defined her existence.

Who was she? What was she?

Maybe the Orb would show her.

***

Both Iliana and Lore stared in shock at the road that led from the town and straight into the forest. An overladen cart, pulled by a team of *rohhas,* made its way out Galion's gates, past them and into the domain of the beast.

"What now?" Iliana asked. "Is the monster dead?"

Lore hesitated. "I do not think so. When it killed the group of merchants, it was set upon by fire, blade, and lance. Even wounded, it never lost its strength, and it did not die." Lore frowned. "I am not sure it can die."

"Then how are we supposed to—"

Lore held up his hand to signal silence.

Iliana sidled Qi over until her leg almost touched Lore's. "If it cannot be killed, how are we to succeed in our quest, and how did these people build a road through its domain?"

"The Goddess provides the answer to the first question. I do not know the answer to the second." Lore scowled. "But if we find out how they travel safely, it might help in our task."

They rode through the unguarded gates and into the town.

Although smaller than most settlements, Galion bustled with

life. Carts loaded with ceramic vases went by Iliana more times than she cared to count. Most people were too busy or too uninterested to pay much attention to two filthy riders. Even Lore, despite the warrior cord that bound his long hair and the sword at his side, bore little but a passing, uninterested glance.

Trailing behind Lore, Iliana watched the people out of the corner of her eye. They did not look oppressed. Neither did they appear to be content. There was a pall that hung over them like a thin blanket. A disturbance that marked their features.

Lore stopped in front of a small building. Although not new, the structure seemed in good repair.

Dismounting, Lore motioned Iliana to do the same. She slid to the ground.

"I know someone we can speak with about the monster and what is going on to make the villagers either so careless or so brave."

Iliana twisted Qi's reins around one of the porch supports and followed Lore up the few steps to the open door.

They were in a small room. Almost barren, there was no furniture other than a desk, a chair and a small table piled high with parchments.

The only occupant was a man with pale brown hair and a beard streaked with gray. He looked up, smiling. "How can I he—" His smile died. "I never thought to see you here again."

"I did not expect to come." Lore nodded towards Iliana. "This is my companion. I have some questions."

With a sigh, the man rose, closed the door behind her and locked it. Returning to his seat, he leaned forward, hands steepled in front of him. Lore did not take the chair but remained standing, his hand on the hilt of his weapon. Iliana stood at his other side and hoped she looked as unreadable as her mentor.

The silence was awkward, the tension high, but Lore waited, as immobile and emotionless as stone.

The other man broke first. "You want to know about the beast?"

Lore gave a single nod.

"We built the road a few years ago, along with the other villages. The time it took to go around—"

"I do not want to know about why you built the road, Jaxon. I know the dynamics of commerce. I want to know how."

Jaxon hesitated, toying with the beaten-metal drinking mug on his desk.

Lore continued. "The beast lives, yes?"

Jaxon nodded.

Lore leaned on the desk, his large hands splayed. "How do you get past? What have you done?"

Iliana raised a dark brow. What had they done? It seemed as if Lore already had an idea of what was going on.

"It was the only way, Lore. The villages were dying. Our people were dying."

His people?

"What did you do?" Lore's voice was lower. Deeper. Frightening.

Jaxon crossed his arms over his chest, defiant. "We made a choice."

"To do what?"

Iliana bit her lip, not wanting to know the answer. Whatever it was, she got the impression it was worse than the creature.

"It is only at the end of the harvest, and even then, we have but a few days before the monster is active again." He babbled now. "It is not just us. We share the responsibility with the other villages so no one is asked to sacrifice too much."

"What do you sacrifice?" Iliana whispered, dreading the reply.

Jaxon kept talking, as if he heard neither her questions nor Lore's. "We tried animals at first. I want you to know that we are not monsters, but the animals did not work. They did not stop the monster from killing our people whenever they tried to travel through the forest."

He paused. "We tried everything. I even gave my best *rohha*, hoping that . . ."

"Jaxon, answer Iliana's question." Lore straightened, his hand on the hilt of his sword. "What is the sacrifice?"

Iliana held her breath in dreaded anticipation, wishing Jaxon would stop talking. If he spoke, then the villagers' decision would be true. Real. Brought to life by admission.

"A person."

"May the Goddess forgive you," Lore uttered as he spun on his heel and walked out the door.

Iliana followed, taking a brief moment to glance at Jaxon. Defiance fled, his head rested in his hands—the epitome of desolation.

She felt nothing but contempt and the urge to take Lore's sword and render justice.

She slammed the door behind her.

Lore was already mounted on Lev.

Iliana mounted Qi. Around them, the village hummed with life as people loaded carts, bartered for goods, and went about their chores.

The smiles were false. The laughter as hollow as their souls.

"They are fools," Lore muttered between gritted teeth. "Fools who would betray their people for a coin. For profit."

Our people. Jaxon's comment ran through Iliana's mind, refusing to be ignored. "Are they your people, Lore?"

He ran a hand over his disheveled hair. "I was not sure you noticed the remark, but yes, they are my people." He turned to her, his blue eyes haunted. "My mother passed over to the Goddess when I was young, and my father sent me away to be a Warrior. We were never close after that. I did not plan to return. At his request, I came back when the beast killed the merchants." He gave a short bark of laughter. "I am sure he would rather that I had not come back now."

She flinched. She had never seen this pain of the heart in him, and she did not like it. She knew his lightness. His darkness. This was different. This was a loss of both. "Jaxon is your father?"

Lore nodded.

"This is not your fault, Lore. As Jaxon said, they made the choice. Not you. Them."

"If I had been here, I could have stopped them."

"Their decision is not your burden. I know what it is like to carry such, and it has only been in the past few days that I feel my burden growing lighter." She hesitated, then took his hand in hers, giving his fingers a quick squeeze of comfort before pulling away. "Do not do this to yourself. Once taken, it is difficult to remove."

He hesitated. "Thank you."

"You are welcome."

He turned Lev back towards the gate and the Forest of Tralane.

"Wait!"

Lore held.

It was Jaxon. "What are you going to do?"

Lore took a deep breath. "I should tell the Warriors. Let them decide your fate and the fate of your people."

"You cannot."

Lore continued as Lev danced beneath him. "Instead, I will

do what you seem unable to accomplish. I will kill this beast."

***

Moments later, Iliana and Lore were well into the forest, traveling down the road the villagers had constructed.

As they began their search, Lore's generous mouth thinned and his eyes betrayed his emotions. He was angry. So furious that Iliana knew only years of training kept him from losing control.

It was only when his expression cooled that she dared speak. "Do you know where we are going?"

"No. I have little memory of my childhood, but I do remember that no one went into the forest. Ever."

"Why is the village so close? If the monster wished, it could reach out from the trees and snap a person up." She gave Qi a pat, wishing the tiny *rohha* were faster in case they needed to outrun a multi-legged, fanged creature.

"The city was close, but it did not touch the forest's border like it does now. Even so, the beast does not leave the safety of the trees."

"How do we find this beast?"

He shook his head. "Look. Pray. The usual."

A high-pitched scream broke the silence. They glanced at each other and kicked their *rohha's* into motion. Their mounts crashed through the forest, wrecking the delicate flowers and undergrowth that lived beneath the trees.

Iliana ducked as they bolted under low branches. Abruptly, the wooded area ended, and they entered a clearing.

In the middle was a tree, unlike any tree Iliana had ever seen. The leaves were so dark they were almost black, but the trunk was bone white, with an almost glossy appearance.

Beneath the dark branches and cowering on the ground was a girl, her eyes wide in terror.

There was nothing else. No beast from nightmares. Nothing. Just the girl, screaming beneath the strange tree.

Lev came to an abrupt halt, and Lore vaulted off his back, drawing his sword at the same time. Running to the child, he put her between himself and the tree.

Iliana slid to the ground and ran to Lore's side, further blocking the girl from any harm. Her stomach tightened. A child. They were sacrificing a child?

Lore handed her the *cuchil* from his boot.

"This is all I get?"

He did not reply but continued to search the area with a practiced glance.

She followed his gaze but saw nothing. The trees rustled. She turned towards the sound, her heartbeat lurching forward.

Nothing emerged.

Lore took a fighting stance.

They waited. And waited.

Time ticked by. Finally, Lore straightened and lowered his weapon, but he did not sheathe the long blade. "I think we must have frightened it off."

"*We* scared *it?*" Iliana asked.

Lore glared at her.

"Am I safe?" The question was asked in a child's voice.

Both turned. The girl crouched among the tree's thick roots.

She was older than Iliana first thought. Her short, dark hair gave her a childlike appearance, but she was tall, with the top of her head almost reaching Iliana's chin.

Iliana noted her threadbare clothes and her bare feet. Was this the reason they chase to sacrifice her? Because she was poor?

Her stomach turned in revulsion, and she ached for Lore. To know his father was a part of such a plot must be unbearable.

"Yes, you are safe." He held out his hand to help the girl up, his large palm engulfing her delicate fingers.

She managed a tiny, half-smile. "Thank you." She nodded towards Iliana. "Thank you both."

Iliana smiled back. "You are welcome." While the thought of battle both excited and frightened her, the myriad of emotions would be worth it if all people would look at her with such gratitude and acceptance. So, this was what it felt like to be a Warrior. "We must ride now." Lore sheathed his weapon. "We cannot fight the beast and guard a child at the same time."

He squatted down until he was eye level with the girl. "Have you ever ridden a *rohha?*"

She shook her head. Lore pointed towards Lev. "Well, that is my *rohha,* and he would love to meet you."

"He looks big." The girl whispered in an awestruck voice.

Lore smiled. His smile was the dazzling one that made all women swoon, no matter what their age. "What is your name?"

"Mari."

"Mari, Lev is big, but he is also kind and would never hurt a little girl." He chucked her under the chin. "Especially one as pretty as you."

Mari blushed. Lore straightened and held his hand out to her. "Ready?"

"What about my people? They told me to wait."

Lore frowned. "They made a mistake to bring you here. We will take you to a safe place and then go talk to them. Make them understand that keeping you safe is more important than anything else."

Mari's frowned. "They need me here. Without me, there will be no harvest."

She backed up. Looked ready to bolt as the realization of what was going on dawned on her.

Goddess. Iliana frowned. Why did not Lore lie and tell the child they were sent to retrieve her? "There will be a harvest. Do not worry yourself about that." She held her outstretched hand palm up, in what she hoped was a non-threatening and sympathetic manner.

Instead, Mari skirted around the tree, attempting to edge past them. "I am sorry I screamed. I was frightened. Father told me not to be, but I was." Her large brown eyes welled with tears. "Father said that it was my turn. I have to do this, and then I can see the Goddess."

Iliana rolled her eyes, half tempted to make a grab for the girl. But if she did and missed, who knew where Mari would run. "As Lore said, we will speak with your people."

Lore pulled at Iliana's arm. "Come, we must talk."

She followed him to the edge of the clearing. "What?"

"I am going to tend the *rohhas*. I want you to convince Mari to come with us."

"Why me?" Iliana asked in an angry whisper.

"You are a woman, and I am a big man with a big sword that might be perceived as threatening."

"She likes you. All women like you."

Lore raised a blond brow in response. "We can talk about that later."

Goddess save her from her mouth.

Lore continued. "You are good with children." He snuck a glance at Mari over her shoulder. "For all her height, she is but a child."

"You are good with children as well," Iliana argued.

"You are better. Now go." He walked over to the *rohhas*.

Iliana sneaked a glance at Mari. How did one convince a child not to be eaten by a monster, when that was what the child wanted? She sauntered towards her, making sure to keep her steps slow. "Tell me about your family."

Peering around the backside of the tree, Mari cast her a wary glance. "There is only myself and father."

"No mother?"

Mari bit her bottom lip. "No."

"Mine is gone, too," Iliana replied, remembering the day her Mother passed. For a flicker, her heart ached with the loss, and her eyes watered with the memory of how safe she used to feel. She blinked back the pain. That was past, unchangeable. In front of her was someone with a future.

Reaching the base of the tree, Iliana sat cross-legged on the ground and motioned Mari to do the same.

Mari edged out from behind the tree and sat down a few feet from Iliana.

Underneath the ragged clothes and the dirty face, she was a lovely child. Even her matted black hair did not detract from her innocence. "Mari, I know you were told many things about why you were left in the woods. What I need you to understand is that Lore . . ." She pointed towards him. ". . . and I do not want bad things to happen to you. Not too any child. We have come to change all this. To make sure no child is ever hurt again. Ever."

"How can you stop it?" Mari asked, her voice soft, like a whisper through the trees.

"We will kill the beast."

"How?"

"With sword. With luck." Iliana smiled. "We also have a special gift." She leaned in, closing some of the distance between herself and Mari. "We are on a quest, sent by the Goddess."

"Really?" Mari's eyes widened at the mention of the Goddess.

Ah, finally, something the child responded too. "Yes," Iliana replied, grasping at the opportunity. "The Goddess came to me in a dream and commanded I do these things. So you must understand that there is no need for you to see her yourself. At least not yet."

Mari smiled. It was a dazzling and infectious grin. Iliana knew she had convinced her.

"Are you two ready to go?" Lore called. Iliana looked over her shoulder. He leaned against Lev, looking for the entire world as relaxed as if he slept, but she knew better. His hand rested next to the hilt of his weapon, and while he leaned, he listened.

She turned back. "Well, are we?"

Mari gave a single nod. "Yes."

"Good." Iliana braced her hand against the tree to stand, and her fingertips touched something cold.

Cold and smooth and it did not feel like bark, but it felt familiar. Metallic.

She peered at the object, but it was difficult to make out as the bark obscured most of it. Still, a flash of sunlight shied off it, and it flashed gray.

Her breath caught. Using her knife, she chipped away at the bark. A chunk fell off, revealing the familiar talisman metal. Her heart rate sped up. "I have found it," Iliana shouted.

"Found what?" Lore called.

"Another talisman."

Mari edged closer. "You should leave that be. We need to go. You said so."

"Do not worry. I will hurry." By the Goddess, the bark was hard. She wedged the tip of the blade underneath an edge, and a large triangular shaped chunk fell to the ground. "Now, go and wait with Lore."

Mari clutched her hand. "I said, stop it."

Iliana shook her off. "I said, go. Wait with Lore."

"What about the monster?"

"It will be dead soon."

"I do not think so." Mari's voice deepened with each word. "The beast will live, Iliana. It is you who will die."

Iliana froze, her thoughts running back through their conversation with Mari.

Never once did Lore speak her name.

So how did Mari know it?

A feeling of dread roared through Iliana. She thought she heard Lore shouting something, yelling at her.

Slowly, she turned. It was not unlike a nightmare—the knowledge that you could not escape, that you had no choice but to watch the horror as it came at you until you woke.

What met her eyes was worse than any dream. Mari grew. Writhed like a thing possessed. Her skin stretched.

Within seconds, the child they planned to save was gone, and the fanged monstrosity from Lore's description stood in front of her, swaying on its hind legs.

Nine

Iliana screamed. The monster roared in response, its mouth opening wide to reveal a black tongue and row upon row of serrated teeth.

Somewhere, in the far reaches of her mind, a voice told Iliana to shut up and run.

She wanted too. Wanted to turn and flee. Flight was impossible. Frozen in fear, her legs were immobile. She screamed again, arms clenched into fists at her sides, eyes wide open and unable to turn away.

"Run!" The voice in the back of her mind thrust its way to the front. "Go. Now!"

It was not her fear shouting at her.

It was Lore. Out of the corner of her eye, she caught a glimpse of him behind the monster, running towards her, towards it, with his sword drawn.

Be calm. Be calm. Be calm. She could do this. Had to do this. She raised the knife.

"Run." Lore was closer now. His voice was louder. More urgent.

Knife raised, she backed against the tree. The monster leaned in. Inches away, its breath smelled of blood.

Her shaking fingers dropped the small weapon.

Tears burned her eyes. She did not want to die. Not now. Not like this. Not with her life and Lore's hanging in the balance.

The beast licked her cheek as if tasting her.

Bile rose in her throat, and for once, she was unable to control it. She wretched, great heaving spasms that dropped her to her knees.

A scream of pain and anger shredded the air around her, and the fetid breath disappeared.

Iliana wiped her mouth with the back of her hand and glanced up through eyes that stung. The beast and Lore circled each other like sparring partners, but this was anything but friendly. The beast bled from a long wound on its side. Despite that, it lunged forward, jaws snapping. Lore danced aside with the speed he was famous for.

The monster was almost as fast. Its front legs shot forward, claws snapping, and ripped the sleeve of Lore's tunic from his body.

Iliana's breath caught in her throat. "Lore! Watch out!" she screamed.

He shot her a glance, telling her with a single look that he did not need her advice, but he did need her to hide. Now.

She took one last look at him. Lore stared at the monster through hooded eyes with a look that made her stomach roll again. He was no longer a Warrior.

He was a predator.

She scuffled through the dead leaves and grass to hide behind the tree.

A sharp pain made her stop.

The knife. It was under her shin.

She grabbed the hilt. There had to be something she could do.

She remembered Mari's—no, the monster's—voice when it told her to leave the talisman be. It was when she tried to free it that the beast showed its true form. There was a connection. Something that scared the beast or at least worried it.

The talisman. It was when she tried to free it that the beast showed its true form.

If she could free the bit of metal, maybe they could use it against the monster.

She turned back to the tree and began hacking away at the bark that imprisoned the dull, silver-colored piece of metal. Behind her, the sounds of battle increased. The snap of a tree rent the air.

The knife slipped, nicking the heel of her hand. She barely noticed.

"Iliana, look out!"

She glanced over her shoulder to see a clawed foot coming at her head. She ducked out of the way and behind the tree, the knife still in her clenched fist.

She pressed herself against the pale bark, trying to make herself invisible.

The clawed fist came around the tree, ripping through her leggings and into her thigh.

Another scream rent the air. Hers.

And the beast dragged her closer.

Desperate, she stabbed downward with the knife, and the monster's scream of pain mixed with hers as it let go.

Her thigh poured blood. Her heart pounded like a fist inside her chest. Iliana yanked her tunic over her head and tied it around the gaping wound.

Clad only in her breast-band, leggings, and boots, she leaned against the tree. How could she have missed the child's true nature? Even without her Trancer powers, how could she not see the monster in Mari's eyes?

Another great crash caught her attention. "Lore!" Her useless leg dragging behind her, Iliana crawled to peer around the trunk of the tree. A sigh of relief escaped her lips. The beast was wounded, its strange blue blood spattering the ground like rain. Lore was dirty and sweaty, but red blood neither stained his skin nor the forest floor. He was unharmed. For now.

Once again, the beast swiped at Lore. He blocked it with his sword, and in a beat, he was behind the monster.

It followed, its teeth gnashing.

Lore ducked under the jaws and ran to the border of the small clearing. The beast followed.

He ducked out of reach. His speed saved him, but for how long? As wounded as the monster was, it did not appear to be weakening.

Iliana gritted her teeth. It was up to her to make this right. Up to her to save Lore.

The short blade still in her fist, she crawled back towards the talisman.

Her wounded leg burned. Throbbed. Unnatural heat crawled up her thigh like an icy flame.

She reached the talisman and propped herself up. She would end this.

The burning swept over her hip and through her abdomen, licking her sides like a sadistic lover.

She raised the knife. "Curse this," she muttered through clenched teeth.

She pounded the knife into the wood and managed to pry off a piece of bark. The searing pain reached her chest and gripped her heart like a fist. She ached with the heat.

The talisman was almost free now.

She raised the knife.

The flames inside reached her throat. It hurt to breathe. Made her want to sob with the effort.

She levered the knife under the talisman and pushed the handle. The talisman popped free and fell into the dead leaves next to her.

The burning reached her eyes. She turned her head and held

out her hand to Lore. He did not see her victory. He was on the ground, his blade out of reach. The monster towered over him, its claws poised to strike.

The burning reached her brain. She fell into the leaves as darkness enveloped her.

**

Will Iliana live?

The question burned in Lore's brain as he sat at the Trancer's bedside. She had slept all afternoon, resisting his efforts to wake her. At one point, he had even doused her face and the soles of her feet with cold spring water, but neither caused a reaction.

The last time he saw such a sleep was when the beast attacked the winemakers. One had lived, if one called being lost in slumber living.

Unable to eat or drink and weak from his wounds, the man had died within a handful of suns.

"Iliana?"

She did not respond. He could no longer wait for the Healer's draught to work. He needed to take her to someone with a more powerful medicine. Tonight.

Moving the blanket aside, he checked her bandaged thigh. Though no longer bleeding, it still looked unhealthy with the area around it reddened and inflamed.

With a worried sigh, he tucked the blanket back in around her. This was his fault. He should have been more cautious. More aware.

Now, Iliana paid the price for his ignorance. He tucked her hair behind her ear. "I will not let you die. Not now. Not ever."

She stirred at his touch.

He stilled.

Her dark lashes fluttered in the candlelight. She opened her eyes. "Lore?"

For a number of heartbeats, it was all he could do to breathe. "I am here." He bit his lip to keep from shouting with joy. With hope.

"Where am I?"

Knowing she needed to remain calm, Lore took a deep breath and beat back his desire to crow with happiness. "We are in Galion."

"Your home?"

"My father's home," he replied, unable to keep the bitterness from his voice.

She nodded, her eyes still half-lidded. "What happened? You were on the ground. Your sword was out of reach."

He remembered the moment all too well. The adrenaline that pumped through his veins. The taste of battle. Then the surge of horror as Iliana's scream broke his concentration, and he watched, helpless, as she fell into unconsciousness. "I know. Your scream drew my attention."

"I screamed?" Even as she spoke, her eyes glazed over in unnatural sleep.

The same surge of horror at seeing her collapse rushed through Lore again, and the brief moment of hope died. This was not a natural sleep. He gave her shoulder a shake. "Iliana!"

She started and opened her eyes. "I am sorry. I am just so tired. I can barely keep my eyes open." She yawned again. "Tell me more."

He hesitated. He should tell her about her condition. He knew it was the right thing to do. What a Warrior would do. What a Mentor was required to do.

Yet, the words would not come. He could not tell her that if she fell asleep again she might never wake up.

He glanced out the low window. The moons grew closer to the horizon. There was little time to waste in the telling of what happened.

Neither could he leave, knowing this might be the last time he spoke with her. The last time he heard her voice.

The last time he could touch her, not as a Mentor, but as a man.

He moved to stroke her hair and stopped. Desire or no, he could not touch her without her permission.

She glanced at him with sleepy eyes.

He held his breath.

With a sigh and a smile, she guided his hand to her.

Not caring if it was the sickness or true emotion that steered her hand, Lore buried his fingers in her hair, twining the strands around his fingers. Letting the black strands fall like so much dark water. His breath caught in his throat. He could neither lose her nor leave her. Not yet.

She leaned into his touch. "Tell me more."

Lore continued. "When I looked, you were lying on the ground, and there was something gushing from the tree. Liquid, perhaps an oil of some sort. I am not sure."

His knuckles brushed the side of her cheek. Despite their

ordeals, her skin was petal-soft.

"And?" Iliana prompted.

"Whatever the connection between the talisman, the tree and the creature, freeing the talisman broke it. Weakened the monster and made it vulnerable."

"I saw you. The creature was poised to strike. How did you get away?"

"Qi saved us." He wound another strand of her hair between his fingers.

"Really?"

Her question was but a murmur, and he knew he was losing her, again. "Iliana?"

"Yes," she whispered.

His eyes watered, and he squeezed them shut. He could take a thousand battles, kill a thousand men, and walk away with his heart intact.

How had this dark-haired Trancer managed to do what loss and death were unable to accomplish?

He continued, his voice tight. "Qi performed like a true Warrior's *rohha*. She galloped in and nipped the creature's tail. When it turned to bite her, I rolled away and grabbed my blade."

Iliana's lips parted, and Lore leaned in to listen.

"Is she all right?"

"She is fine. Much like her owner, she is more than what she appears and carries within her the heart of a Warrior."

Lore wove his fingers through hers and squeezed.

Iliana was asleep.

***

Lore shut the door to the small room and turned to face his father. With a fireplace burning bright, the room looked cozy. Warm.

And much like the monster, this room, this home, was not as it appeared.

Jaxom rose at Lore's approach. "Will she live?"

"I do not know, but I need to take her to a Healer tonight."

"She woke. That must be some cause for hope."

Jaxon sounded genuine, and a part of Lore wanted to believe the sincerity was true. He could not bring himself to trust that Jaxon was concerned with anything other than his wealth. Hope meant little to a man like that. "Why do you ask? Do you even care?" Lore snarled.

Jaxon's eyes widened. "Of course I care. She saved us. You saved us. That is a debt far greater than a simple thank you."

"We did not do it for you." Lore pushed past him. If they were to leave before the sun rose, there was work to be done. The trip to Kythae was a day's hard journey, and the ride would be rough if he wanted to get Iliana to the city before her condition worsened. He wished he could have moved her earlier, but until she woke, he was not sure she would survive the trip—no matter how short.

Jaxon followed. "I will pray for her well-being, if it will help."

Lore pressed his lips together. "Forgive me if I doubt your compassion. You sacrificed your own people. What does a stranger matter?"

"She is your woman."

His woman? Iliana belonged to no one, but his father would not understand such a concept. To him, all was about property— who had it, and who did not.

Jaxon continued, "She matters to me because you matter to me."

"I mat—" Lore clamped his jaw closed. He would not do this. Not argue. Not justify. Not say anything that might assuage Jaxon's guilt. A dark chuckle escaped his throat. Once, there was much he wanted to say. Much he wanted too ask of the man in front of him. None of it mattered anymore.

This was not his father. His blood. This was a stranger who sacrificed his people in the name of profit.

Lore flung open the cupboards and began searching for supplies. He opened a parchment. Within were slices of dried meat. He stuffed the meat into his satchel.

"Take whatever you need. Anything." Jaxon offered.

There was nothing else suitable for travel. Lore slammed the cupboard doors shut and went to load the *rohhas*.

The moons afforded some light. They would not be visible much longer. Dawn would be upon them soon. He tied the satchel to Qi.

Now, to transport Iliana. He picked up one side of the makeshift travois and dragged it to Lev's side. Qi might be brave but it would take more strength than the little *rohha* had to pull Iliana for any distance.

A heavy hand on Lore's shoulder caught his attention. "You may hate me, but I am still your father."

Lore shrugged Jaxon off and gritted his teeth as anger threatened to overwhelm years of training. He took a deep breath. And another. Control returned.

He faced Jaxon. "You gave up the right to be my father when you sold me."

"We were starving. What was I supposed to do? Watch you die?"

Lore did not remember the hunger. All he remembered was the pain at being sold. "You sold me to merchants. Sold your son."

Jaxon's eyes narrowed. "I did what was necessary. It was a hard choice, but there was no other."

As always, there was an excuse. A reason for doing the unthinkable. "You say that a lot," Lore scoffed. "It is convenient, is it not, to say there was no other choice when there is always another choice."

Jaxon's face remained impassive, and Lore knew that his words made little impact. He almost laughed at himself, at the thought that anything he said or did would make Jaxon understand the horror of his decisions. To try was a lesson in futility.

He hooked up one side of the travois to Lev.

The *rohha* danced sideways as the weight of the wooden and cloth frame settled behind him. Lore patted Lev's sleek neck. "Easy. It will not harm you."

Jaxon walked around the *rohha,* stopping in Lore's line of vision, and for a moment, Lore saw himself in Jaxon. Different coloring, but the same jaw. The same hands.

He wanted to be ill.

Jaxon crossed his arms. "Do you think it was easy, watching you leave? Crying that you would be good if I would let you stay?"

Lore did not look up. If he did, what little control he retained would vanish. Neither could he let Jaxon think, for a single beat of time, that what he did was excusable because he had also felt the pain of separation.

Lore tightened the first strap of the travois. "I am sure the weight of gold in your pocket was a comfort." Walking around Lev, he jostled Jaxon out of the way and tightened the second strap.

"It was not about the gold, and besides, you ended up with the Warriors. That is a better life than I could have given you."

"I ended up with the Warriors because Reapers killed my owners." Lore remembered the fear at being taken by the merchants. The betrayal. And later, the horror at watching his new master slaughtered.

Worse, was the memory of Jaxon jingling the small purse of gold. It was not much, just the price of a child.

Hot anger boiled to the surface. "Not about the gold?" Tell yourself whatever it takes to absolve your guilt, but do not expect me to do the same. You never sent for me. Not once."

"What was I suppose to do? I did not know you were with the Warriors. Not until later."

"Did you even look?"

"Who was I to bring you back here?" Jaxon asked.

"You were my father." Goddess help him, Lore's hand itched to draw his blade. Begged to be allowed to take vengeance, not for just the murdered villagers, but for the small boy whose father sold him.

His hands clenched and unclenched as he pounded back the anger. He turned away, pacing. He ran a hand over his hair in frustration, stopping at the Warrior's cord that bound the dark blond mass behind him.

He stopped pacing and took a deep breath. This was foolish. An argument that died many season ago when the Warriors took him in and claimed him as one of their own.

He was no longer a frightened child. He was the Master of Many Swords, and as such, he was bound by honor.

Control washed over him, soothing old wounds and bringing peace to his turbulent thoughts. "Jaxon, when I came to fight the beast the first time, when the winemakers died, I was prepared to greet you with open arms. All forgiven. There was no such greeting from you. No open arms. No tears. Simply a cold man who was more annoyed over the loss of profit than over the loss of life."

Lore took a deep breath. "Until that moment, I was prepared to believe you sold me out of love, but after seeing you and what you were." He shook his head. "Any childhood wish for a happy reunion died that day."

"It was not like that, Lore. You mistook control for coldness."

Jaxon did not understand. Never would. Even Warriors cried over the loss of brethren, and the winemakers that died were Jaxon's friends.

"No, I do not think so."

One last cinch and the travois was ready. Lore wrapped the thick sticks in cloth to prevent excess rubbing on Lev's side. "That does not matter now. The beast is dead, and there is nothing for you and the other villagers to worry about." He moved around Lev to wrap the other pole. "Nothing other than how to count your money."

Ten

Iliana beat on the bars of her cell, as Mako taunted her with the promise of freedom. Cloaked in shadow, he stood on the other side of her cell, laughing.

He kept her in darkness. Utter silence. Alone. She refused to beg for a light, for freedom or anything else. She had not begged when she was his prisoner before. She would not beg now.

A voice broke the darkness. "Iliana, you must fight this. Try to wake up."

It was not Mako. This voice was distant but kind. Mako never sounded kind. Not even when he wanted to.

She shook the door of the cage, but it refused to budge. The shadowed figure strode towards her, its black cloak billowing behind it. Iliana backed away, but it grabbed her, and pulled her close.

The voice caught her attention again. It was louder now. More insistent. "Apprentice, I said, open your eyes. Now."

With a scream of determination, she broke the grip of the shadow. The door to her cell swung open, and she ran through.

With a great sob of relief, she opened her eyes. The room was dim. A hand touched her shoulder.

With a shriek of defiance, she lashed out, fists flailing, trying to make contact with her attacker.

He grabbed her wrists.

She shrieked in frustration and struggled to break free.

"Iliana, you are all right. You are safe. Be calm." A concerned voice broke through the haze.

She hesitated.

"Shh. Be calm."

She recognized it. "Lore?"

The grip on her wrists was released. She took a deep breath, gathering her senses. Her vision cleared.

Lore looked down at her, a smile on his face. The cell was gone. She was free. There was no Mako.

She almost sobbed with relief.

Lore stroked her cheek for but an instant. "Welcome back."

"Where was I?" Her throat was dry as a dune. She swallowed, hard.

"Asleep. Dreaming."

Not a dream. A nightmare. Remembering Mako and his hold on her, she shuddered.

It was over now. Mako was gone. Dead. Best forgotten and left to the recesses of her mind.

And there were other issues more urgent.

Where was she? This was also not the same room she awoke in before. "Where are we?"

"Kythae."

"Kythae?" Had she been hit on the head? The last she remembered was going to sleep at Jaxon's. "When did we arrive?"

"Two suns ago."

"Two suns?" She shook her head. "Why do I not remember coming here?"

"Because you have been sick."

Sick? She seemed to be better now, but to not remember the trip? She must have been gravely ill.

He tucked a blanket around her shoulder and sat down on the bedside chair. "What do you remember?"

She searched her thoughts. "I remember talking to you in your father's home, but . . ." She searched for the words. "The conversation seems hazy. Like a dream. We spoke of Qi. The monster." And there was more than conversation. Her cheeks burned with a heat that was not a fever as she remembered how Lore had stroked her hair, and she had wanted him to. Encouraged it.

"It was no dream."

He gazed down at her, relief in his eyes, and Iliana shifted, both enjoying the attention and wanting to escape at the same time. The heat spread from her cheeks to the top of her head and the tips of her toes.

She continued. "I remember the talisman."

Lore reached into the pouch that hung from the leather cord around his neck and drew forth a piece of metal.

The talisman.

Taking her hand in his, he placed it in her palm and folded her fingers over it.

Heavy and cold, it weighed more than she thought it would. She opened her palm. The same silver color as its brethren, this one was round and marked with three wavy lines.

She stroked it with a fingertip. "What does it mean?"

"It is another sign. A marker of a place."

"Another monster?" She trembled at the possibility.

He shook his head. "No. I think that part of the test is over." Taking the bit of metal from her tired fingers, he put it back in the pouch around his neck. "We travel to the Spring of Kylan."

"How far?"

"Once we reach the far side of the city, we will cross the lake to reach the spring." He stood. "We will leave as soon as you are strong enough to travel."

They had already wasted enough time. She flipped the covers back, realized she wore only a thin shirt, and yanked them back up. "I am strong enough. Bring me some clothes."

"No, you are not, and not until you are well."

She struggled to sit back up and keep the covers about her at the same time. "I am fine." Besides, she wanted to leave the dim room. She needed the warmth of sunlight.

His jaw clenched, Lore gently pushed her into the pillow. "By the Goddess, Iliana, you do not understand. You almost died."

The intensity in his voice caught her off guard. "What do you mean, I almost died?"

He leaned forward, elbows on knees. "I almost lost you. If I had not found a Healer skilled beyond even my hopes, you would still be sleep, never to waken."

Her first reaction was to argue her point, but the look in Lore's eyes stopped her. She had never seen it before. Guilt? Sorrow?

Again, she moved to sit up and flinched as her wounded leg twinged with unexpected pain.

Lore winced. "It pains you. I will not have you using it."

"My leg does not hurt much, and I am quite awake. There is no need to fuss over me." She saw her words made little impact. He looked just as angry. Just as guilty. Did he blame himself for this?

She inched her hand along the blanket, the urge to comfort him overwhelming.

"Ah, you waken." An unknown voice, and the slamming of the door, broke into the argument.

Iliana propped herself up on her elbows, watching as a wizened old man shuffled towards them. His homespun tunic was unadorned. His leggings just as plain.

What little remained of his gray hair stuck out in all directions.

Lore stood, offering his seat. "Healer, I was just explaining to Iliana the gravity of her situation."

A male Healer? Iliana had never heard of such a thing. She tried to keep the surprise off her face.

The Healer motioned Lore to move aside. He held a hand out to Iliana. "Sit."

She ignored his assistance and pushed herself upright, being careful of her thigh.

The Healer shook his head and pulled the blanket away from her leg.

She yanked it back.

He slapped her hand. "None of that. I have seen more flesh than yours, Trancer, and I have no interest other than to heal it."

She met his eyes, and while his voice was harsh, his expression was kind. His blue eyes twinkled as he sat in the chair across from her.

Besides, it was either let him pronounce her well or let Lore keep her in bed until her leg was healed.

She set the blanket aside. "Can I ride?" she asked.

He motioned her to lean away. She watched as he examined her wound. He had sewn it shut, but otherwise, it looked healthy with no tenderness at his touch or redness around the edges.

He leaned back. "I would rather you wait a few days."

"We shall," Lore answered.

Iliana glared up at him. "We do not have a few days."

The Healer shrugged. "Ride slow. In ten suns, you," he pointed to Lore, "will need to cut the threads from her wound. Can you do that?"

"It will not be a problem," Lore replied. "I have seen worse."

The Healer laughed, his voice surprisingly young for such an ancient man. "Battle is different, Warrior. Those are comrades in arms. Not a lover."

Lore's face flushed. "Uh, we are not . . . It is not what you think . . ."

Lovers? Iliana knew her face burned as well.

Did Lore like the idea, or was he appalled?

Lovers. The word caressed her.

The heat deepened. She pulled the blanket back over her bare legs and smoothed it with the flat of her hand.

The Healer stood with a grunt and shuffled towards the door.

***

Iliana gritted her teeth in pain as she and Qi followed Lore through the wide streets of Kythae. They had ridden since the sun reached its peak and had not reached the outer edge of the city.

Perhaps Lore had a point in that she was not ready to ride. Her thigh throbbed in time with the beat of her heart, and she wanted to cry with the agony or at least beg for a short rest.

Her stomach growled. Soon, it would be time for the evening meal. Did he plan to eat or just ride until she broke down?

She opened her mouth to ask but stopped herself. Any admittance of weakness would make Lore more difficult to deal with.

Even now, he insisted on leading Qi through the crowded streets. Iliana tugged on the reins.

Lore held firm. "If she bolts, you could get hurt."

Iliana sighed at his continued attention. It was both comforting and annoying, in equal portions, and she was ready for it to end. "Qi stood up to the beast." She patted the petite *rohha's* neck. What was once a burdensome animal was now her savior, ally and even more important, friend. "I do not think a few people will startle her."

Lore glanced over at her and let the reins go. "Stay close."

She squelched the urge to stick out her tongue, took the reins, and kicked Qi into motion. Slowly, the *rohha* stepped on delicate hooves though the crowded streets.

Despite her annoyance and weariness, Iliana could not ignore the vendors they passed. She had never been one for buying trinkets, but Kythae was amazing. One vendor sold cloths of such hues that she could only marvel at how he managed to create colors that almost glowed.

Next to him, a woman called out that her jewelry was of the finest workmanship, and from what Iliana saw, she thought the woman right. A kirtle, made of what looked like finely spun metal, caught her attention.

Lore glanced at her over his shoulder and slowed Lev until he rode by Iliana's side. "Kythae is known for its artisans, but there is something else I want you to see besides trinkets." He pulled Lev to the left and around a corner. Iliana followed, and what met her gaze astounded her.

The road spread to either side. In front of her, the land dropped away and there was nothing but water—a vast expanse the color of an exotic crystal and just as clear.

Below, a boat crossed her vision, its bright yellow sails

flapping in the breeze. A work of art unto itself with its ornately carved prow, she gaped in awe as it raced towards the pier and came to an abrupt halt just before it slammed into the wooden pilings.

"You will catch bugs if you do not shut your mouth." Lore chuckled.

She clapped her jaw shut and tried to ignore his amusement.

He chuckled again. "Do not be embarrassed. I looked much the same when I first saw the sacred lake of Kythae."

"This is a lake?" She could not see the shore to either side. Only a distant mountain gave any indication of a shore.

"Yes," Lore replied. Dismounting, he took Qi's reins again and walked Iliana and her *rohha* towards a two-story, wooden building that rested on a stone outcropping overlooking the water. "We stop here for the night," Lore commented over his shoulder.

"What about Kylan?"

"There is a ferry across the lake in the morning. It is either that or circle the lake—which would take us more than two suns."

Iliana gave a relieved nod. She might not admit it to Lore, but she was desperate for a rest. "If you say so."

Lore nodded. "I do."

He led her the rest of the way in silence, around the building and to the stables on the other side.

A young boy, busy mucking out the stalls, looked up, shielding his eyes against the sunlight.

Dismounting, Lore flipped him a coin and signaled him to take the *rohhas*.

Rest. It was a splendid thought. Her weariness catching up to her, Iliana slid off Qi. Lore caught her before she hit the ground, his large hands lingering on her waist.

Lovers. The Healer's comment flashed through her thoughts.

She knew she blushed. The heat of it radiated from the pit of her stomach to the top of her head.

A heartbeat passed before he let go. "You must remember to be wary of jarring your leg. If you break the threads holding the wound closed, we will have to find another Healer."

She nodded, mentally kicking herself for her carelessness. She took a step and flinched, wishing for a walking stick. She grit her teeth, determined not to show any pain.

Lore's hand touched her shoulder, stopping her before she took another step. "Iliana?"

She stopped. "Yes?"

"You do not have to be brave for me. I already know your courage, and it is not in doubt." He held out a hand. "Let me help you."

She shook her head. She would not have him think her weak. Not now. "I am fine." She took another step and swayed.

Lore caught her, one arm around her waist. "So fine that you can barely walk." He pulled her close. "Do not let your pride keep you from asking for assistance when needed."

She leaned into him. He was right. As much as her pride hated to admit it, it was pleasant having him hold her, which was even harder to confess.

He walked her back to the front of the building and up the short steps. Painted in gold above the door was the phrase, 'Be content. Be welcome'. Iliana smiled. A well-run, quiet inn was just what she needed.

Lore opened the door with his free hand, and once again her mouth dropped open. This was not an inn unless inns featured half-dressed women and men.

A woman, dressed in nothing but a short, red silken tunic came forward to greet them. "Be content. Be welcome." She bowed her head in greeting, dark curls falling forward to obscure her face.

"Thank you." Lore bowed his head in return and held out a gold coin. "We seek shelter and food for the night."

The woman looked up, brushing her hair back with a pale hand. "As you wish."

Iliana hid her torn, calloused hands behind her back, acutely aware of her less than clean clothes and her dusty, unkempt hair. She was not vain, had not thought about her hair in many suns, but now she wished it once again reached the tops of her thighs, and she cursed Mako for chopping it off.

She tucked a loose strand behind her ear.

The young woman smiled. "You look weary. Let me show you to your room. I am called Gwenlyn." She held out her hand.

Lore accepted the gesture, and a surge of jealousy shot through Iliana as Gwenlyn led them to the stairs. Iliana glanced upwards. The stairs were steep. Too steep for her to climb with her wounded leg. "Is there a room on this floor?" Iliana asked.

Gwenlyn shook her head. "These are all pleasure rooms. If

you want—"

"No, thank you." Lore cut her off. "A room, bath and food are sufficient."

"As you wish, Warrior," Gwenlyn said.

Iliana glanced at Lore out of the corner of her eye. Was he turning red? She tried to hide the smile that threatened to turn her lips upwards.

He caught her gaze and returned it. The desire, the sheer need Lore radiated in his glance, told her that he did not cut off Gwenlyn because of embarrassment.

He cut her words short because they were truth. He desired pleasure. Intimacy. Passion.

But from whom?

Lovers.

Relentlessly, the Healer's comment pursued her, but there was no more time to speculate or protest as Lore lifted her into his arms and followed their hostess up the stairs.

***

Still warm from her bath and clad in a robe, Iliana padded back to her room. With her wound well wrapped, and a numbing salve applied, she felt relaxed and content for the first time in many a sun. The long hallway was lined with windows that not only afforded light but also gave her a view of the sun setting over the lake. She stopped and watched as the deepening rays turned the lake to liquid gold.

Kythae must be a blessed city, as she had never seen anything so wonderful.

Her stomach growled, and she tightened the sash about her waist as she continued onward, past the doorways that lined the second half of the hallway. She hoped the food was as exquisite as everything else.

She opened her door and stopped.

This was not her room.

It was Lore's bathing room, and the Warrior was no longer in the water.

His back to her, he wore but a cloth tied around his hips. His wet, blond hair was unbound and reached almost to his waist. The candlelight in the room, combined with the golden sunset streaming through the large window, created shadows highlighting every sculpted muscle and giving him an ethereal glow.

He was not alone.

Still in her short tunic, Gwenlyn came up behind him with a thick cloth, her slim hands massaging Lore as she dried his back.

They did not know she had entered the room.

Her mind screamed at her to turn around and run. Leave before she was discovered. Instead, her body was frozen in shock and confusion as she stared at the tableau in front of her.

How could he let another woman touch him with such intimacy? How? Iliana's knees threatened to buckle as Gwenlyn reached Lore's waist, and the cloth covering him shifted downward an inch.

"May I ask you a question Warrior?" Gwenlyn asked as she worked her way towards Lore's thighs.

"Yes." He stretched, rotated his head from side to side as if to work the final kinks from his neck.

"Is the woman your mate?"

Lore shook his head, and Iliana's skin burned with the question and his answer. She tried to inhale, but the very act almost doubled her over in pain.

"Why not take pleasure with me?" Gwenlyn continued. "You have traveled long and must desire a woman by now, and I am curious to experience the legendary control of a Warrior."

"I appreciate your curiosity," Lore answered, turning as he spoke. "I cannot—"

He stopped speaking as soon as his eyes met Iliana's.

She shook, knowing she should have left. Maybe. Perhaps. By the Goddess, she did not know anything anymore other than she wanted Gwenlyn to take her hands off Lore.

Gwenlyn reached for Lore's covering, and he stopped her with a touch. "Leave."

She followed his gaze and met Iliana's. The courtesan gave a single nod but otherwise showed no emotion. "As you wish. I shall prepare your meal." Dropping the drying cloth to the floor, Gwenlyn left through a side door.

Lore ran a hand over his damp hair with a sigh. "How long have you been standing there?"

"Long enough." Iliana bit her lip. She wanted to cry, to shout, to find Gwenlyn and beat her until she bled.

It was not her place. She and Lore were partners. Master and Apprentice. Companions on a quest.

And while the lack of more had niggled her brain, it had never bothered her. Until now.

Lore picked up the cloth from the floor and tossed it into a corner. "It was not how it looked."

"It looked like she was drying you."

Lore sighed again. "Then it was how it looked, but that was all it was. It is her position to offer other services."

"Do those services include bedding her?" A tiny voice of reason in her head told her to shut up. It was not her place to judge Lore.

She could not shut up. Could not let it go, let Lore go, without finding out why Lore let Gwenlyn touch him—when it should have been her?

Even in the candlelight, the red heat of embarrassment colored Lore's face. "Whom I bed is my choice." He turned back to the window. "Besides, I turned her down."

Shutting the door, Iliana walked to him. Talking to Lore was more frightening than the beast or any trial, but she needed answers. Without them, she was not sure she could go any further. "Why? She was right. You have not been with a woman in . . ." She stopped, realizing she had never seen Lore with a lover nor heard whispers of female conquests. Ever. She continued. "Anyway, I know it has been a long time. Why deny yourself?"

He turned back to her. The sun was almost below the horizon now, and the shadows were deep. Lore's eyes were dark in the candlelight. "What do you want of me, Iliana?"

"I do not know." She twisted her sash around her hand.

"I think you do," Lore replied. "I would like to hear what it is."

She crossed her arms over her chest and shook her head. Why did he have to press her for answers she would rather not admit to herself much less to him?

She walked past him and over to the window, leaning on the sill, wishing she felt anger instead of the ache that consumed her.

Anger was so much easier to deal with.

He stood behind her, so close she felt the heat of his skin. "I did not mean to hurt you," he whispered. "Letting Gwenlyn assist me meant nothing. Was nothing." He hesitated. "She was not the one I wanted to touch me. There is only one person I crave. A Trancer. And she cannot speak her thoughts, so I do not know what to say to her."

Her pulse quickened and her eyes burned at his kindness of

distancing the conversation so she could say what was needed.

It was so like him. Dark in battle. But in the ways of men and women, he was kind. Thoughtful. So gentle it threatened to break her.

Iliana swallowed hard. "What if this Trancer spoke her heart?" She whispered. "What if she told you of her desire? Her fear that you might not feel the same? Might think of her only as a traveling companion, nothing more? What would you say?"

The silence grew. Lore put his hand on her waist.

She did not flinch at his touch. She welcomed it.

He turned her to face him. Iliana met his steady, dark gaze.

He smiled. "I would tell her that this Warrior feels the same desire. The same fears."

Iliana laid her palm against his rough cheek. "I thought great Warriors felt no such fear."

"This Warrior is also a man." Lore kissed her palm.

Shivers ran down Iliana's spine to the soles of her feet.

He did not move any closer, and Iliana realized what he waited for. He waited for her to kiss him. To show she was ready for what he offered.

His kindness overwhelmed any lingering trepidation.

Standing on tiptoe, she brushed his mouth with hers, and he opened to her, returning the kiss, but letting her set the pace.

He tasted like wine. And she was thirsty for more. She drank of his taste. His scent. His very touch. She nipped his lip and swallowed his sharp hiss of desire. Her hands roved across his chest of their own accord. Testing his flesh. Stroking his muscle.

He tasted her. Nibbled the corner of her mouth. Traced her ear with his tongue. His hands, firm and sure, pulled her closer, fitting her against him. Finally, with a cry of hunger, he slanted his mouth across hers, his tongue tasting her until she grew lightheaded with need.

By the Goddess, she could spend an eternity with him, and it would never be enough.

As if sensing her desire, Lore picked her up and walked through the doorway. Their meal was on the table, and the room was empty.

He laid her on the bed and locked the doors. She watched him as he walked back towards her, marveling at how much she desired the Warrior who came to her.

Until Lore, there was no thought of passion. Only fear. Only dreams of Mako and the darkness he wanted to give her.

Lore was her light.

He stretched out next to Iliana measuring her with the length of his body.

Feeling the power that came with desire, she traced his lips with a fingertip. "Do you want me, Warrior?"

His hand on her hip, he pulled her against him. "Your leg? How is it? I do not want to hurt you."

His desire pressed against her, hard and hot. "My wound is nothing when compared to my need." Her smile broadened as she slipped her hand under the single cloth that covered him, wrapped her fingers around his length, and squeezed.

With a groan, Lore pulled her closer. He had never felt such an urgent, almost painful, desire to sink inside a woman and lose himself in her sweetness.

He took a deep breath. She smelled fresh, clean from her recent bath. He reminded himself that Iliana was also vulnerable—much more so than she wanted to believe or let show. As much as he wanted to ravage her, he would take his time. Treat this as if he were her first.

She rolled on top of him. Astride him, she was a goddess. Her thin robe fell open, and her black hair brushed the tops of her dusky-tipped breasts.

He could not help himself as he rose and took her nipple in his mouth. He had to taste her. Touch her.

She moaned, and he suckled harder while his other hand drew lazy circles on her back.

She writhed against him, and his body responded. He fell back into the pillows before the need to take Iliana overwhelmed all else.

"What is wrong?" Iliana asked. Her eyes were half-lidded with desire, but he heard the fear of rejection in her voice and remembered what had happened the last time they kissed.

How he pulled away.

That would not happen again.

He cupped her cheek in his hand. "Nothing is wrong. I am too eager and fear this will be over before it even begins."

She smiled and relaxed.

He rubbed her thigh, and she flinched in his arms. Goddess, he should be more cautious. "Your wound pains you. Maybe we should wait."

With a tug, she undid the belt of her robe and let it slip from her shoulders. "No waiting."

Carefully, he rolled her over and under him. He knelt between her thighs. "I do not want you to break your stitches."

Leaning over her, he propped himself up on his elbows and kissed her full lips, tracing her bottom lip with his tongue, savoring the soft texture.

Her knees gripped his waist. "Do not be too gentle, Lore," she whispered. "I want to feel the legendary Warrior control." She bit his ear.

He laughed. Gentleness shifting into passion, he took her mouth as his hand traced down her stomach to the warmth that rested between her thighs.

Slick and hot, she was ready for him. He stroked her with his fingertips.

She arched upward, pressing against his hand. Smiling, he kissed a path down her throat, working his way to her breasts, with licks and gentle nibbles.

"This is torture," she moaned, her hands tangling in his hair.

He chuckled. "Torture? Should I stop?" He had forgotten how much fun it was to urge a woman to distraction.

"By the Goddess, no!"

He chuckled again and continued his path downwards. He glanced up. Her hands clutched the headboard, and her body strained for release. He would make sure she received it.

And more.

The heat between her thighs called to him, and he could no longer wait to hear her cries. He took her, kissed her with lips and tongue, loving the taste of her.

With a shriek, she shuddered and arched upwards. He cupped her bottom with his hands, holding her to him as waves of pleasure coursed through her.

She cried out again, bucking against his mouth, and he almost lost control. Only years of training kept him sane. Kept him from taking her.

When she relaxed in his arms, he groaned and let her drop back to the mattress.

Tearing the towel from around his waist, he rose to his knees and gazed down at the beauty of Iliana. The candlelight turned her skin to gold, like a Goddess that few would ever be privileged enough to worship.

She smiled up at him, but it was anything but a lazy, satisfied smile. It was the wicked grin of a woman who had only sampled a taste of desire and wanted more.

He held his hand out. Iliana took it and pulled him to her.

She wanted him like she wanted air. Not even the Given ceremony, when she went from Maiden to Apprentice, compared to her desire to have Lore inside of her. To feel him move with her. Flesh upon flesh. His heart beating in time with hers.

There was just the sound of her breath in his ear as she gripped his hips with her knees, and he slipped inside of her.

An almost painful passion surged through her veins, as he sunk into her depths.

He moaned and stopped, his hands clenching the covers beneath them. He stared at her, his eyes hungry with need. The muscles in his arms and shoulders bunched as he tried to remain in control.

Iliana shifted her hips. "There is no need to hold back. I have waited a long time for you. A lifetime." She clutched his back, pulling him deeper. Closer. Slowly, she pulled away then thrust her hips upwards, almost sobbing in joy as he throbbed within her body.

"Again," he groaned, his voice desperate.

She let his length slide away then back again.

With a cry, Lore gathered her in his arms, rose to his knees, and rocked back on his thighs so she was astride his lap.

Quickly, they found a rhythm, and Iliana held on to his shoulders as he slid his length into her again and again.

His hands still on her hips, he pressed her against him, his lips buried in her hair.

The familiar sensation of release grew inside her, tight and hot. She gasped at the sweet completion of having Lore within as she surged towards satisfaction.

With a cry, Lore pulled her to him and lightly bit her neck, sending her over the edge to join him as he shouted his pleasure and release.

Eleven

Across the street from the brothel and hidden by the shadows, Medea waited, emotions warring within her breast. On one hand, she was pleased that Iliana and her Warrior had managed to overcome the monster. On the other, Iliana lived.

She ran a palm over her skirt, tracing the knife she kept strapped to her thigh. The Trancer's continuing existence was becoming bothersome.

At least Kole was leaving her alone. He also spent the night in a brothel. A less expensive one, to be sure, but a brothel nonetheless. His pathetic attempts to bed her were almost as annoying as Iliana. Almost, but not quite.

Medea ran a hand through her hair and listened as the town came to life with the rising of the sun. It would not be long now. Soon, the Warrior and Iliana would emerge, and when they did, she would follow them.

The door to the brothel opened, and she pressed herself against the wall of the building. It was the Warrior. Alone.

Calmly, she watched as he passed her. He did not notice her.

The quick pace. The solid steps. He was a man with a mission.

She smiled. Not that it mattered if he saw her. He had never met her. Did not know what she looked like. To him, she was simply a dark-haired beauty. In Kythae, dark hair was common.

She followed him. He entered the market, and she trailed him with hurried footsteps. He passed stalls of fruit. Baked goods. His intensity roused her curiosity. Whatever he was after, it was not breakfast.

What mattered so much that he would leave Iliana alone and unprotected?

After all, when the Trancer whore was ill and with the Healer, the Warrior never left her side.

Lore slowed. They were in the weapons district.

Interesting. Medea stopped to adjust her boot, tugging on the leather and keeping her eyes on her prey.

He stopped at the swords-smiths. Why a sword? His Warrior's blade rested against his thigh. She sidled closer, listening as best she could.

"No. Shorter. It is for a woman." Lore waved away the long

blade the smith had presented to him.

"A woman?" The sword smith's eyes widened in surprise. "Since when do women carry swords?"

Lore smiled. "It is strange, I know, but it is truth. She is Apprentice to me, and I would not have her defenseless."

Iliana was a Warrior's Apprentice? The Trancer surprised her. Truly, she did not think Iliana had the courage or the blood lust to wield a blade.

"Apprentice?" The smith shook his head. "The world changes too much when a woman can be an Apprentice."

Lore's smiled widened. "I was once skeptical of the idea, but I have since seen just how strong a woman can be."

Still shaking his head, the smith began rummaging through his inventory.

"Show me that one." Lore pointed toward the upper shelf. "The one with the blue stone set in the hilt."

She did not need to read thoughts to know that the Warrior was smitten with Iliana—Apprentice or not. She heard it in his voice. Saw it in his lovesick grin.

If she kissed him, she was sure she would taste Iliana on his lips.

The Trancer and Warrior were lovers. Of that, there was little doubt.

Medea grinned. Now, there was one more item the Trancer possessed that she could take.

She itched with the desire to seduce the Warrior. Bed him. Show him the ways of pleasure and then slip her knife between his ribs.

She quelled the urge. It was not time. There was still work to be done. Trials to overcome.

She needed him. For now.

Death could come later.

Twelve

Iliana woke to daylight and an empty bed.

Where was Lore?

The thought that he had left her behind flickered through her mind, but only for a moment. Lovers or no, he would not leave her. To think such a thought was the old Iliana.

And she had buried her last night with Lore's help.

Iliana stretched, grinning as she remembered last night's lovemaking. Lore was magnificent. Tender. As learned in the skill of love as he was in weaponry. Her body was sore in the best of all possible ways.

The door opened. Iliana bolted upright, clutching the blanket to her chest.

Lore walked in, a rectangular cloth-covered box in his hand. He stopped mid-step and gazed at her, as if seeing her for the first time.

She blushed, despite their intimacy. There was something unnerving about him being dressed while she was naked beneath the blanket.

He smiled, humor in his eyes. "Shy?"

Her skin burned hot, and she did not need to look beneath the blanket to know that she blushed from head to heel.

Lore kicked the door shut behind him and set both his scabbard and the package on the table before coming to her. "There is nothing to be shy about. Not anymore." Pulling the blanket down, he kneeled and kissed her exposed breasts, taking a moment to tug on a nipple with his mouth.

The familiar surge of desire worked its way through her blood. Iliana pulled him up and to her. Lore resisted and pushed away.

She breathed deep with disappointment. "Done so soon?"

He shook his head. "No, but I have something for you."

She ran a hand up his thigh, stopping to rub him, enjoying the feel of him as he hardened under her touch. "Yes, you do."

His breath hissed through clenched teeth. "That is not what I meant." He took her hand in his, nipped a fingertip, and put it back in her lap. "Do anymore and I will not be able to walk." He straightened with a groan, went to the table, and picked up the package. "Shut your eyes."

She raised a brow.

He shrugged and set the package back on the small table. "As you wish."

Curiosity surged forth, and Iliana leaned forward. "What is it?"

"A present. Now shut your eyes or I will throw it into the lake."

With a sigh of resignation, she rolled her eyes before closing them.

The wooden floor creaked as Lore walked back to her. He stopped. "Hold out your hands."

She held them out, palms up.

He laid the package in her hand. Her hands sank with the unexpected heaviness of her gift. Whatever it was, it was solid.

"Can I open my eyes, or shall I unwrap it blind?"

Lore chuckled. "Go ahead. Open your eyes."

She opened them. It had been many a season since she had received a present. Fingers shaking, she undid the twine that bound the package, unfolded the edges of the cloth, and removed the box's lid.

Her breath caught.

A sword.

She set the box on the bed and pulled the scabbard to her lap. Unable to believe it was real, Iliana pulled the blade free. It was not as long as Lore's weapon nor was it ornate. Simple in style and elegance with a single blue stone set in the hilt in the way of finery.

It glinted in the morning light. Its weight pulled at her arm.

It was real. Not a knife. Not a dagger.

A sword. For her.

She ran a finger along the blade and promptly sliced her flesh. Grinning, she thrust the wounded appendage into her mouth.

Using more caution, she wrapped her fingers around the hilt and raised her weapon. She had never felt anything so perfect.

It was hers.

The bed sank as Lore sat next to her. "There are no finer craftsmen of weaponry than those found in Kythae."

She could not take her eyes off the glint of the metal.

Lore continued. "The stone matches your eyes." He ran a hand through her hair, sending shivers through her skin. "Do you like it?"

She opened her mouth to speak, but only a sob emerged. No one, not even Aria, had ever given her something so wonderful.

He touched her damp cheek. "I take it that is a yes?"

Carefully, she sheathed the sword back in its scabbard and laid the weapon on the floor beside the bed.

She yanked Lore down to her, and they sank into the mattress. Never had she ever wanted a man like she wanted Lore at this moment in time.

Desperate to feel his flesh against hers, she pulled his shirt over his head and tugged on his leather breeches, pulling them over his hips. He kicked them off and to the end of the bed.

Another heartbeat and he was inside of her. It was not enough. She wanted him deeper. Closer.

He moved inside her. Kissed her. Bit her shoulder.

Goddess, she wanted to blend with him. Merge her soul. Within her mind, something cracked. She gasped as her dormant Trancer skills fought to emerge. Teased her thoughts with promises. Twisted through the tiny break in her shield.

Lore moved faster. Harder. As if the very force of his body could break apart anything that kept him from her.

She arched, clawing at the air as the black wall hiding her Trancer skills shook with the force of the power building within. Her heart pounded in expectation.

Lore slowed. Somewhere in the distance, she thought he asked about her leg. Did he hurt her?

With his gentleness, the small gap in the black wall hiding her skills closed.

She wanted to howl with the loss. Until this moment, she was not sure she wanted her talent to return. Now, with Lore inside of her, loving her, she wanted nothing more than to share that part of her with him.

"Iliana." Lore whispered her name as his hand reached between them to caress her.

With his touch, all regret and thought dissolved, and desire took its place. Lore moved within her again, caressing her as he sank into her body.

A wild man, he claimed her mouth, and her desire peaked, erasing any thoughts other than those of Lore as he joined her.

Countless heartbeats later, she found herself looking into his eyes, passion spent, and desire replaced by sweet satisfaction.

He rolled away from her and onto his side. "Next time, I

shall bring you a shield as well."

Iliana giggled. "Do not think I will always thank you like that."

He hugged her to him. "I can try."

Lying in his arms, she let her thoughts float, feeling free for the first time in many a season.

He played with her hair, letting it run through his fingers. Twisting the strands, stroking them.

She shut her eyes, drifting with the tenderness of his touch.

"Iliana?"

She snuggled closer. "Yes?"

"There are some aspects to owning a weapon that I want you to think about."

She sighed, knowing Lore, her lover, was gone, and in his place was her Mentor. She rolled away and into a sitting position.

Standing, Lore grabbed his clothes and dressed. He sat down next to her. "I gave you a weapon because it has become apparent you need one, but that does not mean that I want you to use it."

The old, familiar anger pricked at her thoughts. "Why bother?"

"I do not think you are ready, but I can see now that you need something more than a knife to defend yourself. It is clear that we are going to be in situations that neither one of us can predict, and while I do not think we will come upon another beast, there is no way I can be sure." He glanced at her wounded leg. "It seems that despite my intention to protect you, I cannot always do so and would not see you defenseless."

She bit her lower lip as guilt blossomed. He blamed himself for her being hurt. The desire to comfort him overwhelmed her. He was the Master of Many Swords, and so vulnerable it broke her heart.

She laid a gentle hand on his forearm. "What happened to me was not your fault."

He managed a weak smile. "You are kind to say so."

"It is true." She squeezed.

He removed her hand. "I will not argue. Suffice it to say that I will not have you put in such a position again." He brought her hand to his mouth and kissed her palm before pressing it to his heart. "Especially now."

***

Iliana breathed a sigh of both relief and trepidation.

Relief that the journey across the Sacred Lake was almost

over—the ferry was crowded with people and their goods, her leg ached, and though the boat was well constructed, it made her uncomfortable to be on water with a storm coming.

Trepidation in that Lore worried about her to the point of being unreasonable.

Soon they would be at the Spring of Kylan. Who knew what new monstrosity would greet them, and Lore hindered their mission by worrying for her safety.

He could be as stubborn as a *rohha.*

Leaning against the rail, Iliana watched the whitecaps and prayed she and Lore were ready for the unknown.

A large man jostled her, interrupting her thoughts. Iliana flinched at the unexpected contact.

"Are you hurt, miss?"

"I am fine." The stranger's overripe scent reached her nose, and she took a step back. The railing pressed against the small of her back. "Thank you for your concern."

He grinned, showing a mouth full of uneven teeth. "You are welcome." He inched closer, invading her personal territory. "Do you travel alone?"

"No," she replied, wishing he would back away. She glanced around. Despite the crowded conditions, no one paid the little scenario any heed, and there was no sign of Lore returning from checking on Lev and Qi.

"Then where is your companion?"

"Returning," Iliana replied through clenched teeth. "In but a moment."

The stranger leaned in, closing the gap between them. "I would be more than happy to keep you company, if you so desire. It is not safe for such a pretty girl to be standing all alone."

His words seemed innocent, but his actions spoke otherwise. His leer reminded her of Mako. Iliana set her hand on the hilt of her sword. "I am not alone." The wind over the water whipped her cloak about, revealing the weapon at her side.

The stranger glanced at her hip and grinned. "That is a big needle for such a little girl."

Little girl? She scowled but held her ground.

The man hesitated, as if he wanted to say more, but instead of speaking, he crowed with laughter.

Iliana glared at him.

Still chuckling, he grinned and left, disappearing into the

crowd.

Relieved, Iliana released the breath she had not realized she had been holding and flipped her cloak back over her sword. The ship rocked hard to the right, and she caught herself with her wounded leg, stumbled, and grabbed the railing, almost tumbling headfirst into the lake before catching herself.

"Are you all right?"

It was Lore. For a moment, Iliana was not sure if he spoke of her encounter with the strange man or her near miss at a dunking.

He continued. "You should be more careful. You will pull your stitches."

Another near miss. If he knew she had showed her weapon, he would scold her, despite the stranger's uncomfortable advances. Smiling, she tucked a strand of windblown hair behind her ear. "I am fine. You worry too much."

"Is that a bad thing?"

She shook her head and let him pull her to his side.

Snuggling into his warmth, she gazed over the waters, letting the crowd, the noise, and the stench of bodies fade away.

A wave broke over the edge of the ferry, dousing her feet. Although a brighter shade of blue, the waters that surrounded the craft were not unlike those that bordered the shores of her Tower.

Was it truly herself that was raised in the Tower as a Trancer? She remembered the training, the love that had surrounded her. The Elder Mother, gray-haired but with the fire of youth in her blue eyes. Classes filled with Apprentices, eager to learn.

The Healer who died for her—her throat cut by Mako.

She lost so much the night the Reapers came—her friends, her family, and herself. She shivered at the memories.

Lore wrapped his cloak around her, drawing her against his chest so her back faced the waters.

Iliana sighed in appreciation, and the dark memories faded as he enclosed her in his warmth.

She shut her eyes and let the rocking of the ship, the steady sound of the wind, and the heat of Lore's body lull her.

"Prepare to disembark!"

The call from the ferry's captain broke the feeling of solitude. She opened her eyes to see a rocky shore looming closer. Lore kissed the top of her head. "We should prepare the *rohhas*."

She nodded, took one last moment to snuggle into Lore before pulling away. "I am sure Qi will be relieved to be on dry land once again." The *rohha* faced a monster, but the sharp rocking of the ferry had almost put Qi over the edge. Only when Lore covered her eyes did the tiny mount calm down.

Iliana and Lore went to where the animals were penned and began loading gear onto their backs. "How far until we reach the spring, once we arrive?" Iliana asked.

"I asked the locals when I was purchasing your sword and was told it is a half day journey. There is not much of a road, but what little trail exists is marked."

Iliana gave Qi a pat on her flanks. "Do you have any thoughts on this trial? Before, we had something to go on."

He shrugged. "We have triumphed over the breath and bone of the Goddess. Who knows what blood will bring."

His comment stopped Iliana in mid-step. "You think this is the trial of blood?"

He nodded.

"Why?"

"The order of the prophecy. Breath. Bone. Blood. Heart."

"True." It made sense. A stray thought crossed Iliana's mind. "Do you think we will be required to shed blood?"

Lore shook his head and tightened the straps that held his packs to Lev's saddle. "Required? No. The test of breath and bone did not require a sacrifice of either, but might it happen?" He glanced at her wounded leg. "We know that anything is possible." He turned back to Lev. "Which is why you will not participate."

For a few heartbeats, Iliana could not speak. When she found her voice, it took all her effort to keep it calm. She laid a gentle hand on his arm. "Lore, I am a part of this, and you cannot change that."

He did not shrug her away, but neither did he acknowledge the touch. Still, she sensed the change in his demeanor. He was all Warrior now. Protector. The final word. "You will wait with the *rohhas,* and I will complete the trial."

She took a deep breath, reminding herself that Lore thought with his heart, and while she loved that about him, now was not the time. "When we began this, we knew it was a partnership. You told me that we could not become lovers for fear I would not be able to distance myself."

"It is not about us."

She returned to Qi and tightened the *rohha's* reins, keeping herself moving for fear she would loose her rising anger on Lore. "Lie to yourself if need be, but it is clear that the lack of objectivity is not mine. It is yours."

"I am practical. That is all. All the trials have been physical, and you are not up to the task."

"What if it is not physical?"

Finished with readying Lev, Lore stroked the *rohha's* neck, smoothing the beast's coarse, white hair. "If so, I will rethink my decision, but if it is at all physical, you will only slow me down."

Iliana bit her lip. By the Goddess, he was unreasonable. "This is not your decision to make."

His expression remained stoic. Expressionless. "I will not lose you."

***

The storm passed, and Lore stood outside the small cave where he and Iliana had bedded down for the night.

Behind him, he heard her murmur in her sleep. He thought about waking her but decided against it. After yesterday's ferry ride and the taxing trek to the spring, she was worn out.

Let her dream.

Pulling on a shirt to ward off the morning chill, he walked down the short path to the Spring of Kylan.

He emerged from the trees, and his breath caught.

Yesterday, when they arrived, it was nightfall, and the waters were dark.

Now, the water sparkled in the morning light as pristine and clear as glass.

The beauty was superficial. This was a trial, and trials meant danger. He crossed the clearing to stand at the water's edge. He peered into it, trying to estimate its depth, but there was no way to tell—not with the clarity and refraction fighting him.

At least the bottom was visible, and with nothing but gravel and a few plants, it looked monster free.

Overall, it did not look special, magical, or otherwise holy.

Which made it all the more suspect.

Not that it mattered. The quest brought him here, and myth or falsehood, he would dive in and test the true nature of the trial.

Smoothing his hair back, Lore secured the long strands with a leather thong. A rustling of trees caught his attention, and he whirled on his heel, drawing his weapon at the same time.

Iliana emerged from the forest. She yawned. Loud.

He wanted to go to her. Hold her. Feel her skin against his. Such needs would wait. Now was the time for focus. Decisions.

Not need.

In a few moments, she was at his side, barefoot and tightening a belt around her tunic. "Any thoughts on what we are supposed to do?"

"Other than diving in, no," he replied, glad that she did not risk pleasantries but focused on the task.

She would make a wonderful Warrior.

She nodded. "How deep is it?"

"It is difficult to judge." Still, he had a nagging suspicion that it was much deeper than anyone supposed. What little else he knew, he did not share with Iliana. When he bought her weapon yesterday morning, he had asked questions. While he did not learn much, he did find out that there was one specific rule when it came to the Spring of Kylan.

He eyed a discarded dipper at the waters edge. While it was permissible to drink of the water, no man ever touched it with flesh. Ever. To do so was considered blasphemy, and legend claimed that the spring itself would seek retribution.

It was unfortunate that he had little choice but to commit sacrilege.

He continued. "It looks safe enough." He took Iliana's hands in his and kissed her fingertips despite his decision to remain focused on the trial. Her skin smelled like *ici* flowers from the small bit of soap she carried in her pack. "I shall swim to the bottom and find the next talisman, if it rests there."

Iliana frowned. "By yourself?"

He knew he should release her, but he kissed her open palm. "At the first sign of danger, I shall return to the surface. I promise."

She shook her head. "Promise or not, we are a team. To act otherwise brings us harm. Remember what happened with the trial of breath when you refused to let me help. We lost valuable time and almost did not complete the test."

He both cursed and admired her stubborn nature. He let her hands go, not wanting to hurt her, but knowing it was the only way to make her accept what must be done. "You are too weak."

"I am not!"

"You are. Would you have my blood on your hands because

you are too proud to admit weakness?"

The color drained from her face, and it took all of Lore's will to not apologize and pull her into his arms to comfort her.

"No," Iliana whispered. "But this is about both of us. I fear what will happen if you go alone."

"Fear more about what will happen if you accompany me. I cannot have you holding me back."

She swayed, and once again, Lore held his distance.

Another breath and she straightened, all hint of tenderness gone from her expression. She glared at him, her eyes as cold as the waters. "As you wish."

He nodded his thanks despite the sick feeling in the pit of his stomach. Later, when he found the talisman, he would apologize. Explain that he would die before he put her in harm's way.

He hesitated. She was right about one thing. He was not objective. Not now, nor ever again. Not when it came to Iliana.

Sitting on the grass at the edge of the spring, he took off his boots then stripped until he wore only his breechclout.

He stood, almost naked.

A part of him shouted that this was a bad idea, but one look at Iliana, and he quashed the insistent voice.

He would not risk her.

Despite her quick temper, she held her delicate palm against his cheek. She did not speak and did not need to. Her bright blue eyes spoke volumes.

She was angry. She was hurt. She was frightened and feared for him.

Once again, he kissed her palm.

Her eyes filled at the gesture, but she let her hand drop.

Lore turned to face the water. Short knife in hand, he took a series of deep breaths, filling his lungs, and without a backward glance, dove in.

The water was freezing, chilling Lore to the very core of his body. He ignored the urge to inhale at the shock of the cold. He had to reach the bottom of the spring before he ran out of air and before Iliana gave in to her urge to dive in and help.

With broad strokes, he made his way downward, ignoring the pain in his head as the pressure grew.

Finally, he was at the spring's floor. There was nothing but gravel and rock. Upright, and using small strokes to keep himself from floating back to the surface, he scanned the area. The water acted as a magnifying glass—all was as clear as if he were on the surface.

A small hole in the wall caught his attention. He swam over. His lungs ached. Much longer and he would have to return to the surface and try again.

Knife in hand, he poked at the dark hole.

Nothing.

Still, maybe the trial sensed he used a knife. Bracing himself for a trap, he reached in. His fingers, almost numb with cold, touched something solid.

He grabbed the unknown object and pulled.

He opened his clenched fist. An oblong-shaped talisman lay in his palm.

Thank the Goddess. It looked like this trial was not as lethal as the rest. He pushed off from the bottom of the spring but was stopped by a tap on his shoulder.

Next to him was Iliana.

Naked, her hair like a dark cloud, she nodded towards his hand.

He had told her to wait but was not surprised that she did not. He held his annoyance in check. Later, he would speak to her about what being an Apprentice meant.

For now, he held up the talisman.

She nodded.

The burning in his lungs intensified.

Smiling, she pulled him into her arms, kissing him.

Her lips were not warm. Far from it—they were colder than the surrounding water. A rush of fear, unfamiliar and unwelcome, rushed through him. In his heat, he knew one clear truth.

This was not Iliana.

It might look like her.

But it was not.

Lore kicked hard, trying to swim away.

The creature grabbed his ankle and yanked him back down. *Iliana.*

No. Not Iliana, he reminded himself. He kicked the creature. Its head rocked sideways. It did not release its hold. He kicked it, the heel of his foot connecting with its jaw.

Its grip tightened.

Desperate, the unfamiliar fear rising, Lore slashed at the creature with his knife, burying the blade up to its hilt in its abdomen.

It did not bleed. Neither did it flinch or show pain. It smiled. The sick grin broadened until it reached from ear to ear—a warped caricature of his Trancer.

The creature radiated malevolence like a thick cloak that blocked out all his other senses. It was strong. It wanted him.

And as he knew it was not Iliana, he knew he could not escape. He would try, as it was his nature to fight, but there would be no salvation. Not for him.

The creature pulled him close and put its mouth to his.

He struggled, but all strength fled as the creature sucked the air from his body. Lights flashed behind his eyelids, and he knew he was close to blacking out.

Pulling back, it smiled and once again pressed its lips to his.

The lights behind his eyes expanded, and Lore knew he was at the threshold of death.

As the light grew brighter, a myriad of thoughts spun out of control through his mind. That he had failed. That he did not want to leave Iliana.

The memory of her touch, her rare laugh, the scent of her skin, rushed through him, making him hesitate.

But the Goddess wanted blood. He had always known that.

It had to be his. Not Iliana's. Never Iliana's.

He embraced his sacrifice.

With his acceptance, the warmth and light of the Goddess enveloped him. Loved him.

Lore rose from his flesh and crossed over to the other side.

Thirteen

Iliana knelt at the edge of the spring, watching. Waiting. She was not sure how deep the pool was, but the crystalline water magnified everything, and it was easy to see what was happening below its surface.

Lore poked at the walls with his knife and then put his hand out. His arm disappeared into the hole.

She tensed.

If something grabbed him, would she be able to get to him in time?

He pulled his arm out, his fingers clenched around something.

Iliana breathed a sigh of relief.

Lore hesitated for perhaps ten heartbeats, and then he pushed towards the surface. He jerked downwards.

Her breath caught in her throat. What was happening?

Lore struck out with his knife, but there was nothing there. He struck again. Something was wrong.

Very wrong.

It did not matter that she could not see what attacked Lore, she only knew something did.

She also knew he would soon run out of air. There was no way he would survive much longer.

Iliana jumped to her feet and ran down the short path to their camp. Grabbing her sword, she rushed back. Perhaps the enemy was invisible, but she was betting she could make it bleed.

Standing at the water's edge, she kicked off her boots, poised to dive, and stopped.

Lore floated face down at the bottom of the spring.

Motionless.

"No." She whispered the denial, refusing to believe her eyes. Sword in hand, she took three deep breaths to fill her lungs and dove into the clear waters.

The freezing water almost drove the air from her body, but she resisted the urge to exhale. Her focus was on Lore's still form, and she kicked towards the bottom of the pond.

In what seemed like an eternity, she reached him. Hands trembling with both cold and fear, she rolled him over. His blue eyes, once kind, were dim. Sightless.

It was true. He was gone.

Dead.

Her sword slipped from her fingers and landed on the sandy bottom. He could not be dead. Not now. They had come so far together.

Her eyes betrayed her. They had to.

He was not dead. This was part of the test.

In the back of her mind, all emotion shut down. She wondered if this was what battle was like—an absence of emotion. A cold realization of what needed to be done to succeed.

In this case, the battle was for Lore, and for herself, if she did not get back to the surface before she ran out of air.

She grabbed Lore's lifeless hand, and a small piece of metal fell from his grip and into the sands.

The talisman.

She snatched it up and shoved it into her breast-band.

Picking up her sword, she grabbed him again and kicked for the surface.

Something yanked them back.

She looked downward and saw herself. Naked. Her hair a dark halo. Her double held onto Lore's thigh.

Iliana's brain whirled in confusion. Was this what Lore had seen? What had killed him? Her? How?

The trial.

As if reading her thoughts, the creature grinned at her in confirmation, revealing a mouth of sharp teeth.

Iliana's lips turned downwards at the trial's cruelness of using her image to harm Lore.

Cruelty and unfairness meant nothing. Winning. Beating this trial. That was all that mattered.

Gripping Lore with all her strength, Iliana kicked for the surface.

Her double held onto Lore, keeping her from moving. Then it began working its way, hand-over-hand, up Lore's lifeless body and towards her.

Iliana's lungs began to burn with the need for air, and she kicked again, knowing she did not have the breath left for a battle.

It reached her ankle, gripping her with an unnatural strength. Panic pricked at the edges of her mind. The need to flee was overwhelming.

The need to fight was stronger.

Iliana pointed her sword towards the creature.

She stopped the thrust before completion.

It was already wounded. Probably by Lore's *cuchil.* Its stomach gaped open with a bloodless hole that opened wider with each movement

There was no blood. Just the open wound. It seemed to neither notice nor care. Perhaps it could not be killed.

Her thoughts flashed back to the Test of Acceptance. Not everything was about strength. Sometimes, it was about a riddle. Wisdom. Sacrifice.

Do you think we will be required to shed blood?

The words came back to haunt her. Was blood the key? What the creature wanted? Craved because it had none of its own? Is that why it took Lore's life, because he wounded it when he was supposed to wound himself?

Iliana let Lore go.

The creature was in front of her now—a caricature of herself found in the darkest of dreams.

Raising her sword, Iliana sliced open her hand to the muscle. Despite the numbing cold of the water, she winced.

She held out her hand, palm forward, her blood coloring the water and prayed this was the answer. If not, she was dead as well.

The creature grabbed her hand, latching onto the open wound like a baby latched onto a breast.

It burned. Felt like it was not merely sucking the blood from her body but the life from her soul.

Iliana's lungs ached as she fought to remain motionless. Her heart beat in her ears. One. Two. Three.

The creature let go, and the pain stopped. Its face as expressionless as stone, it floated backwards and faded away.

The trial was over.

Lights flashing behind her eyes, Iliana grabbed Lore's limp hand, and once again, swam upwards.

She broke the water's surface with a gasp, and her thoughts turned to saving Lore. Her Tower had been on the coast, and she was familiar with the techniques to return a drowning victim to life, but Lore's breathing had ceased many minutes ago. There was little time left. She needed to get him onto dry land— something she was too weak to do even if her hand was not sliced open.

"Lev!" She screamed for the *rohha*. "Lev!"

Lev galloped into the clearing, tossing his head and wild-eyed, as if he knew there was a problem.

Qi followed him.

With a push and a cry of pain, Iliana heaved Lore partway up onto the muddy edge of the spring.

He was as pale as wax. Wincing, she managed to pull herself out.

Gripping his arm with one hand, she used her wounded one to pull her wet shirt over her head. Pulling Lore's hands over his head, she wrapped his wrists with the wet garment.

Grabbing Lev, she shoved the ends of the sleeve in his mouth. "Pull!"

The *rohha,* battle-trained and intelligent, pulled his master the rest of the way to dry land.

Iliana fell to her knees beside Lore and fought the urge to cry.

His blue eyes were devoid of life. His mouth open in surprise. Despite the chill of the water, his skin was warm against her palm.

There was hope.

Ruthlessly, she tilted his head back and blew into his mouth. His chest rose.

Another breath. His blue eye remained lifeless.

Again. Again. And again.

She did not know how long she tried to breathe life into him. She only knew that when she gave up, she wished the creature had taken her as well.

***

Kneeling beside Lore, Iliana did not know how much time had passed. A heartbeat. A sun.

She smoothed Lore's hair away from his face. The blond strands were still wet, so she knew it was not long since she had pulled him from the spring.

"It does not matter, anyway," she whispered. Time meant little as she faced an interminable and painful forever without Lore.

She closed his eyes, leaving a bloody handprint. She tried to wipe him clean but instead, succeeded in creating a red smear across his forehead.

He looked peaceful. Almost happy. If she did not know he was dead, she would almost think him asleep.

A high-pitched keening broke the silence. A cry of pain so deep that it seemed as if the air split with the hurt.

Iliana realized it was herself that cried out. Wrapping her arms around her waist, she rocked back and forth, trying to contain the ache before it shattered her into a million pieces.

Not that she cared. She wanted to die. Nothing mattered now. Not the Orb. Not the world she was supposed to save. Nothing.

It was not her world. Not now.

"Lore." She touched his lips with shaking fingertips, shuddering at their lifelessness. "Come back to me. Do not leave me alone."

He did not move.

Lev trotted over, nudging Lore's shoulder with his nose. Sobbing, Iliana hugged the *rohha's* neck, burying her face in his thick mane.

Lore was not supposed to die. "I told you that it was foolish to attempt the trial without me."

She squeezed her eyes shut. "Help me, my Goddess."

There was no answer. Just the soft breathing of the *rohhas* and the breeze through the leaves.

Iliana lay next to Lore, resting her head on his chest and curling herself around him. She was tired. Too tired to think. Too tired to live.

"How can I go on?" she whispered. "How can I finish the quest without you by my side?"

There was no answer. No sign for her to cling to.

The sadness was too much to bear. She had lost too much. Her Tower. Her ability to Trance.

Now Lore.

She could not do this alone. Could not take the grief.

Would not take it. Refused.

She wiped an angry tear from her cheek and sat up.

She pulled the almost-forgotten talisman from her breast band. This was what had killed him. A part of her was tempted to fling the piece of metal back into the spring. Or the woods. Anyplace where it could do no more damage.

But if it was the culprit, it might also be the salvation.

She turned it over. It winked in the sunlight. Etched into its surface was a triangle topped with a crescent moon. The sign of a Trancer.

The first Trancer.

A sign? She rubbed her thumb over it, leaving a bloody print, before she clenched it in her fist. Only a Trancer could solve this. Only a Trancer could make it right.

She was a Trancer once, and by the Goddess, she was going to be a Trancer again and bring Lore back.

With her resolve steeled, and her anger wrapped around her like a cloak, Iliana took a deep breath, crossed her legs, and rested her hands, palms up, upon her knees. Shutting her eyes, she took another breath, letting her lungs fill. She held it.

And searched for the wall in her mind. She did not have to look hard. Like a black fortress wall, it loomed within her, hiding her skills.

Twice before, she had tried to destroy it, and twice failed, waking up on the ground with a splitting headache and racing heart for her efforts.

Failure was no longer an option.

She raised a mental fist and struck.

The wall repelled her, as if she was less than nothing. Darkness danced at the edge of her vision. She refused to give in.

Instead, she summoned her rage, her pain, and her fear. She called upon all that had ever hurt her. Made her cry when she was alone. That which kept her awake at night, wondering if she were fit to live.

She called upon it, reined it in, and held it close. By the Goddess, she would beat the wall down.

She struck.

Ragged pain shot through Iliana, radiating into every bone of her body. Heart racing, she opened her eyes.

Lev and Qi stood nearby, watching, as if they knew she attempted the impossible.

Lore remained lifeless, and her gifts hidden.

Staggering to her feet, Iliana screamed her rage. Both the *rohhas* shied away in fear, snorting and stamping their hooves.

"What is the use in being a Trancer if I cannot Trance?" Iliana screamed at the bright, morning sky. "What do I have to do to find myself? What do I have to do to bring Lore back?"

How was she supposed to break down the wall? It was strong. Invincible.

Hot tears welled up in her eyes. "What do I have to do? Tell me. Please."

She collapsed into the grass. "Please."

Control your rage. Lore's voice spoke to her. *Control it or it will control you. There are other emotions stronger than anger. Than fear.* The memory of Lore whispering her lessons warmed her.

Stronger than anger?

She closed her eyes. There was one time when she felt stronger than her anger. One instance when the wall cracked.

When Lore was with her, loving her.

A weak smile turned her lips upward, as an almost surreal calm swept through her. She was a fool to not have realized it sooner.

Once again, she sat down next to Lore. "I am coming."

Crossing her legs, she shut her eyes again, but this time, she let her thoughts relax. She embraced the anger. Loved it. Transformed it. The blackness flowed out of her.

Only thoughts of Lore remained. How she felt when he kissed her. When he stroked her skin.

How his laugh made up for all the wrong in the world. How she felt when he was inside of her.

Most of all, she thought about how much she loved him.

She laid her hands on his chest.

The wall loomed in her mind, still as black as sin.

Mentally, she touched its surface. A gentle touch. A caress. A kiss. Her love for Lore flowed through her, consuming everything in its path.

The blackness crumbled into dust.

***

The currents of life swirled around Iliana. Dark. Light. Bands of color, like rivers that wrapped the world.

She had forgotten how much she loved to swim in them She opened herself, and the currents swirled through her, multihued, texture and taste—the lightness of the wind and the solidness of the earth.

All life pulsed around her, filled her like water filled an empty cup. For a beat, there was no grief. No pain of loss. Just the gift of life. The beauty of being a Trancer.

It overwhelmed her. Crushed her and rebuilt her.

She looked down at her body. She appeared to be both solid black and a brilliant white. Opposites twisting and turning. Mingling as two halves of a whole.

She felt sorry for the woman she watched. Wished she could heal her. Wished she could help her forget the past. Forget the darkness until only the bands of light remained.

Perhaps, but not yet. There were more important tasks.

There was Lore. His body lay next to her. It was without color.

Lifeless.

It was up to her to correct this wrong. To enter the Realm of the Goddess and bring his life force out—a deed that was sacrilege to even consider.

But to live without him was a worse blasphemy.

She steadied her thoughts, her spirit. Calling upon the earth, she wrapped its life force around her like a cloak, bound herself to it, praying it was enough to remind her of who she was.

For that was the risk in attempting to enter the Realm of the Goddess—being caught up in the beauty and losing oneself.

Left behind, the body wasted away and died.

But better death than a life without Lore.

Funny, before Lore, she had faced that possibility of solitude and welcomed it. Now, the thought was unbearable.

She focused herself. Let her mind fill with thoughts of Lore. His scent—that of leather and sweat. His hair, silky under her hands. His kiss. His mouth.

His kindness.

His life force called to her over the distance. Across the barrier of life and death. Across the separation that spilt reality from that which was reserved for those who were no longer part of the world.

He was far. She sensed it. Distance was nothing to the currents.

Iliana focused her thoughts, her spirit. Listened for Lore, his essence, and in a rush of time and a blinding pain, she was with him.

A being of pure light, he greeted her. Welcomed her. His love, a pure white light, touched her. He accepted his fate.

She did not accept as easily. She reached for him—

What do you think you are doing, little Trancer?

A voice sounded inside Iliana's head. It was huge. Booming. More than human. Bigger than love and just as cruel.

She hesitated.

Trancer, answer me.

Iliana had no choice. Was compelled to reply. *I come in search of Lore.*

Lore?

My lover. My Warrior.

We have many Warriors here. Many lovers.

The voice took shape. Like nothing she had ever seen before. Brighter than a star, it was almost unbearable.

The Goddess.

Iliana held to her resolve. Perhaps, but he was special. *He was not supposed to die.*

The voice chuckled. *I have heard that cry many times. From mothers and fathers. From children. From men and women.* The voice wrapped around her with a mother's love. A touch she had not felt since her Tower fell and she had lost her family. Iliana fell into it. Sank into the omniscient love of the Goddess.

The Goddess lifted her up. *You are not the first, little Trancer. Nor will you be the last.*

The weight of the world tugged at Iliana. The green of life she had bound about herself called her home, and she knew it was not her time to die. Not yet. There was much to do. A life to live.

With Lore.

There was no time left. With each beat of her heart, the call of eternity grew stronger and the earth-force weakened. Much longer and she would forget her body. Her life.

You are right, Iliana. This is not your time. Leave him. He is no longer needed. Not for what I have planned.

She needed Lore. Could not fathom an existence without him.

The Goddess chuckled again. *You think to take him from me?*

I have little choice. I am on a quest to save the world, and without him, the quest dies.

The light of the Goddess brightened. *Quests mean nothing to me. Even if you fail, the world will survive. Nations can crumble. Empires will fall. My world goes on.*

The Goddess was right. There was no argument strong enough, no need strong enough, to justify taking Lore.

There was only love.

It would have to be enough. Iliana knew it was probably useless, but she tried to shield her thoughts.

Turning her back on the Goddess, Iliana reached for the light that was Lore. Pulling him into her embrace, she called herself back to the world before hesitation took hold.

And found herself back at the spring, their bodies below her. Waiting.

Not yet.

Lore?

His spirit touched her. Wanted her. She tasted his need. His desire. It tasted like life.

Her spirit sighed, and he wrapped his life force around her. Intertwined his soul with hers. Joining.

For a brief moment, there was the sharing of souls, the joining that was forbidden between Trancer and Warrior, and then they split apart as they were thrust into their bodies.

Fourteen

Medea stood in the thick of the bushes at the far side of the spring, watching Iliana through the small gaps in the leaves.

It looked as if she was trying to obtain Trancer consciousness. Fool.

The air stirred and Kole appeared at her side. He watched the scene and raised a brow.

"The Warrior is dead," Medea whispered.

Kole grinned.

Medea shrugged. It would have been pleasurable to bed Iliana's lover. While this was not as satisfactory, it would have to do. Watching Iliana's pain. Seeing the Trancer's tears of helplessness gave her a warm glow that radiated throughout her body.

Iliana rose, screaming at the sky. Medea held back a laugh. Iliana had lost her Trancer ability when Mako took her. And what Mako took remained his. She might shout at the sky, but nothing would ever return her powers.

Suddenly, Iliana stopped raging, hesitated, sat back in Trancer position, and closed her eyes.

Medea's warm glow grew cold. Something was wrong.

"What—"

Medea held a finger to her lips.

Kole did not finish the sentence.

Iliana smiled.

Hot rage roared through Medea's veins. She did not need to be a Trancer to know that Iliana had done it—taken back her powers. The rage burned hotter. How dare she?

She reached for the knife strapped to her thigh, pulled it free, and took a step forward.

Kole's hand stopped her. "Leave her be. With the Warrior dead, we need her," he whispered.

Medea tried to shrug him away, but his grip on her arm tightened. "Think, Medea. The Orb is the goal. You can kill her later, after we have retrieved what is ours."

Medea relaxed. He was right. Death could come later. The Trancer had already taken everything that mattered. She would not take the Orb as well.

Kole's grip eased. "Besides, where is the fun in death, if it cannot be combined with fun?"

"True." Medea chuckled. She had such plans for Iliana.

She glanced at Kole, her eyes taking in the erection that betrayed his excitement at the thought of fun with Iliana. "You desire her?"

Kole shrugged. "She is a beauty. I would enjoy breaking her in." He caressed Medea's throat.

She did not stop him. Not this time. Rage burned her and release would be pleasurable.

He continued. "She is not you. She does not have your fire. Your desires. Your needs."

Leaning in, he bit her ear. Hard. "I would have you. Now."

Kole was loathsome, but she needed release. Pleasure to counteract her anger at Iliana' success.

Medea bared her neck. "Take me." She reached down, grasping the hardness between his legs. "Put this to good use, and I might let you have me again. Disappoint me, and you will never touch my flesh again." Running her hand up his chest, she ground herself against him.

With a growl, Kole pushed her to the ground, pinning her arms above her head.

Medea smiled as small stones and sticks scrapped her back and bare arms. This was what she craved. No tenderness. No words of love.

Mako had never given them to her. His passion was enough to let her know how he felt.

She saw that passion in Kole. Not as dark. Not as deep. But it was there.

Her hands still pinned, Kole yanked down the top of her dress, exposing her breasts. With a growl, he bit them with the same force that he bit her ear. She whimpered at the pain, as she gave herself over to the moment. The desire. The need to have a man possess her flesh.

Kole undid the ties that held his leather leggings closed, and pushed them down.

Lifting her skirts, he pushed her legs apart with his knees and thrust himself into her.

It hurt, and Medea sighed as a wave a pleasure washed over her.

Fifteen

First, there was pain. Lore burned. He wanted to cry out, but his voice was mute.

An eternity seemed to pass while he fought to wake from the black dream that tortured him.

Nothing penetrated the darkness that was his world. No light. No caress. No scent. Not even the beat of his heart broke the fire that branded him.

When he thought he could abide no more, sound emerged. Chanting.

It was a woman. He could not understand her words, but he sensed that she called to him—bringing him out of the nightmare and back into the world.

Her words became louder. Clearer. He recognized the voice. Iliana.

He caught a few words, but he did not recognize the language.

Aga'ir . . . balam . . . gurdháya

Her tone grew more insistent, stronger, pulling him towards something—he was not sure what.

Her voice rose, breaking through his darkness, and like the moon breaking through the clouds, he woke and the pain abandoned him.

For a moment, he lay still and reveled in the glory of peace. Slowly, he opened his eyes.

He was on his back in the morning-damp grass. The sun stood poised at the edge of the trees. Disoriented, he blinked at the sunlight, letting his eyes adjust while the world spun off kilter.

What had happened? How had he gotten here?

Another deep breath and the spinning stopped. The sway of the trees overhead mesmerized him. Each leaf stood out in relief. Never had they looked so bright. So alive. Almost as if they vibrated with energy.

Yet, everything seemed unreal, as if he dreamed.

He turned his head, and his breath caught in his throat.

Iliana sat next to him, her legs crossed. Her hands rested palms up on her knees.

Trancer position.

Had she found that which they all thought was lost forever?

He smiled, knowing the truth even as he asked the question. He sensed the Trancer power she held at her command, almost as if he bore it himself.

He wanted to weep with joy.

She was beautiful, like a raging fire was beautiful—bright, warm, and if one touched it, painful. Perhaps even deadly.

He had to touch the flame that was Iliana. Could not resist her brightness.

"Iliana." He whispered her name, not wanting to awaken her too fast. Talon had told him of the danger all Trancers faced. When in the currents, they became lost if not handled with caution.

She did not respond. He whispered her name again, and traced a gentle circle on her upturned palm.

Her eyelashes fluttered like a dreamer's. Her fingers curled around his and squeezed.

He squeezed back. "You have regained your gift."

Half-lidded, she looked at him through her dark lashes and drew his hand to her mouth, kissing his knuckles. "Yes."

Suddenly, hot tears spilled over Lore's hand.

Iliana was crying.

For a heartbeat, he stared at her in shock. He had never seen her tears. Her anger. Her joy. Her passion.

Never her grief. She kept that hidden from everyone.

Until now.

The sorrow was almost too much to bear.

Pulling her to him, he laid her head on his chest. She wrapped her arms around his neck, her pale body shaking with the force of her sobs.

"It is all right, love," he murmured. As he waited for her to calm herself, he stroked her hair, letting the black strands cascade through his finger.

Finally, she quieted, and with trembling hands, she traced his face with her fingertips. From chin to forehead, she ran her hands over his skin, as if memorizing his every feature. Still trembling, she followed the path she had traced with her lips, tasting him with subtle kisses. Letting her mouth tell him what words could not.

She needed him. She feared for him.

With a sudden fierceness, she pulled him to her, taking his mouth. He recognized the intensity in her touch as reassurance that he lived. Recognition that he was real—as he once needed when he experienced his first vision and thought he had killed her.

Much like she had returned his kiss then, he returned hers now. Matching her need, he drank deep of her. Swallowed her cries. Wove his hands through her hair and claimed her as she claimed him.

He had never wanted a woman like he did his Iliana—with both a fierce possession and an almost painful need to merge with her both physically and spiritually.

The desire to be within her burned so deep and fast that it was torture.

Wrapping his hands around her, he pulled her against him until they were matched hip to hip, and he pressed hard against her.

She stopped him by grabbing his hands, her lips pressed against his neck. "Lore." Her voice was warm.

Her hands braced against the cool, rain-soaked ground, she rolled off him.

He forced back a groan of need, knowing that she was not ready for lovemaking.

Not yet.

Her head nestled in the shelter of his arm, she tucked a wet strand of hair behind his ear. "I thought I had lost you."

He heard her words, but all he could focus on was her hand.

She was wounded and bleeding, her palm sliced open.

Sitting up, he took her hand in his, opening it.

She flinched.

Lore grit his teeth in anger. "What happened?"

She shrugged but did not look up. "It is nothing."

It was not nothing. It was deep, and from the way she held it by her side, painful.

Luckily, it was not her sword hand, but if it was not bandaged soon, she might lose its use.

He kissed her knuckles, wishing he had the skills to heal her. "This is not nothing. Now, who did this to you?"

Again, no answer. She hunched inward, as if hiding.

He would have none of that. There was no shame in a wound.

He tipped her chin up, and all thoughts of her sliced hand disappeared.

Her wide eyes were no longer a pale, clear blue.

They were as dark as the night sky.

***

"How?" Lore asked, the shock in his eyes as plain as the desire he had felt just moments ago. "Did your returned powers do this?"

Iliana swallowed, hard, not sure of where to begin, and even less sure that she wanted to.

Despite her reluctance, there was little choice. He deserved to know the entire story. Besides, her eyes gave away the deed, and Lore would know if she lied. He knew everything about her, even if he was not yet aware of that fact.

She wrapped her arms around her knees. There was no possible way to explain the bonding without telling the whole tale.

How would he feel about being brought back from the afterlife? In more than one Tower, she would be put to death, or at least exiled, for such an arrogant act of blasphemy.

Knowing that there was no right way, no kind way, to explain, she let the words fall from her mouth unchecked. "You died, and I brought you back from the afterlife. Upon our return, our souls bonded."

His eyes widened, and for moment, he looked angry, like he wanted to argue her point. Then, his skin went gray, and she knew he remembered the truth of it.

He managed a slow nod. "I am not sure what to say. What to ask." He ran a hand through his hair. "But you speak the truth. I died."

"Yes." She worried her bottom lip, waiting for a response. An emotion. Any emotion. When she reached out with her still sensitive skills, she felt nothing but a numbing sensation.

He looked thoughtful as he absorbed her words. "How long was I gone?"

"It seemed like forever, but in truth, it was less time than it takes to boil water over a roaring fire."

"You used your Trancing skills to bring me back?"

She moved to reply, and he stopped her with an upturned hand. She blinked, forcing back hot tears. "You are angry."

"I am many things. I am glad your powers are returned, but I am disturbed you used them to violate the sacred garden of life." He ran his hands over his body, as if testing its reality. "I am glad to be alive, but I am angry that you broke the laws of life to accomplish this task."

She bit her lip. She hated feeling vulnerable. Hated worrying about what Lore thought or wanted. Yet, she needed to make him understand. "When you died, something in me snapped. I could not go on with life, much less the quest." She took his hand in hers. "I was angry at first. Furious that you were gone. Then I remembered you telling me that not all wars are won by rage, and I calmed. I remembered how much I cared for you and you for me."

"And you came for me." Once again, the silenced lengthened as Lore searched his memories. "It was not you who chose the bonding, was it?"

"No, but that does not make it any less welcome," Iliana replied, remembering the rapture, the sense of completeness that enveloped her when the joining occurred.

Lev trotted over and nudged Lore with his head. Absently, Lore patted the *rohha's* nose. "I need some time to think on this."

She nodded, knowing the conversation was over for now and dreading what would happen when it resumed.

***

Iliana stood at the edge of the clearing and watched Lore.

The sun had set, and still, he had not spoken a word to her since he had said he needed to think over her actions. Nor had he eaten or slept.

He had dressed himself in only his leather breeches and taken a seat by the spring. There he remained.

She squeezed her eyes shut, steeling herself against the sorrow that consumed her. Now that he knew what she was capable of, would he ever look at her the same? Feel for her as he once did?

She shook the melancholy off.

It would grow cold soon.

Blanket in hand, she walked to Lore, draped the rough cloth over his shoulders, and turned to leave.

"Stay."

She hesitated, and he opened up the blanket.

She settled next to him, and he wrapped it around her so that it enclosed them both.

For what seemed like countless heartbeats, both sat as still as stone.

"I remember what happened," Lore told her, his voice low. "The cold, the dark, and the talisman. Even my death." He shuddered. "Whatever it was that took me looked like you. I did not expect such maliciousness."

He took her wounded hand in his and kissed her bandaged palm. "It was not you. I know that."

She breathed a sigh of relief. "I saw her, too."

"How did you get past her?"

Iliana disengaged herself from Lore's grip and held up her hand. "This. I was right. The trial demanded blood."

He nodded. "The talisman?"

With her other hand, she pulled it from a pouch at her waist.

Lore held it up, and it caught the last rays of light. "So small an item."

"Yet so important."

He handed it back to her. "You know what it means, do you not?"

"Yes. It is the first Tower. The first Trancer." She put the talisman back in the pouch, cinched it tight and leaned into Lore's embrace. "It will take us at least two suns of hard riding to reach the ruins of the first Tower." Two suns and their fate would be decided, as well as the fate of the world.

"We shall talk of this, but not yet." He turned in her arms. Rising to his knees, he framed her face in his hand. "We are joined for life, are we not?"

"Yes," she whispered, knowing it was useless to lie. They were joined. He would know an untruth. Sense the wrongness.

He smiled, a soft turn of his lips that she had never seen before. "I want you, Iliana."

She knew he spoke from the heart. She felt it in her blood. Her bones. His need called to her, leaving her unable to resist— even if she wanted to.

She leaned upwards and pressed her lips to Lore's. A small, shy kiss. "I am yours."

Lore pulled her tunic over her head and urged her onto the ground with the blanket beneath them.

Iliana lost herself in his desire.

His fingers teased her skin with subtle touches. His lips traced a path from the nape of her neck to the sensitive spot at the crook of her arm.

The touch of his skin against hers. The way his muscles twitched at her touch. His scent—that of leather and sweat.

It was all familiar. Yet different.

In the back of her mind, she wondered if any two souls had ever been joined so completely.

He murmured her name, low and needful. She could listen to his voice for eternity, and it would never be enough.

His long hair, unbound from the Warrior's cord, tickled a path from her thighs to her breasts, as Lore roamed across her body. She ran her hands through the blond strands, reveling in the texture. The contrast to her own dark strands.

She pulled him to her mouth, knowing that the taking was more than accepted.

It was wanted.

He kissed a path to her neck. "Iliana?"

"Yes?" She ran her hands over his buttocks, pulling him against her. Reveling in the way his desire pressed hard against her stomach.

"You must make me a promise."

"Anything," she murmured, wishing he would shut up and make love to her. "As long as you keep touching me."

He pulled her nipple into his mouth, and she arched beneath him, sensing his desire, his need, as if it were his own.

The joining.

He left her breasts, leaving his hands to draw lazy circles on her sensitized skin, keeping her heated. "You must promise that if something happens to me, you will not try to bring me back. Not again."

"What?" Desire died.

Grabbing his wrist, she stopped him, knowing his touch could make her promise the world, and at this moment, she did not want to promise such.

He leaned up on his elbows, his hands tangled in her hair. "I want you to promise me that you will not take such a chance again."

She did not understand. "You are sorry to have returned?"

He shook his head. "I thought about that today. What you did. What I would have done if you had died and I had the ability to bring you back."

"And?"

"I would have done the same." He kissed her. "I would have moved the world to bring you back to my arms. Given anything to see you breathe."

He kissed her, and desire washed over her once again.

Then he smiled back and continued, "Sitting by the pond, I imagined how my life would feel if you were not in it, and I discovered that I did not want such a life."

He smiled at her, a half turn of his lips. "I cannot fault you your decision, but I must ask you that if it comes down to it, you would not make the same one again."

Knowing she would only sob if she opened her mouth, she rolled away and into a sitting position, legs crossed and her back to Lore. How could he ask this of her, knowing how she felt? Knowing they were joined?

He touched her shoulder. "I know it is not an easy promise, but it is necessary."

She shrugged him off.

He slid closer, wrapped his arms around her.

She stiffened, wanting to pull away and sink into his touch at the same time. "We had this conversation once before."

"Apparently, it was not enough." He kissed her neck. A tender kiss. A kiss of comfort.

"Can you promise the same?" She whispered the question, dreading the answer.

He pulled her closer. "It will never come to that. I promise you."

She trembled. "Do not make promises you cannot keep." Turning in his arms, she touched his cheek. "Can you let me die, knowing we are joined? Knowing that with my death, you will lose half of yourself?"

He closed his eyes. "No."

"Neither can I." She leaned her head against his chest. "For good or ill, we are joined. We are bound. To lose each other would be like cutting out half our heart."

"What if that is what is required to save the world? Can we be so selfish as to sacrifice our friends to save ourselves grief?" He nuzzled her hair. "It is not the Warrior's way."

Aria. Talon. Tarik. Roam. Was the babe born yet?

"I know," she whispered. Closing her eyes, she reached out into the Currents, the strength of her gift surprising her.

Across the void, she felt Aria. Questioned, without words, about Roam.

Aria's reply was as wordless, but Iliana felt the acknowledgment of her question. Roam was fine. Unborn as of yet.

And she felt more. Aria's pleasure at knowing that Iliana was a Trancer once again. That she was joined to Lore and had found some semblance of happiness.

Aria also she wished her success and to come home safe.

Soon.

Iliana opened her eyes.

Could she let all that she loved, let Aria's daughter, die to save herself?

She knew the answer and it broke her heart into a million shards. "I will not save you again, Lore. If you die, I will let you go."

She raised her face to him, knowing that her cheeks were wet with tears and not caring. "Now promise the same. Promise me, and then make love to me."

He nodded, his cheeks as damp as hers. "I promise."

And he eased her back onto the ground. Kissed her. Loved her.

Her mind searched for his. Found it. She twined herself around him and fell into the rhythm of his body, his heartbeat, until she lost herself and death was of little consequence.

Sixteen

Iliana woke with Lore spooned against her back, his left arm draped over her waist. Two days of hard riding and two nights spent making love until late into the night had taken their toll on her body. She was so weary her bones ached, and her wounded thigh throbbed.

Plus, they had another full day's travel before they reached the Ruins. They had hoped to make it in two, but Qi, for all her tenacity, was unable to keep up with Lev.

Iliana held back a groan at the thought of the additional days, and instead, snuggled into the curve of Lore's naked body.

He squeezed her close and kissed her neck. "We should get up."

She nodded but made no move to rise. Weariness dropping away, she wiggled her nude bottom against Lore's growing length. "Can the world wait a bit longer?"

He nibbled her ear. "We should leave. We have a long ride ahead of us."

She wiggled again, smiling as he hardened further. "Give me this morning, and I shall ask nothing else of this day."

He pressed himself between her thighs in reply, and she knew she had won. Her breath hissed through her teeth as Lore sought her heat, and finding it, took her from behind.

It was primal. Sensual. Animal. She rocked against him as her Trancer senses expanded.

Once again, the forces that joined them sprang to life, linking their minds.

She felt his pleasure. Desire coursing through his veins. She knew he felt hers.

Moans and soft sighs filled the morning air. Skin stroked skin. Iliana did not know if the sensations were hers or Lore's, and she did not care.

All she cared about was one more morning of freedom. One more morning of loving her Warrior, of savoring his life, and tasting his love upon her like a kiss.

One more moment where she could be Iliana, the lover.

Not Iliana, savior of the world, Warrior in training, or even Trancer.

Just Iliana.

Forces built, and her body tightened in anticipation, blotting out any other thoughts.

Sensation folded over her, and she crested, crying out, arching against Lore as he joined her.

For an endless count of heartbeats, she laid sated, hair damp against her cheek and Lore still within her body. Iliana sighed. If the world ended at this instant, she would depart this plane of existence content in body if not in spirit.

Lore kissed her neck and rolled away, breaking not just their physical link, but also their emotional one. She winced at the loss.

"It hurts me as well," Lore whispered.

She nodded, but both knew this was the way of the joining. Better to suffer the pain than forgo the pleasure and bonding that happened when they made love.

He ran a gentle hand through her hair, guiding the damp strands so they lay against her back. "The *rohha's* grow restless. It is time to leave." He made to rise, but Iliana grabbed his hand and pulled him back to her.

She did not want to go.

Perhaps it was childish, but the closer they came to the end of their quest, the more she wanted to run the other way. Or make time stand still. Stop. Anything, but find the answer to the question that burned in her mind now that she was bonded with Lore.

What would happen afterwards?

If they failed, death awaited them.

Success was almost more frightening. What would their future be? Lore was accepted. Loved. Respected. When he returned to the Keep, he would be welcomed with open arms.

She, on the other hand . . .

She remembered the night she sat on her windowsill and listened to the men discuss her. Would saving the world be enough to change their hearts?

Would it matter? Lore would stay with her, regardless of how others felt. He would stay because of the joining and never regret the decision, of that she was sure.

And she would live with the knowledge of what he scarified to be with her. His status. Perhaps even students.

The chance to lead a normal life.

She rubbed her cheek against his arm, his muscles flexing at her touch.

A normal life? Lore was her life.

Weaving her fingers through his, she pulled him closer. Would they ever have this again?

"You are troubled." Lore snuggled back into the curve of her back. "Tell me what bothers you. Let me share the worry."

She turned in his arms, loving that he cared so much for her, even when she was being silly. Selfish.

There was nothing to tell him. Not yet. Afterwards, when either success or failure was upon them, she would speak her thoughts. Until that moment, Lore could do nothing, and she would rather have him focus on the upcoming trial. She traced his lower lip. "It is nothing. I worry about the test. The outcome."

The corners of his mouth turned down. "Are you sure there is not more?" He kissed her fingertip. "We are joined. There should be no secrets between us."

"I am sure. For now."

He nodded. "As you wish."

Kissing her one last time, he stood and stretched.

She sighed at the sight of him in the morning sun. He was beautiful. The sunlight turned his hair to gold, and he looked like a God.

A well-muscled, well-loved God.

He extended his hand to her, and she took it, letting him help her to her feet.

She wrapped her arms around his waist, breathing him in. His scent. His life. Everything that he was.

She could stay like this forever—wrapped in Lore's embrace.

It was not to be. Not yet. Maybe never.

Not even when she wanted it so much she ached with the need.

With a shake of her head, she made herself let go of him and took a step back.

Lore brushed a strand of hair away from her cheek. "You do not need to go if you would rather wait. The last test was difficult, and we have been riding hard for days."

She smiled at the offer. "The last time you tried to attempt a trial alone, you died." She kissed his palm. "Perhaps we promised to let the other go if it comes to that again, but I am not eager to put that promise to the test."

He smoothed her hair. "I know, but I worry for you."

She leaned into him, taking one, last deep inhalation. "Do not worry. It will solve nothing."

Lore rested his head on top of hers. "Spoken like a Warrior."

***

The Ruins stood like a skeleton against the late afternoon sky.

The final trial. Iliana took a deep breath. Soon, the world would know its fate.

So would she.

She pointed Qi towards the largest structure. Or what appeared to have been a structure.

It was said that the Ruins were once magnificent. White pillars of stone that glowed and were known throughout the land as the Tower of Hope.

Now, it was a pile of stone, with only a vague shape to indicate its former glory and a grim reminder of where all Trancers came from.

The Tower fell thousands of seasons ago, in the Great War of the Sceton. A time of legend, when a tyrannical warlord attacked the first Tower, wanting to claim the Trancer's powers for his personal use.

He was defeated, but in doing so, the Tower was destroyed. The white stones blackened by smoke and fire.

Now, a few stone walls surrounding some crumbling buildings were all that were left. The Ruins were devoid of all plant life, as if nothing would grow where the First Trancer, the Great Mother of them all, gave her life in killing Lord Sceton with her powers—sacrificing not just her body but her sanity.

Iliana's skin prickled at the story. For a moment, it was as if she smelled the burned air and tasted the tears and blood of not just the Great Mother, but also all her Apprentices who died in that battle.

The taste and smell were familiar.

Her Tower.

Except at her fallen Tower, there was no great battle. Just a massacre. Death with no purpose. Regret and anger murmured in her mind, familiar in their touch.

"Do you feel it?" Lore whispered.

She started.

"Power," Lore continued.

Iliana calmed herself, and the touch of power closed over her. "Yes. I feel it."

They grew closer, and the energy surrounding the Ruins roared through her veins, making the hairs on her neck and arms rise.

Lore stopped.

"Are you all right?" Iliana asked, reining in Qi next to him. He shook his head. "I am not sure. I feel strange."

She felt much the same, as if she were filling up with energy. So much that it threatened to shoot out of her fingertips and the ends of her hair.

Iliana kicked Qi back into motion, the power calling to her with familiar strength. With Lore following, she entered the Ruins through what appeared to have once been a massive archway. Now, the top was rubble on the ground, ruined by battle and time.

The *rohhas'* hooves clopped against the stone walkway as they followed the power, letting it guide them. They passed one dilapidated building after another, each telling the tale of war.

They turned a corner. Iliana stopped.

Before her lay a building of white and crystal. A thing of legend. Of secrets. Of myth.

It looked as if all four walls still stood despite the destruction surrounding them.

"The Temple of Light," she whispered. "I did not know it survived."

"Do we dare enter?" Lore asked.

"I do not think we have a choice." Iliana slid off Qi and walked to the Temple with Lore at her side, drawn to its voiceless call. Desperate to walk its floor.

They entered through an open archway, and the Temple opened in front of them. Austere. Pale. Silent.

And not empty.

In the middle of the enormous room was a statue. A large, crystalline structure carved into a likeness of the Goddess in Trancer position. Shafts of light broke through the decaying ceiling, making it glow.

Lore clasped her hand in his, and together, they approached it. Iliana fought for breath. To know that this Temple was once alive with Trancers. Her ancestors. Her people.

The power they had commanded was not dead. It lived in the air and stone, growing deeper and richer, as they drew closer to the altar.

Stopping at the base, Iliana dropped to her knees before the carved crystal. "My Goddess."

Lore dropped beside her, head bowed in worship and

supplication.

"So much power," Iliana murmured, as heat rushed through her veins, giving her strength and humbling her all at once. "To think they commanded all this." She gestured at the Temple surrounding them "When I think what we did at our Tower, I know it was but a pale shadow of what once was. Of this Temple. Of its Trancers."

"Your Tower sacrificed itself. The women, your family, were just as heroic." Lore took her hand in his and kissed her bare knuckles. "While you do not always see it, so are you."

Heat stained her cheeks, but she did not argue. Not here. Not in this holy place.

"Look." Lore ran his hand over the base of the white stone altar supporting the statue.

Iliana caught her breath. There were carved holes—each unique. Each formed an indentation that matched one of the talismans that she carried at her side. Four carvings. Iliana touched the pouch at her waist. Three stones. So far. One more test. One more chance at either failure or success.

"Iliana?"

She looked up. Lore stood. She shook herself. She had not heard him rise.

She stood, and they walked back to the *rohhas,* leading the animals out of the Ruins.

This last test. What would it require?

Her gut told her this test would be the most difficult. Granted, the others were hard. Who would have thought that breath would have involved jumping into a wind or that blood would insist on actual blood.

She rested her palm against her chest. What would the test of the heart demand?

They passed back through the archway, Lore leading the way towards where they would make camp for the night.

On the horizon, the moons began their trek that would carry them across the expanse of night.

"Today is spent. Tomorrow, we will explore the Ruins and see if we can figure out what the test involves," Lore commented over his shoulder.

Iliana opened her mouth to speak, but instead, a man's cry pierced the air. She looked across the small field to see *rohhas* carrying men, wielding swords, roaring towards them.

***

"Run!" Lore shouted.

His command broke Iliana's immobility, and she wheeled Qi about to make for the Ruins.

Behind her, the clash of swords broke the evening's peace.

Her breathing loud in her ears, she flashed back to the night her Tower fell. The sound of women screaming. The swish of a sword as it cut through the air.

The deafening silence of impending death.

She stopped a few feet from the archway.

She was a not that girl anymore. Not scared. Not innocent. She was a Trancer, and more importantly, she was a Warrior.

Warriors did not run.

With a scream of fury, she whirled about and galloped back to the fight. Pulling her sword from its sheath, she glanced at the unfolding scene, making a quick estimate as what needed to be done.

There were four men. All armed. Two on *rohhas*; two on foot.

Lore was outnumbered, but she did not think he was out-skilled. If she killed even one of them, he might be able to handle the rest.

Sword held up for defense, she called upon all her skills, running Lore's training words through her mind even as the Currents opened up to her, drawn by her power and fear.

Wrapping their energy around her, the Currents weighed on her, like a suit of armor, protecting her and amplifying her strength. Making her more than a Warrior. More than a Trancer.

A bandit on foot came at her, his upper lip curled to reveal missing teeth, as he swung his sword in a wide arc. Her senses heightened by the Currents, she watched the sword come at her throat. With what seemed like all the time in the world, she parried, slicing the bandit's throat instead.

He fell, the droplets from his spraying blood hanging in the air like liquid jewels.

Her stomach rolled, and she swallowed to keep from getting ill. Now was not the time. Later, when they were safe, she could get sick.

She turned back to watch Lore.

His face was grim, emotionless, even as he was in the process of gutting one of the men who rode.

There was more. She shook her head, unsure of what she watched. Darkness? Shade? Her Trancer sense saw a black cloud unlike anything she had seen before.

It covered Lore.

The darkness was not as important as his impending death.

Behind him, another bandit stood, his sword poised overhead for a killing blow.

Iliana's heart sped up.

Not again. She would not lose him.

With all her strength, Iliana galloped past Lore, and before the sword was halfway to his skull, her blade was beneath it, deflecting it.

Without a second thought, she ran her sword through the bandit's chest and watched in morbid fascination as he keeled over in slow motion, screaming.

Out of the corner of her eye, she caught more movement and turned to see Lore's blade cleave the skull of the last bandit, splitting it in two.

Iliana's blood sang with adrenaline, even as her stomach rolled over once again.

Lore spun Lev towards her, sweat dripping from his brow, his chest heaving.

His gaze met hers. His eyes narrowed.

The hairs on the back of Iliana's neck rose. Something was wrong.

The darkness. It grew. Covered Lore like a cloak.

He raised his weapon, pointing the tip of the blade in her direction, as if he would skewer her through the heart. In the fading light of the sun, Iliana met his hard gaze, but the eyes that met hers were not the ones she knew. There was no blue left in them. No white. Just blackness.

Her heart skipped. She had tasted this shadow before—in the Reapers.

In Mako.

And it was unforgiving. Filled with a hate that spanned Danu.

Lore grinned, and the death wish behind it frightened her more than the weapon pointed at her chest.

Worse, the urge to use her weapon was just as strong. She resisted. She would not fight Lore. No trial could make her.

Heart pounding, Iliana wheeled Qi about. Something hit her, knocking her to the ground and the sword from her hand.

She ended up on her back.

Lore straddled her, his own weapon dismissed, left in the dirt beside her. His knees pressed into her ribs, and his hands pressed her wrists into the ground. "Submit!"

"No!" Iliana bucked, trying to throw him off.

He laughed, a dark, sinister sound. "Not good enough. Try something else. Save yourself, Trancer." His black eyes stared into her as if they saw her soul. "If you can."

Iliana bucked again.

Whatever this was, it was not Lore. It was evil.

Laughing, he gripped her waist with his knees and squeezed, crushing her ribs.

As fear threatened to turn into panic, Iliana's mind raced. The Currents still surrounded her. They were hers to command. She gathered more around her, thickening them. Using them to read her lover and the darkness that blotted his soul. To see how to stop it without severing his life, and before he took hers.

The darkness was dense. Complete. Blending with Lore's spirit like a parasite.

There was no way to destroy it. Not without killing Lore.

She tried to scoot out from beneath him, but he tightened his knees.

Goddess help me.

She did not want to hurt Lore, but neither did she want to die. Not here. Not like this. And if it had its way, she knew that death waited. Her death.

Opening her mind as wide as possible, she used the Currents of Life to amplify her strength. They filled her, surging through her veins like fire. Giving her strength.

With a roar, Iliana reared back as much as she was able and then threw her head forward, hitting Lore's nose with her forehead.

He shouted in pain, let go of her, and rolled away.

She scrambled to her feet, ready to run if needed.

In the glow of the setting sun, he looked up at her. His eyes were once again the clear blue that she loved.

He was returned.

But what of the other?

Lore leaned his head back, trying to stop the flow of blood.

The other, whatever it was that had possessed him, could wait another breath. Lore was hurt. Iliana unwrapped the Currents from around herself, letting them fall away like a cloak from her shoulders.

Her senses returned to normal.

And with the return, pain.

Unbearable, burning pain that radiated from the very core of her body and seemed to emerge from every pore in her skin. Overwhelmed with its intensity, she fell to her knees.

In a distant part of her mind, she heard Lore calling to her, and she knew she must be screaming because she could barely hear him over her shrieks.

The screaming and burning seemed to last forever, until blessed blackness claimed her.

Seventeen

When Iliana woke, the camp was clean. The bandits' bodies had been removed, their *rohhas* were tethered to stakes, and she was lying by the fire, wrapped in a blanket. She tried to rise, but she couldn't move more than an inch. Her body felt mangled. Beaten.

She had thought she was tired when they set out this morning, but that was nothing compared to the bone-deep weariness that plagued her now.

She was tired. Tired of fighting. Tired of being tested.

She turned her head. Lore sat near her. Lost in thought. Silent. Staring into the fire. The flames created shadows, highlighting the muscles in his arms and the furrow in his brow.

As always, he astounded her with his quiet strength. "Lore?" Her voice sounded hoarse. Her throat was raw—as if someone had rubbed it with grit

In a heartbeat, he was by her side.

"Iliana." Lore bushed a strand of hair away from her cheek and pulled her partway up, cradling her against his chest. "I thought I lost you." His arms wrapped around her, and the familiar sense of safety washed over her. "What happened? Why did you collapse?" He asked, his free hand stroking her head.

She hesitated. What had happened? Did he remember attacking her? It did not seem so. "I . . . I am not sure. I was fighting. When it was all over, there was the pain."

"I did not find any wounds."

She pressed her lips together. Wounds? Pain? They meant nothing. Minor problems when compared to what was happening to Lore. She needed to tell him about The Other, about his possession, before the presence exerted itself once again. "Lore. My collapse can wait. There are other, more important issues at hand."

"It cannot wait."

"Shh." She placed her finger over his lips. "Please. Grant me this."

Lore ran a hand over his hair, and she sensed his frustration. He wanted to help her. Heal her.

He would need to cure himself first. She wanted to scream, to fight, knowing what was happening to him. Knowing that the trial was upon them—the test of the heart.

Hers and Lore's.

And it stood to claim more than Lore's life. It might claim his humanity.

Their love.

She had not imagined it would be so personal. All the other tests were difficult, even deadly, but they did not affect them like this. Even the test of blood would have been of less consequence if Lore had not tried to go it alone.

This was more difficult than even she imagined, and it had to be solved as soon as possible—before The Other grew in power and overtook Lore completely.

Once again, she tried to rise, groaning as her muscles protested the small movement.

Lore reached to help her.

Taking his hands, she used his strength to rise to her knees. Grateful to be upright, she settled against him. Test or no, shadow or no, she felt safe in his arms.

"Are you all right?" Lore kissed the knuckles of her hand.

"Tired, but otherwise fine." She smiled, despite the gravity of what needed to be said. "I know what the next test is."

"Really?" He glanced down at her, one dark blond brow raised. "We arrived but a bit ago. How can you know?"

She worried her lower lip, not wanting to tell him but knowing there was no choice. Not if they planned to succeed. Not is she wanted him free. "When we were fighting, I was in Trancer state. I saw something. A dark something. I think it is our test to banish it."

"A dark something?"

She met his steady, curious gaze. "Yes. I believe it feeds on fighting. Suckles on the fear generated when blades are crossed and pain permeates the air."

His brow furrowed. "Are you sure?"

Her lips thinned, and she bit back an impatient retort. "I might be out of practice, but I still know how to wield my gift. I know what I saw."

He nodded, the Warrior in him receiving her story with cool eyes. "What do you suggest?"

Suggest? Turn back time so none of this had ever happened. Run away as fast and far as their *rohhas* would carry them.

Let the world go on without their sacrifices.

She sighed. She wished she could run, but she was more than the girl who ran.

She was a Warrior. Perhaps not in skill but in blood. "I suggest we kill it, but first, there is another issue that you must be made aware of."

He took her hand. His large palm engulfed hers. His thumb stroked her skin.

"Lore, the other is more than evil. It is a parasite."

"A parasite?"

"It is not living in the Currents. It has a host. It wanted to kill not just the bandits but me. It attacked me."

Lore stiffened. "It must die."

She continued. "I struck its host in the nose to stop it."

She looked into his eyes as realization dawned in all its horrifying glory.

"It is in you, Lore. It possesses you, and I have no idea how to get it out."

***

Lore froze. A parasite living within him? Evil lurking under his flesh?

Iliana stared at him. A single tear slid down her cheek.

As stunned as he felt, her grief was stronger. He sensed it within her breast, no matter how brave she acted. He pulled her to him and held her when she finally cried, hoping his touch was of some comfort.

He knew he needed hers.

The calmness of his action was the opposite of the myriad of thoughts racing through his mind.

He was possessed.

It was not as surprising as it should have been. Both he and Iliana had been through so much already. An obstacle such as this was just one more step in their progressively hard journey.

He had already died. What was a little evil?

Lore drew small, slow circles on Iliana's back until she gave her last, teary sigh. Snuffling, she rubbed her eyes and gazed up at him, her eyes black in the dim light. "I do not know what to do. I have never heard of anything such as this. Never. Not in the stories. Not in the legends."

Lore took a deep, calming breath. As always, she took too much responsibility upon herself. "I do not expect you to know what to do." He tilted her chin up and placed a tender kiss on her still trembling lips. "You told me that we were to take on these trials together. As a team." He kissed her again, tasting the salt of her tears. "This is no different. We will solve this together."

She managed a small nod.

He wrapped his arms around her, feeling her pulse beat against him.

She softened at his touch, wrapping herself around him as if she feared he would disappear. He swallowed, remembering her comments about their skirmish with the bandits.

She said it fed on pain. Fear.

He did not remember that.

Neither did he remember attacking his beloved—he wrinkled his still sore nose—but the proof was in the pain.

If they did not banish this creature, would it take over his body and create a situation so it could feed?

He did not want to find out. Especially when the only other person in the vicinity was Iliana. He tightened his hold on her. If he hurt her, he would never forgive himself.

She sniffed, and he loosened his grip long enough to capture one last tear that rolled down her cheek.

As much as he worried for her, there was no more time for tears. The trial was upon them, and they needed to kill this parasite before it hurt Iliana. "Tell me what you saw. What you know."

She took a deep breath. "There is not much to say. I know it feeds on fear. Pain. All that is dark." Moving back, she took a breath, gathered her thoughts, crossed her legs, and shut her eyes. A few heartbeats later, she opened them. "As of now, I do not feel it." She ran a hand over her hair, tucking it behind her ears. "But I gave the Currents a cursory touch, nothing more."

Lore nodded. "You believe this is a creature of the Currents?"

She nodded. "If I had not used my Trancer senses when we fought, I would never have known it was there. Of that I am sure."

Lore frowned. He might be joined to Iliana, but that did not give him her abilities. He could no more fight a creature of the Currents than she could defeat a seasoned Warrior.

That meant Iliana would have to banish this creature that infected him. Go into the void and fight. Alone.

This was unacceptable, and every fiber of his body fought against what he knew needed to be done. It was his duty to protect her.

Not the other way around.

She continued, "I think the first course of action is to find out what it wants. If I know more, I might be able to come up with a plan." Iliana hesitated. "I think I can do this without putting either of us in jeopardy."

His brow rose. "You think?"

She managed a weak smile. "There are no guarantees. I do not know what this creature is, but if I can find out, we might have a chance to kill it."

Lore remembered Talon's warning that a Trancer's talent was not without risk. He could not take a chance on her meeting this creature in the Currents. "There has to be another way."

His thoughts raced. If she had not brought him back from the dead none of this would be happening. She would be safe. Or at least safer.

But to not know her touch? Her kiss? Her warmth? He could never regret being brought back to his Iliana. Waking up to her smile was worth any price.

Yet, she was strong. His Apprentice. A skilled Trancer with, what he suspected, was more power than any other Trancer alive.

A sigh escaped his lips, and he took Iliana's hand in his, squeezing it, trying to ignore the conflicting emotions that tortured him.

They were on a mission that was bigger than them both. He flashed back to his vision. Straddling Iliana. Taking her life.

She stared at him, waiting with a look of quiet expectation.

He squeezed her hand again. "Promise me that if there is any, and I mean any, danger, you will get out."

She squeezed back. "I promise."

Taking her in his arms, he kissed her mouth. A kiss of promise. Need. Forever. Breaking contact, he touched her cheek. "We might as well get on with it."

She let go of his hand, crossed her legs, and placed her hands, palms up, on her knees. "I will be in a deep Trance," she explained. "Do not try to wake me."

"I will not."

With a deep breath, she shut her eyes.

He felt as if he was going to fly apart. Standing, Lore paced in the firelight. He hated this. Hated putting her in danger.

There was no other choice. They had vowed to do what was needed to complete the quest, and now it seemed that vow was being put to the test.

***

Iliana entered the Currents, all her Trancer senses at the ready. Around her flowed innumerable colors—the Currents of life.

Magnificent.

The Currents were not what she came for. Casting a mental glance at the bright white that was Lore, she sought the shadow she knew dwelt within his breast.

No darkness met her Trancer gaze.

Was it gone?

She did not think they would be so lucky. That meant it was hiding deep within Lore's soul—so deep that she could not see it.

With a mental request, she called the creature. *Other. Changeling. Whatever you are. I demand you show yourself.*

A bright blue patch of color appeared in the light that was Lore. He was worried about her. The blue grew.

Very worried.

It could not be helped.

Focusing her powers, she sank deeper into the Currents. Calling upon all her strength to pull the creature forth. *Creature of shadow, I demand you come forth.*

Still, nothing.

It was as strong as she, and she dared not pull any harder. To do so might hurt Lore. Deep in her soul, she knew what she needed to give the creature. Fear. Pain.

She could do that now if she wanted. Manipulate the Currents. Bring forth Lore's anger. His fighting instinct.

However, in her psychic state, her body was defenseless, and Lore could hurt, or even kill, her before she saved him.

With a single mental wish, she was back in her body, eyes open.

Lore rushed to her side, clasped her head between his hands, and kissed her hard.

His mouth was rough with need.

"You are unharmed?" he asked, his lips but a breath away from hers.

"Yes." She laid her hand on top of his, taking a moment to lean into his touch, his tenderness touching her heart. "We must speak."

He sat down across from her, legs crossed, and his elbows resting on his knees. The firelight danced across his features, creating both shadow and light.

She relaxed her spine, leaning forward to mimic his pose. "I entered the Currents and called to the creature, but I did not find it."

"I would suggest that it is gone, but I doubt the test would be so easy," Lore replied.

Iliana rested her head in her hands for but a moment, preparing for the upcoming argument. Finally, she looked up. "I agree. The shadow is still in you, and there is just one way to bring it to the surface."

Lore frowned, as if he knew where the conversation was going.

She continued. "We must spar to bring out your fighting instinct."

Lore's frowned deepened. "Last time I almost killed you."

Her small hope crashed. He was right.

Lore rose to his feet and paced.

She laid her head back in her hands. Was she doomed to lose all that she loved? What was the purpose of this test? It was the test of passion. Heart.

They had passion. In fact, they shared more. They were joined.

Why was it not enough?

Lore stopped. "You say fighting brings the creature forth?"

"Yes."

Grabbing the leathers they used to tie the packs to the *rohhas,* he handed them to Iliana. Turning on his heel, he found a sturdy tree, leaned his back against it, and put his arms behind him. "Let us hope my pain brings it forth as well. Now, bind me."

Pain? What was he planning? Wary, she wrapped the leathers around his wrist, tying the ends of the long straps around the tree.

"Do not forget my feet."

She nodded, grabbed what was left of the straps, and bound his ankles.

She stood back, understanding that he meant to keep her safe when the creature emerged. But she was unsure how he planned to call it forth. "Now what?"

"Hit me."

Her jaw dropped open. "What?"

"Hit me," Lore commanded.

By the Goddess, was he insane? "I cannot."

He frowned. "Do you care for me?"

"You know I do." How could he question her feelings? They were joined. He knew she cared for him.

More than cared for him.

He jerked his arms, testing the bonds. "You said that it suckled on pain. Do as I say or I will be doomed to live my life in shadow."

The sweat of fear and loathing dampened her palms.

"Iliana, as you love me, you must do this," Lore shouted.

Shutting her eyes, she slapped him.

When she opened her eyes, there was a bright red imprint of her hand on his cheek.

"Again," Lore demanded.

She slapped him again, her hand continuing the motion, even as tears ran down her cheeks.

"Trancer whore."

Iliana stopped her hand before It made contact with Lore's cheek again. It was back, and Lore's eyes were as black as sin. His lips were drawn back in a sneer.

She lowered her hand. "I see you have returned."

Lore spat at her. "Let me go. Now."

Automatically, she reached for him but stopped herself. "You are not Lore," she replied, her voice more savage than she intended. "Leave him."

"You are insane, and I was insane to think this might work. You seem to enjoy the giving of pain. Too much." His sneer deepened. "Did you learn this from your Reaper lover, Mako?"

"Mako? How can you—" She cut herself off with a reminder that this was the creature, not Lore, and there would be no reasoning with it. Not like this. While speaking through Lore, it used his memories. Played on her fears with half-truths.

There was only one way to deal with a creature of the Currents.

Moving away, she sat down, took a deep breath, focused her thoughts, and entered Trancer consciousness.

Once again, colors swirled about her. She turned her mind's eye to Lore and almost cried out. The bright white light she loved was all but gone, shadowed by the creature that inhabited her lover.

She moved towards it. *What are you?*

I am that which does not belong, the formless black replied.

Iliana moved closer, ready to fly away at a moment's notice.

Lore might be tied down, but the creature was perfectly capable of movement in this realm, and that meant it could harm her as long as she was within its territory. *I do not understand. What are you? Why are you doing this?*

I am that which does not belong. In a surge of power, it rushed towards her, threatening to engulf her, drown her in darkness.

Iliana gathered her power and the Currents around her, shielding herself.

It backed away.

Cautiously, she moved closer. *Are you part of the test? Is your death my goal?*

All are part of the test, Trancer.

It figured.

The shadow continued. *As to my death? I am already dead. My salvation is your goal.* The blackness burned hotter, blinding in its intensity.

Iliana held her ground. *I do not understand. If we—*

Not we. You. The Warrior is but a vessel to give me substance and make my presence known.

If I am to save you, why do you attack us?

Us? There is no us. There is no attack. There is only my desire for salvation. Once again, it approached her.

You attacked the bandits. Closer now, she could reach out a mental hand and touch the shadow if she desired.

They were in the way on the path to you.

The creature spoke in riddles, frustrating her. *I still do not understand. You want to harm me, yet you say I am to save you.*

I mean no harm. Only attention. The creature moved a fraction closer. *We are in a place of power. A place where I have the energy to make my presence known to she who took me.*

He spoke of herself, of that Iliana was sure, but it still made no sense. *Took you? You are a creature of the Currents. How could I have taken you from anyplace?*

From the Goddess. From my home. You took me.

From the Goddess? A sick realization rolled over her.

The shadow was from the other side. When she took Lore, she must have pulled it along.

Her shield wavered in her distress. The abomination that was happening to Lore was her doing.

The creature moved closer. So close that it touched her shield. Wrapped itself around it in an attempt to reach her. A chill ran through her being, colder than the spring where Lore died. She flinched.

Return me, Trancer.

Its demand was like a scream for help. A plea for mercy. A threat of death.

Return it? She backed up. *How?*

Death is the path. The creature clung to the Currents that surrounded her. *Take me home.*

Eighteen

Lore woke to Iliana's screams.

Warrior instinct taking over, his eyes flew open, and he surveyed the situation in a beat of his heart.

He was still bound to the tree. The sun peeked over the tops of the trees as it began its trek across the sky. The *rohhas* were close, nervously shuffling, and their only company.

Iliana lay on the ground, out of his reach, curled into a ball and keening. Her hands thrashed about her head as if she kept something away. Her eyes were closed. He did not think she had come out of her Trance yet.

Her cries grew louder, as if someone, or something, tore at her.

Instinct told him that if he did not help her now, she might never come back to him.

And he was helpless.

Fear and anger roared through him. He pulled at his bonds, but the leather was as thick as a finger and simply stretched, cutting into his wrists.

Iliana stopped crying, her voice cutting off, as if clamped down on by a fist.

Lore's heart pounded in his chest as he waited to see if she were waking. His lips moved in silent prayer.

Instead, she rolled over onto her back and all her muscles went slack. For a moment, she appeared almost peaceful, and then she started to shake. Convulse. Her frame jerking as if shaken by an unseen force.

He had to free himself.

He snapped at the bonds that bound his wrists.

Nothing.

He pulled harder, not caring that the leather cut into his flesh.

Iliana's convulsions grew wilder, her torso coming off the ground and her legs kicking uncontrollably.

Lore grit his teeth, forcing himself to keep the pressure on his bonds.

Something wet and sticky soaked his fingers.

Blood.

He did not care. The blood served to spur him. He had to get to her. Now.

With a great cry, his arms bulging, straining from the stress, he gave one last pull.

The strap snapped, and he fell forward, his legs still tied to the tree.

Ignoring the damage to his wrists, Lore unbound his feet and ran to Iliana.

He reached for her and stopped, instinct telling him that trying to restrain her might do more harm than good.

In what seemed an ageless, powerless agony, he watched her suffer. Waited for her convulsions to slow.

Finally, with one last heave, she stopped.

A sheen of sweat covered her body. Her muscles were lax. Her eyes remained unopened.

But she breathed, thank the Goddess.

He pulled her to him, cradled her in his arms, his blood staining her tunic. "Iliana, beloved." He whispered her name, his plea, as he pushed damp strands of hair away from her forehead.

She remained silent to his touch. Lost. He stroked her cheek with his palm, the pain overwhelming him. The thought that she was lost to him was unbearable.

Was this what she had felt when he died? If so, he wondered how she found the strength to push the ache aside and seek him.

A hot tear dropped onto her skin.

Tears were nothing compared to the breaking of his soul as he lost a piece of himself. He buried his face against her neck, rocking. "Please, waken," he whispered.

"Lore?"

His head shot up.

Iliana stared up at him through half-lidded, bloodshot eyes.

They were the most beautiful sight in all of Danu.

Once again, he buried his face against her neck, wetting her skin with his tears, not caring if he appeared weak.

If his need for her was weak, so be it.

"Why do you cry, my Warrior," Iliana asked, her voice hoarse.

He kissed her neck. "I thought I had lost you."

Still cradled in his arms, she reached up and stroked his damp cheek.

He smiled at her, knowing words were useless—unable to convey the depth of their need for each other and the connection that bound them.

Rising with her still in his arms, he carried her over to their pallet next to the now dead fire. Laying her down, he covered her. He was not a Healer, but he would care for her as well as he could. "I will prepare the morning meal, and when you have rested, we will eat."

"I need to tell you—"

He placed a finger over her lips. "Rest. The telling can wait."

She nodded and closed her eyes.

Tucking the blanket around her shoulders, he sat next to her. Almost immediately, her breathing grew steady. She slept.

"Never again," he whispered. "Never again will I allow you to put yourself in harm's way when I can prevent it."

***

The morning meal was ready, and Lore stared into the fire's flames, contemplating a plan of action.

Unsuccessfully contemplating a plan of action.

Until he knew more of the creature that dwelt within him, he could do nothing.

He glanced at Iliana. She lay next to him, huddled under the blanket. She looked as vulnerable as the innocent girl he knew she once was.

A piece of him wished he had known that girl. Known her before her Tower was destroyed and she lost herself to self-imposed guilt.

He would have liked to see her free.

Now, there was no freedom for either of them. Not from duty. Not from fear.

Now he knew what fear was. True fear, not battle jitters.

The fear of living in a world without Iliana.

The fear of losing himself in her—knowing that the fear of not losing himself in her was greater.

He sighed, resting his head in his hands. When they started this journey, he had envisioned many outcomes, many paths— this was not one of them.

Iliana groaned, catching his attention.

Immediately, all thoughts of himself dissipated. Turning towards her, Lore took her hand in his, intertwining their fingers as he waited for her to awaken.

Eyelashes fluttering, she opened her eyes, and her dark blue gaze met his. She smiled.

He squeezed her fingers.

She squeezed back and inhaled, long and deep.

For some time, he stared at her, amazed at his luck. Her strength. The silence of the morning was broken only by the occasional shuffling of one of the *rohhas*.

He kissed her knuckles.

Her stomach growled.

Grinning, he gave her fingers one last squeeze before he rose and gathered the morning meal—a meat broth that he knew would give her strength—and the last of their flatbread.

They ate in silence.

Finally, Iliana set her bowl down and stretched. "I feel much better."

"Good." As much as he hated questioning her, Lore knew he could put it off no longer—not if he wanted to keep her safe. "Are you ready to tell me what happened?"

With a nod, she folded her hands into her lap. "The creature was strong. Stronger than I imagined."

"I thought as much." Only a creature of enormous power could affect a Trancer while she swam in the Currents of Life, much less cause a physical reaction as well.

He set his bowl down, trying to distance himself emotionally, even as his hand crept over to hold hers. "Did you manage to communicate with it? Find out its purpose?"

"Some." She hesitated but met his gaze.

In her eyes, he saw not just love, but trust. Need.

She continued. "Enough to know that I was right. The creature is part of the trial, and it does not belong inside you, or even in this world."

He nodded, puzzling over the small piece of the riddle she had given him. "Did you find any clue as to how we can extract it from my body?"

"No." Tucking a strand of hair behind her ear, she turned her head.

Something in the innocent gesture made him pause. Perhaps it was that she turned away, not meeting his gaze, or simply instinct, but he knew there was more to her story. Something she was not telling him, and now was not the time for secrets. "Iliana, you are hiding something. What is it?"

She shook her head, obviously aware that he saw through her sham.

"You must tell me," he insisted, hating that he needed to pressure her so soon after her ordeal.

"I was close. So close." She swallowed hard. "I . . . I need to go back in, to learn more. I am not sure I can do that. Not again." She turned back to him, her blue eyes wide and filled with unshed tears. "I know I am a coward, but I am afraid that if I go back I will never emerge."

That was what she fought so hard to hide? She thought herself a coward when she was the strongest woman he knew? "You do not need to hide your fears from me, and you are not a coward. You are wise. The creature almost killed you." He ran a hand over his hair. "I do not see how another altercation will change the situation."

"There is no choice. Not if I want to save you. Save us." Iliana pressed her lips thin. "If only I were stronger."

"You are as brave as any Warrior I have ever seen," Lore replied. "I watched what the creature did to you. We will not take that chance gain. Besides, even you agreed that these tests are to be dealt with as a team. To try another way only brings disaster." He tipped her chin up to kiss her, and she stopped him with a gentle touch, her fingertips resting on his wrist.

The bandages.

Her face became ashen and horrified. "Lore. How . . . ? She pulled his other hand to her. "What did you do to yourself?"

"I had to get to you. You were convulsing on the ground." He placed a gentle kiss on her lips.

"You broke the straps," She began unwinding the thin, narrow wrappings. "I forgot you were tied to the tree."

"This is nothing. A mere sliver of a battle wound." He tried to stop her, and she slapped his hand.

The right wrist was the worst. His hand in her lap, she stared at the inch-thick bloody welts. "I know how thick the leather straps were," Iliana murmured.

He shrugged.

She continued as if she did not see the gesture. "You freed yourself to get to me."

She placed a gentle kiss on his palm. When she sat back up, all sympathy was gone. She gave the wound a critical eye. "These need to be cleaned, and if no salve is applied, they will become infected."

Lore paused, remembering that as a Trancer, she was also a Healer. He had never seen her so commanding. So sure of herself.

He liked it.

But he was right in that his wounds could wait until the more pressing issues were resolved. "Later."

She rewound the bandage. "No. Later, we shall talk of what is to be done. In the meantime, I am going to collect herbs."

"Herbs?" He shook his head. "You almost died this morning. You will go nowhere. You will rest."

She did not show any sign of compromise. "I am recovered, and you are in need of medical attention."

Pulling away from her, Lore finished binding his wounds. "I have received worse injuries training my Apprentices, of which, might I remind you, you are one."

She shrugged. "I am also a Trancer and your lover." Standing on wobbly legs, she took a deep breath then straightened herself, shoulders set back. "I shall return soon."

Lore rose as well, but he did not follow her. He had seen enough to know that there would be no dissuading her. Any efforts he made to stop her would be met with anger, and he would end up giving in to her requests anyway.

He signaled Lev. Pulling the *rohha* close he patted the animal's nose. "Follow her."

With a snort, the *rohha* tossed his head and went in search of Iliana.

***

As soon as she cleared the tree line and escaped Lore's view, Iliana sank to her knees. It was not her physical weakness that brought her to her knees.

It was her lies.

The other said that death was the path.

That it meant Lore's death was of little doubt. There was also little doubt that if she had told Lore of this, he would willingly sacrifice himself in order to complete the quest.

She was not so willing.

But to lie to Lore. Deceive him. To use his trust against him with barely a hesitation. The ease at which falsehoods spilled from her mouth sickened her.

"It is for his own good," she murmured, searching for solace.

The words were little comfort as a louder, stronger voice pushed through.

You are what you feared. You are what Mako claimed you to be.

"No." When she was Mako's prisoner, he had told her she was not as different from him as she thought. He had told her that she would lie if it suited her. That she would do what was necessary to accomplish her goal.

"This is not the same," she whispered into the silence of the green. "This is to save. Not harm."

Yet, it came so easily.

She shoved the insistent voice aside. Squelched it with a strong mental fist.

The deed was done and set into motion. Self-recrimination could come later. After she had done what was needed, and if she lived.

Rising on shaky legs, she began searching for what she would need—the *barra* root. She was sure she had seen its stunning red flowers when they passed through the forest on their way to the Ruins.

She followed her and Lore's trail—still clearly marked by broken twigs and the earth that had been disturbed by the hard hooves of the *rohhas*.

In her mind, she ran over her plan.

Death carried many forms, some more permanent than others—she had proved that.

If the trial were so simple as to only require Lore's death— a dark chuckle made its way past her lips at the thought of a simple trial—then it was not a trial devised by the Goddess.

No, there had to be more. Another option. Another way.

She hoped that her plan was enough. That it would succeed. If not, they were all doomed.

A patch of bright red flowers caught her eye, diverting her thoughts.

The *barra.*

She pushed past the surrounding plants, being careful not to disturb the vegetation any more than was needed, until she reached the flowers.

The *barra* was a beautiful plant, prized for not just its sweet scent but also for its brilliant colors.

For a Trancer, the beauty was secondary when compared with its medicinal properties. She inhaled their fragrance, and with a ruthless yank, she pulled one of the plants from the ground. With a sure hand, she dusted the damp earth from the cluster of thin, finger-length tubers that hung from the base.

They looked innocuous. Just a root.

The tubers effects were anything but harmless. One root, boiled and drank as a tea, brought instant relaxation. Two brought sleep. Three paralyzed the user, keeping their heart pumping and their lungs breathing, but that was all as they lay on the ground, unable to move a limb for a hundred heartbeats.

She had seen three roots used but once. An Elder had to restrain a man who had lost an arm in the fishing nets and was out of his head with pain. Only by using the three roots was the Elder able to apply herbs that would ease his suffering. By the time the man emerged from the paralysis, his arm was numbed and bound.

Still, there were risks. Too much did not bring paralysis. It brought death, not paralyzing the muscles, but shutting down the lungs and the heart and suffocating the user.

She shuddered. She did not want Lore dead—merely so close that she could convince The Other to leave his body. Force it back to the Goddess, even if she had to take it herself.

She would be careful. Ever so careful.

She plucked off the head of the flower and stuffed it in her pocket. If it came to it, she would administer the antidote found in the petals.

She hoped it would not come to that. If so, all was lost because the Warrior in Lore would never allow her to do what was needed.

Breaking the tubers off, Iliana let the rest of the plant fall to the ground. She stuffed the tubers into her side pouch, patting them with her hand, sending a brief prayer to the Goddess for guidance in their use.

Now, she needed something to soothe Lore's wrists. He might claim the wounds were insignificant, but she knew better.

Besides, he might become suspicious if she returned with nothing but the tubers.

A rustling in the leaves caught her attention.

Bandits.

Grabbing the knife from her boot, Iliana whirled, ready to fight or run, depending on what was needed.

Instead of bandits, Lev looked at her from across the clearing.

Iliana shook her head, crooked her finger, and signaled the *rohha* to come closer.

Cautiously, the great beast made his way to her.

She laughed. If ever an animal looked guilty and uncomfortable, it was Lev. She wrapped her arms around the great beast's neck and kissed his soft nose. "Did Lore send you to watch over me?" She asked, already knowing the answer.

The great animal leaned into her, rubbing his head along her arm.

"Do not worry," she whispered in his ear. "I will not tell Lore that I saw you."

She was not sure if he understood her, but she felt better in the telling.

Letting him go, she motioned him to follow her. Deeper into the surrounding forest, she searched for a *cascarri* tree. When peeled, its bark could be shredded and used as a bandage, and it had the added advantage of being a natural fighter of infections.

The shade deepened into gloom as she traipsed further, the *rohha* at her heels.

The silence of the surrounding woods deepened, until she heard neither animal nor the rustle of leaves in the morning breeze. There was only the shuffle of her feet along the forest floor and Lev's breathing.

She was debating whether to look elsewhere when she came into a clearing, a single *cascarri* tree in its center—as if it waited for her and for this moment.

Thank you, my Goddess.

Taking the knife from her boot, she carefully peeled a strip of bark as wide as her hand and as long as her arm. Rolling it into a cylinder, she gripped it tight.

Turning back the way she had come, she hesitated as her resolution faded.

She steeled herself once again.

There was no other way. No other path.

It was time to return and betray her lover.

Nineteen

Iliana wrapped the boiled *cascarri* bark around Lore's left wrist, the softened fibers molding to his skin and making a protective bandage.

He tried not to flinch. The wounds were not the worst he had received in his career, but that did not negate the fact that they burned at the slightest touch.

"Does that hurt?" Iliana asked, looking up at him through her lashes.

As always, she worried. "I am fine," he replied.

She raised a dark brow in disbelief.

As always, she saw through his deception, no matter how minor.

Reaching behind her, she picked up a cup and handed it to him. "Drink this. It will both help numb the pain as well as speed healing."

Their fingers brushing, Lore took it from her hand and sipped the hot liquid, grimacing at the bitter taste. "It tastes like boiled hide."

Iliana smiled. "That is why it is called medicine and not wine." She nodded towards the cup. "Drink it quickly, and it will not be so bad."

With a determined frown, Lore tipped the cup and drained it. His stomach rebelled, but he managed to hold the medicine down.

Iliana took his other hand in hers and began applying the fibrous bark. "It might make you a little sleepy, so do not be alarmed."

"Sleepy?" Now was not the time to nap. Night would fall soon, and if more bandits attacked, he would need to be at the ready. "Why did you not tell me before I drank?"

Iliana did not look up but molded the bark to his wrist. "A said a little sleepy, not unconscious. Nothing to worry about."

He relaxed, knowing she did not mean to alarm him. "Next time, please tell me prior to drinking."

"Of course." She finished bandaging him. "There. That should serve until we can find a real Healer."

"You are a real Healer," he countered. Holding up his hands in the light of the late noon sun, he surveyed her handiwork. The binding looked primitive, but the boiled bark felt as soft as an expensive hide.

Iliana blushed. "Barely. I know the basics. I was training for more before my Tower . . ."

He squeezed her knee. She did not need to complete her thought. He knew what she lost at her Tower's death. Opportunity. Generations of knowledge. Family. Friends.

Lethargy washed over him, and he yawned.

"Perhaps you should lie down while I keep watch." Gathering their blankets, Iliana laid down a pallet beside Lore. "I can shout if trouble arises."

Lore shook his head, yawning so wide his vision blurred. A little sleepy? His eyelids felt weighted. He shook his head to clear it. "No. I am fine."

"Are you sure?" Iliana asked.

Lore paused, the hairs rising on the back of his neck. Her tone contained more than concern. There was a curiosity about it. Perhaps it was the joining, but he had the distinct feeling that she was up to something.

He moved to stand. His legs did not obey.

The lethargy felt familiar. The immobility. The mind's desire to move, and the body's inability to comply.

The combination of feeling both foolish and betrayed.

Once, when he had tried to keep Aria from following Talon, she had drugged him.

Now, it seemed, Iliana had done the same.

In the span of a heartbeat, the immobility spread throughout his body, and he slumped over.

Catching him as he fell sideways, Iliana lowered him to the blanket, laying him on his back with his arms at his sides.

"Why," he asked, forcing his jaw and tongue to move. He could barely form the words. His thoughts seemed as if they were wrapped in thick yards of cloth. Even his bones were heavy.

The question nagged. Why had she done this to him?

Iliana stroked his hair, and while he was immobile, his sense of touch did not seem affected. "When I was in the Currents, the other told me what I needed to do to free it. It said that death was the path. Your death. You know I cannot let that happen."

He listened, though his consciousness slipped away as the drug worked its way deeper into his body. Even Iliana's touch was little more than a hum.

She continued. "Do not worry. The effects will not last long. A hundred heartbeats at the most. Just enough to give me time to enter Trancer consciousness and take the other back where it belongs, to the Goddess.

No. Lore fought to scream his denial, beg her to stop, but the words would not emerge from his paralyzed mouth.

"The creature wants your death. I cannot let that happen. Not again," she said, as if she had heard his thoughts. And with the joining, perhaps she had. If so, she also knew he did not want her to risk this.

Once again, he tried to speak. To shout at her to stop.

She pressed a palm against his cheek, her eyes soft. "If I do not return, I want you to know that you are the reason I wake in the morning. You are the reason I breathe and my heart beats." She kissed him and a flash of emotion washed over him.

She was not frightened. She was committed to her actions. Determined. A Warrior to the core of her being.

And the love she felt, the depth of commitment to him, it both humbled and honored him

"I love you, Lore. No matter what happens, know that I love you." She deepened the kiss, her lips molding to his mouth. Warm. Soft. Full of promise and courage.

Then the drug took that away as well.

***

Sitting next to Lore, her sword on the ground in front of her, Iliana took a deep breath and entered Trancer consciousness before resolution gave way to hesitation.

Once again, the Currents flowed around her, bright as the sun and as deep as the moon.

She turned her mind's eye to Lore. His color was dim.

Dim but not extinguished. The drug was shutting his body down—not to the point of death but close. Cautiously, she watched, making sure it went no further or she would have to reemerge and give Lore the petals of the flower to bring him back.

Finally, his light stopped dimming and relief flowed through her. It was time to finish this trial.

Going to Lore, she searched for The Other, but it was still so deep within that it proved invisible. Summoning her strength, she called it. *Creature, I call upon you to come to me.*

To her surprise, instead of either fighting her or ignoring her plea as before, the creature did as she bid and emerged from Lore like a dark cloud of thick smoke.

Her body and soul remembered the pain the creature had

put her through, and her first reaction was to awaken. Run. Anything to escape.

She held the urge to flee at bay. This was not about her. This was about Lore. The trial. And a world that needed her. *It is time for me to take you home.*

The dark that was the creature neither wavered nor broke its attachment to Lore. *Death is the path. He lives.*

He is close to death. Close enough for you to leave. Come with me, and I will show you the way home. Iliana insisted. *I have been to the other side. Walked the path.*

The creature did not reply but waited.

It waited for her to prove her words. If she had been in her body, she would have rolled her eyes. Quickly, Iliana searched her mind, looking for the memories that would guide her to the other side. They were elusive. On the tip of her mind, but without Lore's soul to channel her energy they were without substance. She saw them, but trying to use them was like trying to hold a shadow in her hand.

An instant of panic made her hesitate. She shoved it down inside her soul, ignoring the sharp distraction.

She focused. Reached deep within. Felt the pain of Lore's death. Her desperation to find him.

Loss overwhelmed her. It was not enough.

The way was gone. Invisible to her Trancer eyes.

The creature did nothing. Waited. Its animosity and its desperation, tugged at her. *You have failed, Trancer. Now do as you must. Death is the path. The only path.*

Iliana's anger flared, tinting her vision red. She had seen enough death to last her until she breathed her last breath. Death was not the path. She would not allow it.

There had to be another way.

She searched her memories of training. Of healing. Of death. Of life.

All the death that had touched her. Her friends. Her family. Lore. Herself.

So much suffering.

Her mother's words came back to her. Memories from so long ago she had all but forgotten them.

When she was but a child, she had a pet shabar. One day, it grew ill and died. It was her first taste of loss, and she had cried until she thought she had cried all the tears in the world.

Her mother, an Elder and a Healer, helped her bury the tiny

creature in the garden. It was at the tiny graveside that she first heard the Healer's thoughts on death. *The wheel of life turns, daughter. Death. Life. All are the same. Do not fear death. Embrace it for what it is, both the end and the beginning.*

Her mother had passed away not long after that, dying from a blood disease that no one could cure.

Still, her words lived within Iliana's breast.

Death and life. Both beginnings. Both ends.

So much death.

Still, so much good came from it. A friendship with Aria that was deeper than a blood-bond. Her emerging skills as a Warrior. Her love for Lore.

So much good had come from so much sorrow. Life from death.

Death was the path, but not as she thought.

She glanced at Lore. His light was growing brighter. The drug was wearing off. Not that it mattered now that she understood the truth of it all.

Still, he might try to wake her.

Death. Life.

Thoughts of the Goddess washed over her.

The Goddess was both death and life. The end and the beginning.

She was The All, and Iliana had been as close to her as any living being ever got. Once again, she focused her thoughts, but instead of Lore, she thought of the Goddess.

Her light. The way she had touched Iliana's soul with a love that was as unconditional as a mother's. How she made her feel, totally accepted.

No worries. No doubts. Just complete.

The Currents deepened, glowing brighter as Iliana opened herself up to the Goddess and all that she offered. Opened her heart. Her mind. Her very soul.

The path to the other side emerged, a ribbon of color both beautiful and awesome, to guide her.

It was time to take the creature home.

Death is the path, Iliana thought. *Death and Life.* No longer afraid of the pain, she opened her mind. *Creature, it is time. Join with me.*

In a flicker, it was within her.

Although the creature held no physical form, it weighed on her soul, almost suffocating her with the intensity of its emotions.

It suffered. It mourned. It needed to return from whence it came before it shattered into nothingness.

Her body flinched at the pain and shock, but she kept her focus on the path and where she wanted, needed, to be.

Goddess.

Another breath, a flicker of thoughts, and she was back with the Goddess. Floating in the bright void that was the other side.

With a great shout, the creature left her body, the darkness replaced by light. The pain by joy.

Bondage by freedom.

Thank you. It touched her, leaving a piece of itself as a gift in her thoughts. A sliver of love to soothe her weary mind.

She had done it. Brought the creature back. Freed the creature. Freed Lore. Freed herself. Relief rippled through Iliana. It was time to go home.

She turned her mind's eye to the path. It was gone. Dissipated as if it never existed.

For a moment, she panicked. Being lost in the Currents was a fate that all Trancer's feared.

This is not the Currents, she reminded herself, reining in her fear. *This is the other side. Part of the test. Focus and return home.*

She concentrated on Lore. How he made her feel. The strength of their bond. The joining.

Nothing happened. No path appeared to lead her home. Only the void remained. Black. Unknown.

She tried again, remembering life. Lore's kiss. His courage. The feeling of being safe in his arms.

Nothing.

She was lost.

Fear overwhelmed her, and she let it take her over as she screamed into the dark.

***

His sense of sound was the first to return.

Lying on the blankets, Lore heard Iliana's deep, even breaths. He knew she sat near him.

He fought to emerge from the paralysis that gripped him, but his limbs refused to move.

Sight returned next. He opened his eyes and blinked at the sun above. It did not look like it had moved, so she must have spoken true when she said the drug would last for only a hundred heartbeats.

His sense of touch returned—a blade of grass tickled his cheek. A few more heartbeats and the drug wore off as fast as it had taken him over. All sensation returned.

With a groan, Lore sat up.

He glared at Iliana where she sat at the end of the blanket, legs crossed and eyes closed. She was oblivious to the low fury that coursed through his veins.

He hoped her trick was worth taking such a risk. He searched his soul for the creature. Was he free? He felt no different, but it was not as if he had sensed the creature prior to Iliana's deception.

He would have to wait for her to return and tell him.

Lore rose, both anxious for his beloved's safety and angry enough to turn her over his knee like a child.

Pacing, he wondered what he would say to her when she woke; what she would say to him. How would she justify her actions?

He had never been as angry with another person as he was with the beautiful Trancer in front of him. How could she have drugged him?

Drugged him!

Even Talon would never have gone so far.

Lore raked a hand over his hair in frustration. Worse than his anger was his pride in her decision. He knew she was strong. To have suffered as she had and transformed that pain into life was an accomplishment that few, if any, could manage.

But strong enough to lie to him and hide it? To do what she felt was needed, despite what he said? He had never suspected so much.

She was magnificent.

Still, his pride did not change the outcome. When she woke, she was in trouble.

His skin itched with both worry and impatience as he waited for her to wake. A hundred heartbeats passed, and she did not stir. Did not blink. "Should she not be returned by now?" He muttered, widening the line in the grass as he made another pass.

How long should he wait before he tried to wake her? Or would trying to wake her harm her?

He stopped and kneeled down. Carefully, he curled his fingers around her upturned palm.

The anger remaining in his heart faded. Her body was empty. There was no life-spark present. No soul. No light. Just a shell.

A part of him shouted that he was wrong. She was fine.

However, deep in his bones, he knew this lack of soul was not his imagination. He and Iliana were part of each other. Bound closer than any two people would ever know.

It was the joining that told him that her life-spark was not in her body.

Despite the warmth of the sun on his back, Lore shivered at the implication.

"Perhaps this is part of the process," he murmured, but speaking his hope aloud to the wind did not make it any truer. He knew the words were false. She was in trouble.

His skin clammy, Lore felt as useless as wings on a *rohha*. Iliana could enter the world of the Warrior, but he could not enter her world. Not even to save her.

He was helpless in the face of her trouble.

He did the one thing he knew to do. Pray. "Please, my Goddess," he whispered. "Do not leave me alone. Not like this. Never like this."

He clasped Iliana's other hand and squeezed. "Come back to me."

He remembered the early days, when her guilt and anger engulfed her. Even then, a part of his soul knew that they were going to be important to each other. That one day, he would wake up with Iliana by his side, and on that day, he would never be alone again.

Somehow, he had known.

He was not going to give that up. Not for anyone or for any reason.

He gripped her hands tighter. "By the Goddess, Iliana, come back to me. Find me."

Leaning forward, he kissed her, willing her to feel his touch. To use it to lead her home.

***

Iliana floated in the void, sinking into her fate like one sank into a feather-stuffed blanket.

A spark of light caught her attention. A call from someone familiar. The feeling that Lore called to her. Pulled her to him.

It came again. Lore?

She held on to the feeling, tethering herself to it with a mental fist, but it was not enough. The void's call was stronger.

The strand of life slipped from her grasp and disappeared into the void.

***

"Iliana," Lore whispered her name in prayer and cupped her cheek with his palm. He would give anything, anything, to see her deep blue eyes open. "I cannot go on without you. You said that you breathed for me. Lived for me. Loved me." He kissed her again, his breath mingling with hers. "Know that you are the same for me. Know this and come back."

***

Like a strand of light, the connection to life appeared again. Iliana sighed in relief, once again grabbing hold. This time, she would not let go.

She heard Lore's thoughts. His need. His call for her to come home.

Home.

He was her home.

She wanted to go home. She wanted Lore.

The void slipped away.

Twenty

Iliana opened her eyes. Lore kneeled in front of her. His hands clutched hers, but it was his eyes that touched her at a deeper level. Although she was no longer in the Currents, it was as if she saw the light that burned within his breast.

It flickered with concern. With a fear it had never felt before. A fear brought on by her action.

She placed her palm against his cheek, and the fear was replaced with relief.

With a sigh, she leaned forward, her forehead resting against his.

She was home.

Lore tilted her head upwards and pressed his lips to hers in a gentle kiss. "If you ever drug me again, I shall never forgive you," he whispered.

"Of course," she replied, hearing the meaning beneath the words. If she ever put him through such pain. If she ever took such a chance. If she ever lied to him again, there would be a heavy penalty to pay.

She kissed him, inhaling his warmth.

He returned the kiss, sat back on his heels and waited.

Her eyes locked with his, she opened her palm. In the center rested the final talisman. Unlike the others, this one was made of white glass with no decorations adorning it.

Lore stroked it with a finger. "Where did it come from?"

"The creature gave me thanks. Left a piece of itself as an offering." Iliana took his hand in hers, clasping the talisman between their palms. "I think this is it."

"Amazing."

"Yes," she murmured. "We have done it."

"Almost." Lore turned his head towards the Ruins.

Iliana followed his gaze with her eyes, remembering the altar and the indentations for the talismans. There was no longer any doubt that the portal would open. She closed her fingers over the glass, making a gentle fist. They were almost done. Free. The quest finished.

Either way, their world would never be the same. They would never be the same.

She had never been more afraid in her life. Not even when Mako held her captive had she shaken as she did now. Her courage was as tenuous as a thread.

She was not ready. She wanted another night with Lore. Another kiss. Another moment to lay with him. She wanted this, all the trials and tests and fears, to stop.

She wanted it all so much that she knew she would lose her nerve if she spoke her wants. "We should finish this."

Lore opened his mouth, as if he wanted to say more. Instead, he rose and offered her his hand. Taking it, she let him help her to her feet.

Her legs, cramped from maintaining Trancer position, wobbled beneath her before she gained her balance.

Lore wrapped his arm about her waist to steady her and pulled her close. "Are you ready?"

She was not, but she would not give her fear a voice. It was all happening so fast, too fast, but they had come too far to stop.

She glanced at the *rohhas* grazing at the opposite end of the small field. "What about Lev and Qi and the other *rohhas?*"

"We will leave them untethered. Lev will keep them all in the area until our return."

Iliana worried her bottom lip with her teeth. "What if more bandits come? Lev might be trained for battle, but Qi is not, and without us to protect her—"

Lore squeezed her close. "Qi braved a monster for you. Do not doubt her ability to care for herself. Besides, if we succeed, we will need mounts. If not, the better for them to leave unencumbered."

Other worries tumbled through Iliana's mind. "How will they know when to leave?"

"Lev will know." Lore kissed the top of her head. "Your thoughts seek to keep you safe. It is normal for a new Warrior to search for reasons to ignore his sword, especially when battle has been tasted and death is no longer something that happens in stories." He kissed her again. "The key is to realize this and press past it."

Her cheeks heated. He was right. She straightened her shoulders. "I am ready."

Arms around each other, they walked to the Ruins.

The hair on Iliana's arms rose, her skin prickling at the power that surged through her, the closer they drew to the tumble of stones.

She took a deep breath, breathing in the light that seemed

to flow through her very being. Finally, when she thought that the power was about to reach an unbearable level, they reached the Temple of Light. The power stilled to a steady beat that thrummed through her body.

They stepped into the Temple, and silence followed them like an ancient shroud. They crossed the stone plaza, reached the base of the altar, and knelt at the feet of the Goddess.

Still holding the last talisman in her hand, Iliana pulled the other stones from the pouch at her waist.

She held them out on her open palm, offering them to Lore.

He shook his head. "This is a Trancer Temple. This is for you."

"Are you sure?" she asked, not sure she wanted the responsibility.

"Yes." Lore clasped her hand, the talismans pressed between their palms. "I am sure." He let her go.

Iliana put the first stone in the appropriate space. "Breath."

In unison with her words, a wind blew through the temple, making her hair dance around her shoulders.

The second stone. "Bone."

The ground beneath them started to shake, growing with such violence that it threw Iliana sideways and to the ground.

Lore grabbed her arm and helped her back to her knees.

She shoved the third stone in place. "Blood."

Water, as red as wine, gushed from the once-dry channels that flanked either side of the altar and spilled at their feet.

Her hair now whipping about her shoulders and face, Iliana glanced at Lore. One more stone and they would be at the final stage of the quest.

He nodded. "Do it!"

She set the last talisman in the final space. "Heart." Her voice echoed through the ruins.

All movement stopped. The wind died. The shaking of the ground stopped as suddenly as it began. The blood-red water ceased flowing.

It was as if the world waited, holding its breath to see what would happen next.

A crack sounded above the altar. Both Iliana and Lore looked up to see a rip forming in the air above them. Light poured through the ever-widening slice, spilling an unearthly radiance into the temple.

"I always believed you could do it," came a comment from

behind them.

The voice was familiar in both sound and the way it made the hairs on Iliana's arms rise.

She turned.

At the edge of the plaza, knife in hand, a smile on her lips, and a Reaper by her side, stood Medea.

***

She looks shabby, was Iliana's first thought. What was once a fine gown was patched. Her hair, while still striking in its deep, black color, was in disarray—as if she had tried to comb and style it but was unaware of how to accomplish such a mundane task.

Her gaze shot over to Medea's companion.

The man from the ferry, Iliana realized, even as Lore jumped to his feet, unsheathed his blade and raced towards Medea and the man.

With more skill and speed than Iliana thought possible, the Reaper drew his sword and sidestepped Lore, raising his blade for a killing blow.

Lore rolled, coming up on his feet at the Reaper's opposite side, his blade at the ready.

Medea's lips curled in a sneer. "Kill him, Kole. Kill him now!"

Her screech broke Iliana's paralysis. She jumped up, drawing her own blade as she made her way towards Medea. She had had enough of the Reaper whore. It was time to end this.

Medea raised her knife. Barely longer than her palm, Iliana knew it was no match for her sword.

She did not care.

There was no time for right or wrong. For fair or unfair.

There was only time for winning or losing.

For death or life.

The memory of the pain that had crippled her when she killed the bandit flashed through her thoughts. Iliana dismissed it. Any amount of suffering would be worth the satisfaction of having Medea dead at her feet.

Blade above her head, Iliana screamed a battle cry and brought her blade down, the Currents gathering towards her power.

With a move not unlike Lore's, Medea dodged Iliana's sword, rolling aside. But instead of turning to fight, she ran for the portal.

"No!" Iliana ran after her, her vision of Medea as the Dark Queen gripped her heart. Leaping forward, she managed to snag her rival's collar, yanking her to the stone floor.

The crack of bone was audible above the sounds of blades clashing, battle yells and labored breathing.

With a howl, Medea rolled away, kicking at Iliana.

Iliana rolled to her knees, grabbing her own wrist and hissing at the pain. When she looked, it was undamaged, but Medea's hand hung from her wrist at an unnatural angle.

Something had finally gone her way.

Despite the pain in her eyes and voice, Medea managed to regain her feet and stumble away.

Iliana ran after her and, once again, managed to grab the Reaper and throw her to the ground. This time she kept her own footing.

Another flash of light from the portal washed over the once beautiful temple. It bathed everyone in its bright light, negating shadows, and washing out all color with its brilliance.

Pulsing with life, the portal ceased growing.

"Iliana, go. Now!" Lore called out, even as he blocked a lunge.

Medea smiled.

There was no time for Medea's death, no matter how much she desired to be the one to kill the whore.

There was only the portal and her mission.

Her quest.

Her destiny.

Spinning around, Iliana ran the rest of the short distance to the altar. Quickly, she climbed up, hand-over-hand until she was level with the hole in space.

She glanced over her shoulder at Lore. He and the Reaper from the ferry still fought.

The Reaper stumbled, but he regained his footing before Lore had time to thrust his blade home.

She opened her mouth to call for Lore to be careful and to watch his back, but she stopped before sound emerged. He did not need the distraction.

Below, her broken wrist cradled against her chest, Medea tried to climb after Iliana.

She would not make it. Iliana's lips curved upwards. She had beaten her. Beaten her enemy. She glanced at the split in the air. "Let us hope my victory is not my death," she whispered. And dove into the portal.

***

Iliana came out the other side of the portal and the ground rushed towards her. Tucking into a ball, she tried to roll, but she hit the ground hard, knocking the breath from her body. For the first few moments, she fought to breathe. Finally, the spasms passed, and her muscles relaxed.

Relieved, she looked up at a bright blue-sky overhead.

A person, shadowed by the sunlight from above, blocked her view. "Welcome to my garden."

Iliana's heart sped up. This was not what she had expected. "Um . . . thank you. I am glad to be here."

She sat up, the shadows disappeared, and the stranger came into view. It was a woman. Young. Perhaps her own age.

Clad in a white robe, her black hair fell over her left shoulder and past her hips in a thick braid. Delicate featured, with a small cleft in her chin, she smiled, revealing perfect teeth. Her eyes were the color of the sky that first greeted Iliana.

Though there was no way Iliana could know her, she seemed familiar. "Do I know you?" she asked.

The woman shrugged. "No and yes." She motioned Iliana to rise to her feet.

Iliana stood, straightened her clothes and touched her sword for comfort. Whoever this woman was, her presence seemed as comforting as sitting in front of a warm fire on a cold day—and as frightening as being pinned by a hungry *katah'*.

The woman continued. "You may call me Amarjaa."

"The first," Iliana whispered, recognizing the name.

Not the first Trancer.

Amarjaa was She Who Created All But Herself.

The one with no beginning and no end.

The Goddess.

Amarjaa grinned, her smile dazzling, and took Iliana's hand in hers. "Come. Walk with me."

In silence and awe, Iliana allowed herself to be led down a pebbled path.

Slowly, they walked through what appeared to be a garden, but it was unlike any garden Iliana had ever seen on Danu. Everything was intensified. The flowers more vibrant. The scents sweeter.

And the sounds. Almost indescribable, it was as if the

universe sang, striking the chords of her soul.

They stopped at a *tala* tree. Its long branches touched the ground, creating a shelter. Amarjaa parted the thin, whiplike branches and stepped inside. She sank to the grass, her legs crossed in Trancer position. Iliana followed, letting the branches close behind her and waited, unsure of what to do.

Amarjaa patted the ground next to her. "Come. Sit with me, my sister."

Iliana sat, her head bowed. What was she supposed to do? Say? This was the Goddess.

"I have waited a long time for you, Iliana." The singing of the universe intensified, as if focused through Amarjaa's very being. "Longer than I thought I would." She patted Iliana's hand. "And not as long as it could have been."

"Longer than you thought?" Iliana echoed, confused by the comment. She dared to look up. "I do not understand. You are the Goddess. You know all."

Amarjaa laughed, and it was both like water flowing quietly over smooth pebbles and the wind whipping through the leaves. "True, but even a Goddess likes to be surprised every now and then." She brushed a strand of raven hair away from her eyes. "I suppose we should talk about why you have come here."

"Where is here?" Iliana asked, curiosity making her bold. "Is this the garden we go to after we die?"

Amarjaa nodded.

The garden of the dead.

Her friends were supposed to be here. Her family. Iliana worried her already raw bottom lip. Instead, the garden was empty. "Where is everyone?"

"They are here," Amarjaa explained. "I simply shielded them from your eyes. It is not for you to see the dead. Not yet."

Once again, she patted Iliana's hand. "Now, ask me."

"What?"

"What you came for. Ask me for it."

Iliana took a deep breath, a part of her wanting to end this and go back to Lore, but her other half did not want to leave. Not now. Not yet. Once she had the Orb of Dalis that was what would happen. She swallowed hard and gathered her courage. "There is so much I want to ask you, not just about . . . why I came."

Amarjaa gave a single nod. "Ask. Time means nothing here."

Iliana's mind was jumbled as she sorted through the myriad questions that plagued her. One rose to the top.

The one question that kept her awake at night. The one that she asked herself whenever a townsperson treated her as if she were of no importance. The one that plagued her heart, with the only balm being Lore's strong arm around her. "Why did you let Mako take me?"

The Goddess sighed. "This is the problem with knowing all. I knew you were going to ask that."

"Could you have prevented it?" Iliana asked, already knowing what the answer would be, but wanting to hear it for herself.

"Yes, but that was not the point."

Tears of anger and pain filled Iliana's eyes. She wiped them away with the back of her hand. It was true. None of this—the pain, the suffering, death—had to happen. "Why? Why did you let him hurt me? Kill my family? My friends?"

Again, Amarjaa sighed, her breath blowing over Iliana like a warm breeze, sweet with new buds. "I created Danu, but it is not my place to control it or its people. I had hopes for you, and once I saw what was happening, I watched. Hoped."

Her voice growing stronger, her presence more commanding, Amarjaa continued. "While you may not understand, everything that happened to you was needed, and the universe pushed you to it. Had you not been taken, you would be a Trancer, but nothing more. Granted, you would be a good Trancer, one of my chosen, but you would not have the strength you do now. You would not have been able to do what was needed to endure the trials. And not just endure them, but to thrive and grow in the process of becoming both Trancer and Warrior."

Iliana snorted in derision. Then, as she realized who she was deriding, she clapped her hand over her mouth.

Amarjaa raised a dark brow. "You have a comment?"

Heat rose through Iliana, and she did not need a looking glass to know her cheeks were stained red. "Being both Warrior and Trancer has done me little good. If I use my blade to hurt another, I feel their pain." She shuddered. "Even their death."

The Goddess gave a nod of agreement. "As it should be. You are the first of your line, Iliana. The beginning of what will be a long line of Warrior women, but there is always a price that comes with the shedding of blood. That is what the pain is for.

To remind you to not draw your blade lightly."

The pain worked as planned, but it also made her less of a Warrior.

"Less and more. Forget neither." The Goddess, straightened, and her eyes flashed fire despite the shade of the tree. "Ask me for the Orb, Iliana. It is time."

Iliana shook her head in denial. "There is so much I need to know. Will I ever be whole? How do I get past the blackness of my own soul?"

Amarjaa frowned. "Ask. Now."

Her command was undeniable. Iliana sighed. There was no winning a fight of wills—not with the Goddess. "I ask for the Orb of Dalis."

Amarjaa held out her hand and blew across her opened palm. Like a cloud materializing out of the air, the Orb of Dalis appeared. Faint, translucent.

She blew harder, and the Orb grew in tangibility until it was as solid as the ground upon which Iliana sat.

Floating a finger's width above the Goddess's palm, it glowed with a blue light that was almost blinding.

Amarjaa's frown faded, and she nodded towards the Orb. "Here is your answer. All your answers. The Orb can take away your pain, if you wish. All pain. Do you wish your memories of Mako to disappear? Your Tower's death? Your friends' screams?"

The Orb spun in time to Amarjaa's words.

She continued. "If you want to be just a Warrior, it can take away your Trancer powers as well. But be warned, if you choose to take away your powers, the rest in the Warrior line of women will also be powerless. They will be great women who will command nations, and they will feel no pain for what they cause. No hesitation for the lives they will take."

The Orb stopped spinning. "No consequences for their actions."

Amarjaa dropped her hand to her side, and the Orb remained suspended in midair. "It is yours."

Iliana reached out and cupped her hands around the shining sphere. It pulsed, warm and solid, in her palm. Not be a Trancer? She would lose her joining with Lore, and that was unthinkable. "I thought the Orb was all powerful. Can I take away the pain caused when I fight but still keep my Trancer powers?"

Amarjaa shook her head. "No. There is always a price to

pay for gaining the Orb, Iliana. This is yours."

So much power, and yet, not as much as she had hoped. "What do you think I should do?"

"That is up to you. You have completed the quest, and it is your right to do as you wish with the power I have given you."

"Up to me?" Iliana's cheeks flamed hotter, the question emerging as a squeak. "How would I know what to do? What is right? What do you want?"

"It is not about me. This is about you. You have earned the right to choose. To become whatever you would want. To be the woman you wish."

She smiled, and once again, it was as if Iliana looked into the sun.

Amarjaa continued. "Just ask, and the Orb will grant it."

Iliana lost her breath at the thought. To become whatever she wanted?

The fiercest Warrior. The strongest Trancer.

The leader of Danu.

Once again, the vision of the Dark Queen flashed through her mind, but it was not Medea who sat on the throne. It was herself. A Queen who commanded millions, not out of love and courage, but out of fear and anger and an unyielding power.

She shook with the vision.

Amarjaa touched her hand. "You are wise. Do not let the thought of rule fool you into thinking that it would not come without a price."

Iliana nodded, ashamed that she had even entertained the thought, however briefly.

There were so many other choices and no perfect answer.

She stared into the Orb. To not choose was almost worse. To be a Warrior who could not fight. A Trancer with a blade.

The responsibility was overwhelming.

Amarjaa squeezed her hand. "You will do the right thing, Iliana," she said, her voice as tender as that of a mother. "Of that I am sure, but now it is time to go."

With a fingernail, she drew a line in the air next to her. Once again, a portal opened, and light spilled out into the garden.

Time to leave Paradise. Iliana rose and walked towards the light. She did not want to leave, but neither did she want to stay. She was safe here. Back in the world, there was pain. Suffering. Doubt.

And Lore. Her strength. The one who always believed in

her.

What if his belief was mistaken? What if she chose the wrong path?

Iliana stopped at the edge of the light and turned around. "What if I choose wrongly?"

The Goddess smiled. "I have faith in you. Now go."

Iliana nodded and turned back. If only she had as much faith in herself. She took a step forward, glancing back once again even as she entered the light.

The light was in her eyes, and she blinked.

She was not alone. The garden was not empty. Her sisters, as beautiful in death as they were in life, watched her.

Standing behind the Goddess was the Healer who had died at Mako's hand to save Iliana and Aria's son.

She smiled at Iliana. Not with malice or hate, but with love.

And understanding.

Twenty-one

Iliana stepped onto the stone floor of the temple as if walking through a doorway. The portal closed behind her with a snick.

Quickly, she assessed the circumstances.

It was as if but a brief moment had passed during her time with the Goddess. Medea crouched at the base of the altar, howling in rage at the space where the portal had first opened, and she was oblivious to Iliana's return.

Lore and Kole still battled at the edge of the plaza. Swords raised. Muscles straining.

Only now, there was blood.

The question was whose?

The men turned as they fought. Iliana caught a glimpse of Kole's side. His tunic was stained red. She breathed a sigh of relief.

"Lore!" She screamed his name, trying to be heard above the clanging of metal upon metal.

He glanced at her in brief acknowledgment before Kole thrust his sword towards Lore's chest. Lore had to step aside to avoid the killing blow.

Did he know she had succeeded? Iliana could not be sure. Not wanting to display her treasure to either of her enemies, she thrust the Orb into the pouch at her waist and unsheathed her sword.

She glanced back at Medea. Still oblivious to her return, the Reaper whore lay on the stone floor, curled into a ball and pulling at her black hair.

A mixture of hate, shame, and fear tugged at Iliana. Without the love of Lore and others that might well be her. She shuddered. It had been so close. Closer than anyone would ever know, except, perhaps, herself.

Those were memories she would like to forget.

The weight of the Orb pulled at her pocket.

She touched it through the fabric for an instant, and then she turned her attention back to the fight. Watching, looking for a moment when her skills might turn the tide. Parry. Thrust. Turn. Lunge. Another lunge.

The fight was more evenly matched than she might hope. Lore had the form, skill, and years of training, but Kole fought dirty. Dirtier than Lore would ever consider.

She touched the Orb again. Its power pulled at her. Whispered to her. Reminded her that with its possession, she could do anything. Even end this battle. Finish Kole and Medea, and the world would never remember their existence.

It was tempting. She shuddered at the idea. This gift from the Goddess was too tempting. Too powerful. It brought out her darkness and all the bad thoughts, petty wants, and small evils she had pushed to the back of her mind and locked way.

How would she and Lore ever keep it safe? Protect her people, and even Danu, from others who would use the Orb's power for ill?

"You should have watched your back," a voice whispered, as the point of a blade broke the skin at Iliana's waist.

Iliana inhaled a sharp breath, cursing her lack of attention. "Medea."

Medea dug the knife in deeper. "Drop your weapon."

Iliana flinched and let her sword fall from her grasp. She should have kept a closer eye on the Reaper whore—should have realized her pain and immobility would not last long.

"Tell the Warrior to lay down his sword as well," Medea demanded, her voice low.

Iliana watched the fight. It looked as if Kole were beginning to tire.

If Lore won, there was nothing Medea could do to harm her. She shook her head.

"Do it."

"No."

Medea dug the knife in, and Iliana cried out. It was not a loud cry, but nonetheless, Lore turned at the sound.

"Stop or she dies," Medea called out.

Lore did not hesitate. He dropped his sword, and the clatter as it hit the stone floor was bright in the sudden silence. Kole raised his weapon above his head.

"No!" Iliana screamed.

"Not yet," Medea barked the command at the same moment. Kole hesitated. "Why?"

Medea chuckled, her voice low. "We might need him."

Kole lowered his sword until it was level with Lore's chest. "We have her." He gestured towards Iliana. "This is a piece of Warrior meat that deserves to die by my hand."

Iliana met Lore's glaze. He was fearless, even as he faced death.

She was not as calm at the thought of his murder.

The Orb called to her. Begged her to use it. To end this and put the world right.

She wanted to. Even as she listened, waiting, she could visualize Medea and Kole's deaths. Bloody. Painful. Permanent.

She also saw herself laughing. The Dark Queen. Beautiful and terrible. If she killed her enemies, would it be enough to turn her into the monster she feared?

And the Orb beckoned.

Her every nerve shrieked. Her blood screamed. Every inhalation was a reason to cry out. Denying her desire, denying the Orb, was almost more than she could bear.

"Perhaps the Warrior deserves death," Medea continued, her lips next to Iliana's ear, distracting her from the pain. "But without him, she will do nothing."

Kole's lips thinned into a flat line, but he gave Medea a curt nod. "As you wish." He did not lower his weapon. "For now."

The Orb let Iliana go, and her muscles relaxed. Thank the Goddess.

"Do not think that he is saved," Medea whispered. "Do as I say or it will be the worse for him. Do not have any doubt of that."

"I do not," Iliana replied. She had seen Medea's handiwork when she was Mako's captive. The whore had a talent for causing suffering.

Medea pulled the knife from her body, leaving Iliana to bleed.

Iliana clutched her side, but she refused to cry out. She had done so once. There would be no second time.

Lore shot her a glance, his eyebrows raised in question, silently asking her if her wound was serious.

She shook her head.

"Now, Trancer." Medea ran the tip of her blade from Iliana's wrist to her shoulder, leaving a thin trail of blood. "Give me the Orb." Iliana hesitated. "Orb?"

Medea's lips turned downward, and Iliana knew her ruse, however futile and foolish, had failed. "Do not test me, Trancer. Give it to me." She held out her hand. "Now."

"Do not," Lore said

She met Lore's gaze, and he shook his head.

"Why, Warrior." Medea let the tip of her blade rest against

the skin just below Iliana's ear. "You sound positively frightened."

"Frightened?" Lore sneered. Kole poked him with the tip of his sword, but Lore continued, "Disgusted by you and your actions would be more accurate."

Iliana watched, the Orb whispering to her as her worry for Lore exerted itself once again.

"By me?" Medea laughed, her laughter melodic, despite the insanity of her actions. "I am but a poor girl out to make the world a better place."

Iliana shot Lore a glance that she hoped conveyed one message, Shut up. Do not let her push you to answer.

He either chose to ignore her, or he did not understand. "You are a witch. An animal. No better than the lover you murdered."

Medea's pale skin darkened to red. "You are not allowed to speak of Mako. Ever."

"He was a tyrant," Iliana whispered through tight lips, drawing Medea's attention back to her. A part of her prayed the inane conversation would end. Another part begged her to continue it, because if she continued, then Medea was still talking and they were both alive.

And where there was life there was hope.

End this, the Orb whispered in her mind. The desire was present in her thoughts. Heavy. Thick with need.

Once again, the vision of herself as the Dark Queen passed before her eyes.

She knew the truth of it. The potential.

She would not be that woman. Not today. Not ever.

She would not listen to the Orb's whisperings.

Iliana continued the conversation while she worked to regain control of her dark emotions. "Lore is wrong about one thing."

"What is that?" Medea whispered, her cheeks pink with anger.

"Animals are better than you. They do not kill for pleasure." The Orb's call grew from a whisper to a roar.

Why did Medea not just take it from her? Instead, she toyed with her. Played.

Iliana knew the answer, and her anger taking control, she said, "You are cruel. Crueler than a man. Crueler than any Reaper I met. Except, perhaps, Mako."

"You wanted him for yourself." Medea's knuckles whitened as her hand tensed and the blade pressed into Iliana's throat.

Medea continued. "He was dark. Powerful. He made decisions that no one else could." Abruptly, Medea pulled the knife away, her eyes bright with tears.

One hand on the hilt of her weapon, Medea gripped the blade with the other. Blood dripped from between her fingers. "I loved him. Worshipped him. He made me better. Made me strong."

A twinge of unexpected pity plucked at Iliana, and the Orb faded into the back of her mind. Her body relaxed at the release.

She would have to be careful and not provoke it.

Medea continued. "You made me kill him. You took him. Clouded his vision with your Trancer powers and made him want you."

Iliana took a step back, mesmerized by the blood that ran in thin, red rivulets down Medea's forearm.

Medea matched her step, her eye wild and desperate. "He was my creator. My Master. I could not let him go to another. He gave me no choice."

Use me.

Iliana bit her lip, took a breath, and denied the desire.

Use me. It was stronger now. Deeper. It focused on her need for death and burned her like a brand.

But herself as the Dark Queen? It was her greatest fear. Her strongest desire.

She would not allow it to rule her. Not like this. Would not allow it to command her will.

Use me.

Iliana took a deep breath. *No.*

The call stopped. Iliana smiled, amazed at the simplicity and complexity of the success. One word. That was all it took. No hedging. No asking herself, What if? No playing scenarios through her head, trying to determine the outcome.

Just one, strong word.

"You find your impending pain amusing, Trancer?" Medea took another step towards her.

"No." Iliana tapped into the Currents, even as she took yet another step back. She would not use the Orb, but the Currents were hers to command. If she could use them to manipulate Medea just a little, it might be enough to get both herself and Lore to safety.

Granted, it was against the Trancer code, but the safety of the Orb was more important. Now that she knew its power, she knew she had to keep it safe. Keep it secret.

Carefully, she reached out a tendril of thought, touched Medea, and hesitated. Most people were head-blind and would not notice the touch, but with the insane, one could never be sure. Medea kept talking. Alternately babbling about Mako's strength. His love. Screeching about how he ruined her. How she hated him, and he deserved to die.

Iliana ignored the urge to react, much less comment, and instead reached inward, wrapping tendrils of Currents around Medea. Binding her.

Medea raged, and Iliana breathed a sigh of relief.

She turned the tendrils to Kole even as she maintained a hold on Medea. He was easier to enter. He was not insane. Just a brute with dreams of grandeur.

Now, to stop them. Iliana glanced at Lore. He waited patiently, but his every muscle was at the ready.

Did he know what she was attempting?

His eyes bore into hers. He knew. She was sure of it. Their bond gave him an insight that went beyond anything of which she had dreamed.

He would be ready to take advantage of any situation she presented, of that there was no doubt.

Iliana focused her thoughts. She did not want to kill Kole and Medea. Not yet. She wanted to change the situation. Make Kole careless. Loosen the grip of his sword.

As for Medea, all she needed to do was keep the Reaper whore talking. The more she ranted about Mako, the less she talked of the Orb.

Medea first. Iliana reached in, seeking memories. Darkness that came with Mako.

She pushed past the pain. The passion. Saw the past.

A Tower. Healers. Elders. Laughter. Apprentices. All that was familiar and loved.

The Tower fallen—blackened and smoking. Women slaughtered. Mako's black and white mask.

And a single survivor. Medea.

"Oh my Goddess." The whispered words slipped past Iliana's lips. She saw not who Medea was, but what she was.

Medea was a Trancer.

***

For a heartbeat, Iliana stared at her enemy. A Trancer?

"Praying will not help you," Medea sneered, breaking Iliana's stunned immobility.

Iliana pulled her thoughts back from both Kole and Medea, breathing a sigh of relief. Medea was still unaware that she had touched her.

Medea was a Trancer? Iliana would never have thought that possible. But in the instant she had touched the deepest recesses of Medea's thoughts, she had seen it all—even if Medea had forgotten, chosen to lock her past away behind a wall of insanity, pain and hate.

The young girl—the strongest Trancer born since the First Trancer—taken by Mako when he destroyed her Tower.

First, he had coddled her. Told her he loved her. Desired her. When she refused to use her Talent to help him, he finally turned to torture. A branding of the soul so deep and harsh that the young Trancer went insane, bonding with her captor and losing her Talent.

And her name was not Medea. It was Myrina.

Iliana wanted to cry. Not just for the girl who was once Myrina, but for herself. Medea's insanity could have been her fate. Had almost been her fate. She remembered the darkness that Mako had found in her soul and released. She felt it every time anger or pain or fear folded over her.

She bit her bottom lip. So close. If not for Lore . . .

She glanced at him. He had helped her find that part of herself that was able to defy her baser instincts. He had given her the love she needed to accept herself.

Given her the courage to face the Orb. Iliana brushed her hand against the pouch that hid the gift. Once, not too long ago, she would have used the Orb to kill her enemies. To take life. A part of her still wanted to give in to that urge.

But love, and hers and Lore's joining, had made her stronger than instinct. Tougher than dark urges. Given her the courage to not wield power like a blade.

She glanced at Lore, standing steady with a blade pointed at his chest, waiting for her to act. Thank you, my love.

For a brief moment, his gaze softened, and she knew he felt her love as well.

"The Orb, Trancer. Give it to me now." Medea brushed a strand of her dark hair back and held out her hand.

Iliana glanced at the scarred palm and wrist, knowing it

was Mako who had branded her. Once again, she saw the innocent girl Medea used to be.

Instead of the hate that burned in her heart, there was now only pity. Deep, unwielding sorrow for Myrina.

So close.

Again, Iliana reached out with her mind, shifting the Currents, and making a connection to the woman in front of her.

She sought the past. The exact moment Medea changed from Trancer to the twisted woman standing in front of her.

She was not sure what she would do, but there had to be a way to fix this. Lore had pulled her back from the precipice. Perhaps she could catch Medea. Save her. Force Medea to remember the girl she used to be.

The tip of Medea's blade broke her concentration. "Trancer, I will not ask again. You live for my pleasure. The Orb."

The Orb. It whispered to her again. *Use me.*

It no longer called to the darkness within. Instead, it called to her Trancer half. The Healer.

She could heal Medea with the Orb.

Yes.

A warmth spread through Iliana. This was her mission. Her quest. It was to save Medea. To bring back Myrina. This was what the Goddess had meant when she said she trusted her to do what was needed. What was right.

You can still save yourself, the Orb whispered to her, tempting her one last time. *The girl is nothing. Embrace the Warrior. Kill the Trancer within. End the pain.*

Iliana shook her head. She was what she was, for good or ill. Both Trancer and Warrior. The first of many. Warmth spread to her limbs at the decision.

"It is time," she whispered. She pulled the Orb from its pouch and held it up on her palm.

Medea's eyes brightened and she grasped the Orb, her broken wrist ignored.

Iliana stood ready, and in an instant, grabbed Medea's other wrist and twisted until the knife fell from her hand.

Snarling, Medea yanked at the Orb, but instead of letting go, Iliana held tight. She pulled Medea closer, clasping the Orb between them.

With a release of power, she let the Currents fill her, opened up Medea's mind and called upon the Orb to do what it was meant to do before men corrupted it.

"Be healed," she whispered into Medea's ear.

Light—bright, brilliant, and holy—consumed them. In the back of her mind, Medea screamed. Iliana clung tighter, making sure the woman who was once her enemy could not break free.

Be healed.

Medea's screaming grew louder, more frantic, and Iliana expanded her thoughts with a cruel precision. Like cutting off an infected limb, she gathered the cruelty, the pain, and the rage that was Medea, and sliced it free.

Agony shot through her.

Medea slumped in her arms, and Iliana fell, unable to support their combined weights.

Lore! He was her final thought as the pain overwhelmed her.

Twenty-two

"Stop her, Warrior. Stop her or they both die."

Kole jabbed the tip of his sword into Lore's chest, his eyes wide with fear.

The same alarm raced through Lore, but he kept his expression passive. Calm. To show fear to a Reaper was to admit defeat.

He glanced at the women. Locked in combat, a bright light consumed them.

"Go." Kole jabbed at him again, beads of sweat dotting his dirt-streaked face.

Lore glared at Kole. He did not need to be told what to do. Even without the Reaper's advice, he was going to end this. He did not want to take a chance with Iliana's life.

Shielding his eyes with him forearm, Lore walked towards the light. The women were obscured now by the intensity, and he had to walk with his hand out, feeling his way.

His foot hit something soft.

Without warning, the light died, like a candle snuffed by the wind.

Lore blinked and lowered his arm. At his feet lay Iliana. One hand still gripped Medea. The other held onto the Orb.

"Iliana." He dropped to his knees and pulled her into his lap. "Love. Speak to me."

She blinked slowly and opened her eyes. "Did I do it?"

"I am not sure. What did you—"

"Witch! What did you do to her?"

Lore raised his eyes to see Kole advancing towards them, sword raised for a killing blow.

A growl rumbled low in Lore's throat. He had had enough of the Reaper who posed as a man.

In less time than it took to inhale, he spied Medea's blade on the ground, gripped it, and with all the skill that behooved a Warrior Trainer, he threw it at Kole.

The Reaper stopped mid-step, looked at the knife hilt sticking out of his chest, and fell over, even as he tried to take another step.

"Who was that? Why did you kill him?"

Iliana turned at the question.

Medea was awake, leaning on one hand as she tried to rise.

At least she thought it was Medea. Her hair was no longer black; it was as white as the silver moon. Her eyes had also changed. Once black in both color and hatred, they were a pale gray and filled with confusion and fear.

The eyes of an innocent. Iliana hesitated, hoping that what she thought was right. "That was Kole. Your traveling companion. Do you not remember him?"

Medea shook her head. "I have never seen him before. Why did you kill him?" She shrank back. "Are you going to kill me?"

Iliana glanced up at Lore. "I have my answer," she whispered. "I did it. I succeeded."

"Did what? What did you do to her?"

Iliana rolled onto her knees, acutely aware of her need for rest. "To put it simply, I changed her back to who she was before Mako took her." She kept her voice low so only Lore could hear. "I took away all her memories of being Medea."

Lore raised a blond brow. "All of them?"

Iliana nodded. "Everything. She remembers nothing. Not the men and women she hurt. Killing Mako. Nothing."

"Who is Medea?" A quiet voice asked,

Both turned. Her pale hair about her shoulders like a silver cloak, the girl stared at them, her eyes filled with confusion.

"You are," Lore replied, before Iliana could stop him.

"No, I am Myrina."

Lore hesitated then managed a slow nod. "As you wish." He turned back to Iliana. "It seems you did succeed." He ran a hand over his hair, his expression stunned. "So, who was she before she became a Reaper?"

"She was a Trancer."

Lore's eyes widened in shock. "A Trancer?"

"Taken by Mako and broken. Changed into the monster that was Medea. Now she is saved."

Iliana moved to stand.

"Let me." Lore rose and helped her to her feet.

Myrina scooted backwards, trying to get away.

Iliana took a step towards her.

"Please," Myrina begged, her gray eyes filling with tears. "I do not know who Medea is, but I am not her. You must believe me. Please, do not kill me. I have done nothing."

Iliana held out her hand and smiled. "We mean you no harm, Mede . . . Myrina. We know who you are. We are friends, and we mean you no harm," she repeated soothingly.

The girl hesitated, and Iliana felt a tendril of her touch. "You are a Trancer." The fear in her eyes died and a smile curved her lips. "We do know each other. I felt a familiarity when I touched your mind, but why do I not remember you?"

Iliana shrugged. "It is a long story."

Lore caressed Iliana's shoulder, and she felt his continued confusion at Myrina's change and the new name, but stronger than his surprise was something more.

Pride. In her.

She warmed.

"You did a great thing," he whispered. "Amazing and unheard of, but great." He kissed the curve of her ear. "And compassionate."

Iliana turned into his touch and stroked his cheek. "Thank you. I could not have done it without you. Without your strength."

He kissed her palm. "Do not fool yourself. The strength was in you. It always was."

Her smile grew into a grin. "Perhaps."

Laughing, Lore hugged her, picked her off her feet, and swirled her in a circle. "You are amazing." He set her down.

Once again, she shrugged, but for the first time since before Mako took her, she felt free. Light. Not even Lore's love had been able to fully lift her burden of guilt and self-loathing. It was gone now, with the acceptance of herself as she was—both Warrior and Trancer. A beginning of what would be a line of sisters who could wield both sword and Currents.

As for the Orb . . . Iliana picked it up. Blackened and burned, it was useless—its true purpose filled. Why all this to change a Myrina back to a Trancer, only the Goddess knew, but Iliana was willing to bet it was for an interesting reason.

"What shall we do with her?" Lore nodded towards Myrina. "We cannot leave her here."

Iliana leaned into him. "I know, but neither can we take her back to Talon's Keep. The memory of who she was runs deep. They will never forgive her for her past sins." Her own situation had been strained. Myrina would be dead within days. "I have an idea, if you are willing to listen."

"Always," Lore replied.

"Let us start our own Keep. One were I can train. Where Myrina will be safe. Where others like me can come. People who have a past and nowhere else to go. Others who need to start anew." She held her breath, waiting for his reply. If he denied her, she did not know what she would do. He was her light. Her life. But she had a responsibility to her future and those of her sisters. To Myrina.

"You realize that if we do this, Talon will be truly angry and Aria will miss you?"

Iliana nodded. "We can establish a Keep a few days ride away from them. It might seem far, but it would not be. Not really. If something happened—"

Lore laid a gentle finger on her mouth, silencing her. "You are babbling, my love." He glanced over her shoulder at Medea. "Your burden is my burden. Your responsibility mine." He glanced down at her. "Death could not part us. What makes you think I would abandon you now?"

"You would give up your life, your title, for me?" she whispered, humbled.

"I give up nothing, Iliana."

"You are Talon's Destro."

Lore shrugged. "He will be peeved, but you can always drug him if he protests too much."

Iliana blushed at the joke, both embarrassed and amused.

Lore grinned. "I cannot deny his anger, but he will see the wisdom in establishing another Keep." He tilted her chin up. "Even if he does not, it will not stop me. We may not have an easy life with this Keep you envision, but it will never be boring. I love you, Iliana, and I would move both Danu and the sky to prove it."

Standing on her toes, she hesitated but a breath away from his mouth. "I know. And you already did," she whispered as she kissed him.

Printed in the United Kingdom
by Lightning Source UK Ltd.
101253UKS00001B/510